KAY BO

was born in St Paul, Minnesota, Cincinnati Conservatory of Music Institute where she studied architecture. Her first marriage to a Frenchman took her to Europe where she remained for twenty years. Much of that time was spent in Paris where she knew Robert McAlmon, Djuna Barnes, Nancy Cunard, Gertrude Stein, Ernest Walsh, Sylvia Beach, Ezra Pound and James Joyce. Her experiences are recorded in *Being Geniuses Together, 1920-1930* (1968), which she wrote with Robert McAlmon. Kay Boyle returned to America in 1941 and soon afterwards separated from her second husband, Laurence Vail. She then married Joseph von Franckenstein, an Austrian Baron who joined the US Armed Forces in 1943. During the McCarthy era he, then a Foreign Service officer stationed in Germany, was subjected to a Loyalty-Security Hearing—Kay Boyle was one of the charges against him. Although both were cleared of all charges, Kay Boyle was temporarily blacklisted as a writer and her husband lost his Foreign Service job, but was reinstated nine years later.

Kay Boyle has had a distinguished academic career, with posts at numerous American universities, including fellowships at Wesleyan University, Connecticut (1963) and the Radcliffe Institute for Independent Study (1965). She was Professor of English at San Francisco State University from 1963-79, and has received several honorary degrees and been Writer-in-Residence at two universities.

She has written, edited and translated over thirty books including novels, short stories, essays, poetry, and children's books. Her first collection of short stories was published in 1929. Her first novel, *Plagued by the Nightingale* (1931) is published by Virago who also publishes *Year Before Last* (1932) and *My Next Bride* (1934). Kay Boyle was awarded Guggenheim Fellowships in 1934 and 1961 and won O. Henry Awards for the best short story 'Wedding Day' in 1935 and for 'Defeat' in 1941. In the 1960s Kay Boyle was imprisoned for protesting against the Vietnam War. More recently she has been involved in American Civil Rights and anti-war movements and in Amnesty International. She is a member of the American Academy of Arts and Letters. Kay Boyle's most recent works are a collection of essays, *Words That Must Somehow Be Said* (1985) and a collection of new poetry, *This Is Not A Letter* (1985). She has six children and lives in Oakland, California.

MY NEXT BRIDE

KAY BOYLE

———— ✣ ————

"Knife will be my next bride"
–Laurence Vail

With a New Afterword by
DORIS GRUMBACH

Penguin Books—Virago Press

PENGUIN BOOKS
Viking Penguin Inc., 40 West 23rd Street,
New York, New York 10010, U.S.A.
Penguin Books Ltd, Harmondsworth,
Middlesex, England
Penguin Books Australia Ltd, Ringwood,
Victoria, Australia
Penguin Books Canada Limited, 2801 John Street,
Markham, Ontario, Canada L3R 1B4
Penguin Books (N.Z.) Ltd, 182–190 Wairau Road,
Auckland 10, New Zealand

First published in the United States of America by
Harcourt, Brace & Company 1934
This edition first published in Great Britain by
Virago Press Ltd 1986
Published in Penguin Books 1986

Printed in the United States of America by
R. R. Donnelley & Sons Company, Harrisonburg, Virginia
Set in Caslon No. 540

FOR
CARESSE

Part One

S O R R E L

CHAPTER ONE

Victoria was in Neuilly by afternoon, watching for trees in the bare gardens. When she saw the biggest ones, and the sign at the gate, and the old house standing back on the drive, she put the bags down and pulled the bell at the wall. The two Russian women heard it ring in the house and they laid down their sewing. The air out of the city was clean and sharp and they could see her very well through the machine-fashioned mesh of the curtains at the window.

The servant in her old slippers ran out, her back bent, limping: the short leg and then the long, and the locks slipping free in back from the dark slap of her knotted hair. They saw the gate undone, and the servant and the girl came up the walk together. The servant had never put out her hand to help her, and the girl's face was hanging sideways from the weight of the two bags in her hands. They would remember this, and for a long time after they would not take the mud from their shoes at the door outside but bring it in with them. The girl was passing close to the window: they could see her head riding past the glass.

Her face was small, and the cheeks white, and the eyes set high and deeply in it as the face of a Russian might have been. But when they heard her voice speaking in the hall, they knew better. They were as alike as prisoners, dressed in black silk waists and fitted skirts, with shawls of crimped black lamb across their shoulders. The hair on their heads was wrung tight from their necks behind, and under their neat pompadours their brows swelled full and bare. There could be nothing new in the cold for them, for their slavic cheek-bones were veined with antique roots, and the small nails on their fingers set in stony blue. Their eyes were bright and identically bewildered; their narrow hands were shaking in the bedroom cold.

They went to the panels of the high double doors, their feet quiet, invisible under their hems, and, harking, they laid themselves against the wood. But even in curiosity they upheld a pride: hickory canes might have stood upright down their spines for the demeanour of shy austerity they bore.

"It's dark here," they heard the girl say evenly in French. "Wait a moment," said the servant's voice, blameful that any one should have come. "I'll go for the key."

The girl said yes, and it might have been anything, a new coin flung down in an empty plate, or the beginning of something longer she was thinking of. The two Russian women, no longer young, touched each other's hands at once because they could not run boldly out and touch the voice that spoke.

"Wait here," said the servant, farther, dimmer, wearier now. "I'll strike a match and light the gas and you'll see."

"Gas?" said the quick voice, moving off. The women could hear the blue wings of the light beating and gasping out in the cold.

"How much do you think you'd pay for a big room like this if it had electricity in it?" the servant asked.

"I don't know at all," the girl's voice said. It was certain that she did not believe yet in the cold or the poverty or the dark. She was fresh from somewhere else and she did not know yet how it would be. And the Russian women understood whence such ignorance and power came: not from England, not from Ireland even. It was a voice speaking out of a bodily, a national ease that had never been betrayed. It had purity, and it had an edge of insolence, almost. But insolence was their own thing as well, they who had been ladies too; it was their distinction and their blood replied to the sound of it. The English they knew as well as they did their own people, and this voice had nothing of England in it.

"American," whispered one sister to the other.

"You're not allowed to cook in the room," the servant said.

"No, of course," said the girl, and they could see at once how things must have been for her: a bedroom with clean sheets turned back for sleep-

9

ing, and a kitchen with a stove in it where servants were. The one thing never mixed up with the other. "Where do I wash? Is there a bathroom?" she said.

They did not hear the servant speak in answer, but she must have raised her arm and pointed to the end of the room where they knew the table was standing, stained with the mixtures and remedies of other people's ills, pointing out the tin pitcher and basin on the oil-cloth and the pail on the boards beside it.

"Yes," the girl said. "I think the room will do." The handle of the window ground, and they heard its cry as it opened. "It's come off in my hand," the girl's voice said.

"You can see the house is old," said the servant sharply. "You can't pull at things without reason."

"The trees out there are older," said the girl's voice with the dignity and the contempt they had come into exile for. When the girl and the servant walked into the hall, the two Russian women started back as though the panels of the door no longer shielded them from sight.

"If you want the room," the servant said, "you'll have to see the lady."

They heard this, and their souls went quiet in their flesh. Each could feel the terror of the other trembling like a single dewdrop in the heart of a shrivelled, faded flower. The Russian women stood halted, without breath, without act, but step by step their trepidation mounted the stair-

way with her, their thin hands riding the bannisters after her and their black skirts shaking
the motion out in dust-tufted seams behind. The
sound of the landlady's door opening upstairs
roused them from this apathy of hollow, separate
sleep. "Now she is sitting down. Now she is
waiting. She can't be twenty years old."

Victoria sat straight on the chair the servant
gave her. There were chestnut-trees outside in
the garden, but even turning her head she could
not see from the window because of the velvet
hanging through brocaded bracelets, thick and
untouched as it must have hung untouched for
years. Now it was winter, and in the spring there
would be a difference; in the summer there would
be in the evening when she came home to it the
leaves pulsing soft and dark with untongued
sound.

It was dim as twilight in the room, and the
furniture stood in monuments to death and age
and things that had gone before. These were the
tombstones kneeled and cried before by the
woman who would come, whoever she was, and
whether or not she was old or young. Hoarding
old paintings, mahogany, porcelain figures, velvet,
thought Victoria, sitting tired in the cold. She
had been a long time travelling and carrying the
two bags in her hands. In them were what belonged to her: clothes worn three years, a piece
of soap and a silver-backed hairbrush with her
mother's letters on it; shoes with the heels walked
aslant in Montreal, a water-paint box, and under

the books in the bottom the faces of three women separately framed.

She said: "I didn't want it cold like this, not the first time anyway," and a door at the far end opened and the woman took shape in the recess of cornered dark.

She came lifting her own weight from the obscurity, bearing her own flesh forward like a burden, manipulating as if under water the speechless, slow advance. Victoria stood up before it, knowing it was a woman from the wheeze and cry of the breathing and from the following of the garments that clothed the immensities of flesh. One hand came first, floating upon the tide of dark, swollen and bleached upon the handle of a cane. When she had come to the desk, the other hand lifted and rode along the edge of wood. She had not even seemed to look towards the girl standing in the room. Her pure white, bloated fingers felt across the chair-back, ascertaining, and then the woman sank down in exhaustion on the seat.

"It was about the room you have to let downstairs," Victoria said, hesitant in the silence. "I wanted to know the price."

She could see the woman's face clearer now, immobile, the mouth still gasping for breath, the loose, dry, powdery folds of age, the cinnamon rings of ailment drawn around her eyes. The full lids were fallen almost to the rim, and under them stood motionless two marble threads of eye.

"This is my home," she said in a rich, blinded

voice. "It's not a place for just any one who comes along. I can't have *n'importe qui*." Her hair was strong and beard-like, springing as white as ivory from the scalp, with a great tail of yellow staining the smooth topknot on her head. "Why did you come here?" she said, and her invisible gaze seemed ready to burst through the swelling lids.

"I'm looking for a room away from the city," said Victoria, speaking high and clear. "I stopped to look at the trees in your garden and then I saw the sign at the gate."

"What are you doing in Paris?" said the woman. These things, because of her supremacy, she had a right to know. All about in the room were scattered the remains of what life had been: relics of carved and brass-handled wood, upholstery ready to shred to lace, portraits of ladies with bared, lovely breasts facing full-length and booted military men. They had a mask of dust across their faces, and a gravity born of all that was theirs to honour and remember, even in time of war or even in their cups.

"I'm going to work in Paris," Victoria said, and she saw the pale, slack mouth sag open at her words.

"Work?" said the woman. "What kind of work?"

"I don't know," said Victoria. "I have to look for work. I've just come from Montreal."

The woman waited a moment, sunk white and lax, suspicious, in her chair. The men of the family were dead now, having been of a time that took its wives by arrangement and the women it loved from the stage; but what they had been was left in the remnants, stopping the veins as thick as port, making of those who followed after monuments in halted flesh and bone.

"We have two Russian noblewomen downstairs," she said, and behind the featureless, blind presence wariness and eyesight seemed to move in stealth. "We had a Spanish count for several months on the second floor. I've never had a working person."

This is no ordinary place, was the collapse of her flesh saying. The trees here are as old as your country. The walls are ready to fall away in despair. The stairway has carried down the footsteps of young men too sick ever to remount them. There has been war and invasion in this place, and women running blind up the stairs hearing their men were dead.

When they heard her coming down, the two Russian women went quickly to their bureau and fetched the box of jewellery out and put their rings hastily on their fingers. Then they turned around in trepidation and waited for Victoria to reach the hall.

They had no idea of the thoughts in her head, or where she was going, or why she had stopped at the gate with her two bags in her hands. The middle west of the States or Montreal or no work to be had, these things were as good as nothing to them. Behind them there was nothing but Russia

as it once had been, and they did not know what
promise it is that can woo the blood from one
country to the next one. They had spent their
youth as rich young women did in Russia once,
with the winters passing slow and elegant at
home. Young men had been nothing at all but
callers, for there was always too much of the family
present, either in the room or seated there doing
embroidery in their faces, hindering what the calls
might have come to in the end. Whatever they
had, had never drawn but had driven the chaos
of a loving man away.

They did not know why she had come to this
end of Paris, but to enter this house and take the
filth and the menace in it, the ruin and rack and
the wall-paper tearing off in ribbons, the paintless
sight of the panels and wood, the mildew, the
blisters of varnish, they knew that the heel of
despair had fallen. Almost because of the strong
unheeding trees outside and the great pillared
chambers that were by nature no habitation of the
poor, this house was the application of defeat. It
had them fast. Poverty had made grotesques of
them, for in their ladies' bearing and their speech
there was no difference, but they were living in
the shadow of what had happened somewhere else,
a long time past, when their fur jackets and their
boots and stays were new.

They did not believe that they would end here,
for they scarcely believed their true living had
begun. It was only a time of hardship they were
passing through in preparation, and then justice

would be done. They spoke and ate as carefully as birds, and neither saw the fifty years marked in bewilderment upon the other's face; nor the frayed stuffs, nor recognized hunger or stint, for within them their pride had never cringed.

They heard Victoria's steps upon the tilings in the hall, and although they moved quickly to the door, neither had the strength to lift a hand. They looked at each other in a spasm of queer, helpless fright, and then the elder sister boldly seized the handle of the door and drew it back and open. The girl had been leaning to pick up her bags again, and at the sound of the door she paused and watched the two little women who stood there quivering in the bluish wintry light. She saw them standing, eager as ferrets, against the arch of late afternoon, their heads raised as if on the whale-boning in their chokers, the ears on each side of their neat skulls spread big and delicate against the light.

The sisters did not speak, but the elder one lifted her hand and motioned quickly to the stranger. "Go away," she said, whispering the absolute English words as if they were a direction pointed to. "Go away. Don't stay here," she said across the shallow hall.

It was a late November day, it was almost at an end, but in what remained of it they could distinguish her face still, turned in curiosity to them, and the felt hat over it, strange like a grown woman's hat set on a startled small head. Her skirt did not come far below the knees and her legs stuck out from under it, not as if the dress were made too short, but as if the girl had grown too fast.

"Go away," said the younger sister too. "Don't stay here."

They waited, their heads jerking quickly in agitation; then the elder of the sisters took a step forward and the other sister ran behind. They came forward into the tiled hall, their fear hastening in soft, fluttering waves of warning toward her. The wide, ballroom-like doorway of their bedroom was left empty in the light behind.

"I've taken the room here," said Victoria. She moved her hand towards the cold abyss of darkness. But the two little women might not have heard her speaking. They hastened on over the split stained tiles.

"Go away, please," said the elder, whispering. "It's too dirty and cold here. Don't you see it?"

"They won't make the fire," said the other sister, whispering wilder, her lips drawn back and quivering. "They won't give you any hot water. They make you pay for the gas yourself when the meter-man comes."

"They change one sheet on the bed once in the month," whispered the elder sister. "There are bugs in the wood."

The girl opened her mouth to speak, but the step of the servant came down the stairs. They all raised their heads to it, to the uneven beat of the short leg and the long leg hastening down. At the turn in the stairs she came in sight, and when she saw them she cried down: "Miss Fira, Miss Grusha, what are you doing?"

The heads of the Russian women reared up like puppets pulled; their hands fell into their skirts at their sides, and their rings clicked aloud as they struck one against the other in the cold.

"Go back into your room," said the servant, with her face gone yellow as wax. She lifted her hand and pointed straight into the fading arch of snow-whitened light. The two Russian women turned and went, side by side and their skirts following behind, their heads borne high, identically unfaltering into the vast desolation of their room and closed the door against the dark.

CHAPTER TWO

Victoria took the three photographs out of her bag and set them on the chimney, watching their faces separately as she brought them out. When they were there she turned and looked at the other things in the room, looked long and unpityingly at them, as if now she could bear to see. The bed had a thick whitish cover spread over it, the arm-chair had split its wine-coloured plush and gave out its entrails in coils of dust-bleached hay. There was a rug on the floor with the paths other people's feet had made worn on it, and a sofa to one side, not to be sat on for fear of the curls of its undone springs or what was living there. The tall glass over the chimney-piece, in residue of splendour, was spangled with black needles that reflected only in pieces here and there. The women in their frames had not altered it, but neither had their faces altered in this place.

The first one had her bare head back against the wooden post of a piazza in the country. Her neck was thin and in the lifted attitude the short jaw had a sharp, pure edge. Her eyes were narrowed hard against the sun or air, but looking forthright from her face. Her hair was taken back, and the ears showed close and round and henlike

19

against the skull. It was the diminutive ears, maybe, that had kept her to herself and made a stranger of her. She had never given even a word of herself away. Even the photograph had not been given, but had been made large from a snapshot some one else had taken, pasted on cardboard and framed without her ever knowing. She was the one who taught painting in the middle west, teaching it without surrender to the people taught, unyielding to the good pupils as to the bad, so that every morning for three years, winter and summer, was like meeting the quiet, manlike eyes of some one passing in the street, seeing the tall slight bones over and over until they became the designation of some one scarcely recognized.

(I left the west because of you. You were nothing. You were a stranger, you spoke less than a hundred words to me. But I went east because of you. I went on foot, day after day, week after week, pretending the rain was your tears coming after me. You were a tall, ugly woman, not young any more, but your silence sent me out looking for whatever there is.)

The one in the middle was Victoria's mother. Her hairbrush was on the stone top of the chest of drawers and her face was on the chimney, and that was all that was left of her. She had a full, loving mouth, and her hair was waved low like a *prima donna's* on her cheeks. There was an orchid pinned in her furs, and one shoulder was bare. The fine velvet hat on her head was faced with a rolling mole-skin brim. But her dark, nostalgic eyes besought that love be purified by faith, and sensitivity not stabbed to death a thousand times a life by fear.

(Everything I do you began somewhere and didn't have time to finish—dancing alone to the sound of music before strangers until I could have died of shame for you, speaking of poetry and sculpture as simply as if the coloured servants loved them best. If ever I see the faces of Brancusi, or Duchamp, or Gertrude Stein, I shall look the other way because of the history of courage they made for you.)

The third one had been cut from a paper, and on the back of it the newspaper cutting was pasted. It said: this is Mary de Lacey, Australian songbird, formerly well known to vaudeville audiences here, there, and the other place. She committed suicide last night in a furnished room in Montreal.

The woman was smiling wildly out in her terror of the camera. She was a stricken, thin madonna, with her hair divided through the centre and knotted loosely. Her brow was high and her mouth drawn up in a sharp, sweet, acid, smiling sorrow. The cheeks shrank back from the bone and the shape of the teeth could almost be distinguished in them, the defiance in the eyes mitigated by the panic in them for what the camera might reveal.

(You never gave me a minute's peace when I went to work in New York, typing in wholesale houses, serving in restaurants. You had no patience for it. You said life was an obligation in arrogance, talk an experiment in insult. "If you can't live hard, die holy like a piece of cheese,

Victoria." I never said some things to you, I never said love because of the shy sound it had beside you. You took me to Montreal, freight-hopping with you. We lay all night with our coats stuck under our heads for pillows and the wheels crying out and grinding under us. I said, "Lacey, you're good, bad, rain, wind, thunder, sun, everything." "Where did you get it?" said Lacey. "How much does it cost a yard?")

She said it to Victoria lying there in the freight-car, and the boards were so loose in the floor that the night air came through in clear fresh blasts on their faces. They went into each other's arms for warmth, and the words were better spoken and heard while the bodies kindled each other.

"Whenever it gets to be too much," said Lacey, "I get out from under. That's the way things happen. Everything in you gets good and ready, knowing before you know." Except for the sacks of grain propped up like dead men in the corners, the car was empty and long, leading narrow and hall-like to what they were going to. "I always had a lot of natural colour in my face making me be taken for something I wasn't," said Lacey. "That was in Australia, when I first began skipping out. I took my kid, he was three then, and my mother, and we got by car to Brisbane. We had two weeks to wait for the boat and we had no money, or hardly any. We took a room in the cheapest end, near the wharfs, in hiding like, because we knew my husband would be after us. Every night in that place we played out the cards to see how things would turn out for us, and there was the blooming death card coming up on the right-hand side every time. I was so fed up with seeing it there, that I poured my palm full of ink one night, and I waited. After a bit the moon began shining on the ink, and it might have been moonlight shining on the ocean all right, except that the rain was falling cats and dogs outside. I called out for mother, and she was standing right there beside me watching, when the sharks started jumping around in the ink in my hand. They were fighting like mad over something or other, and mother said 'they've got hold of something they like this time, all right'. We could see it just as plain as that light," Lacey said, and she pointed at the strip of lighted station that was showing through the crack in the freight-car door. Then the train went slowly, completely out into the darkness, as if drawn by the will of its destination past the scattered fires of the smelting town.

"We knew the old man was after us," Lacey said. "The cards said so. I bought some cyanide in the afternoon because if he got there I was going to take it instead of going back with him. Suicide's for the young," she said. "Autumn's a good time for it. Now that I'm forty you don't catch me wasting my time with it any more."

Victoria felt the small, frail body of the other woman in her arms, the wings of the shoulder-blades sharp in her fingers, the necklace of the spine exquisite and perishable in every link, marvellously curved in the stuff of the worn wool

23

dress and the sweater ravelling out. Every breath Lacey took was thin as shallow water; the weight of a hand laid quietly on her throat would be enough to take her life away.

"Three days before the boat was to sail, mother got sick. She had a bad liver, and this was the end of it. She had to put up with bad food, coming off like that with me. But for me she'd never have been there. It was me took her to Brisbane and sent her running to pawnshops with her garnet brooch and her garnet drops and her string of coral. It was the night before the boat sailed, and she died. They were going to take her away and bury her in the paupers' field in the morning. I was thinking of that, and I went into the room where we washed and I took out the package of cyanide and I emptied it down the wash-bowl. I let the paper fall on the floor, or I left it on the wash-stand, I don't know where I put it. But when the doctor came in with the death certificate, he went to wash his hands, and when he came out he said 'I'm not prepared to issue it. There has to be an autopsy made.' "

The whistles of the trains mourned slowly through the night, separately widowed over the wide plains. The cold of the early morning hours was coming in with the white line of sky at the door, and it gathered quietly about them in the freight-car, present as a crowd hushed by a sight or sound is present, voiceless and fixed before the two women in attitudes of awe.

"The bastard had picked up the little paper

left from the cyanide," Lacey said. "He had it in his pocket. So they locked me up for the night in the jail there until the autopsy was made. They took mother to the public cutting-up theatre, and the kid stayed the night with the matron, and by morning they knew there was nothing. They let me out and the kid and I went running down the wharf, and the boat was all set and the gangway being lifted. We skipped into the steerage at the last minute and we stood up at the railing watching the last of Australia. The public hospital where they'd taken mother apart was standing up at the end of the city, right out over the water. There was a man standing next to us on deck, and he started in talking. 'There's the municipal power works over there,' he said, 'and there's our tallest building to date. And up there', he said, 'is where they feed the sharks from!' He said this with a laugh, but I couldn't keep from crying out. 'The sharks!' I said, and everything came back to me. 'Sure,' he said, 'they pitch your innards right over the edge there when they're through cutting you up in the hospital there. Maybe you're not familiar with the city.' "

(Lacey, you sent me away from Montreal. You said, "I don't need any one, don't kid yourself. I don't need any one at all." You said, "Don't fall for the skirts, Victoria, not till you've given the boys a trial. You'll come to it anyway in the end. The best of us do. And another thing, Victoria. Don't go looking for jobs in every city. Go looking for something else. Maybe you'll find it.")

Victoria went to the bed and sat down on her hands to warm them. The ceiling was high, and the light far and dim in it, like lights late at night in the waiting-rooms of small stations. The piano had begun playing before, but only now that she sat down did it seem to come to her hearing. As if shaken in the cold in the next room it came through the wall to her in tentative complaint. The wall-paper was a dark green, spotted with islands of black fir with a gondola beside the shore. This would have been the dining-room of the old place, set to the back and leading off from the front parlour. Three couples dancing in formation could have passed easily through the arch of the open door.

The piano duet came under and through, without any strength but only tenderness to it, as if being played by hands too small to reach the octaves or else too abashed by what the overture implied. Victoria watched the tears hit her skirt, quiver a moment, and end there. What I need is my supper, she said. Lacey was looking straight out of the photograph, writhing away from what the camera might find and set down on paper. And what about the thing they can't get hold of? Victoria said suddenly, jumping up in passion. What about the trees growing in spite of them, pictures getting painted, words that will be there for ever, what about it, what about love anyway, she said.

"Sure," said Lacey's voice, high as a boy's voice, jeering. "Sure. Call it love if you want. Call it that for a couple of years."

CHAPTER THREE

By the end of the week she had begun to space
the meals at longer intervals, to wash in
cafés where soap was found, stale and hard
as a bit of cheese beside the basin; in a week she
could see the city in all its sections, divided as if by
the clarity of hunger. This, not Montreal, not the
middle west, not spring, or summer, demanded
something stronger. It was unlike other places,
but in its unlikeness the mystery and wonder lay
untaken, as such things for a man lie in the still
untaken flesh. This asked for a rich male music in
the blood to play down what was misery and la-
ment and what was walking back alone to Neuilly
in November.

In the right season there might have been many
people walking under the trees here, but the cold
left only a few passing quickly. The horse-show
was on at the Grand-Palais across the park, and
chrysanthemums bearded and golden-locked stood
tall as men in the light at the palace doorways:
blond men with tittering leaves in the cold, the sap
stopped in them, watching the lighted limousines
drive smoothly to the steps, lion-maned flowers
gone toothless and tame in their captivity. Behind

in the dark, small quick river-ferries docked with a soft murmur of water, and went swiftly on again.

"This is the way things begin," she said, walking fast. "Maine, New Hampshire, Vermont," past the elegant wrought-iron gates, the walls of Passy given speech and motion in the ivy that died on them in the cold. "A long time poor and their stomachs moving empty in their skins. China, Australia, crossing alps, walking cold," the houses altering block by block from grace to indigence as factories or storage-houses. Old grass lay dead under the lamp-posts here, and the ribbons of advertisements hung from the board fences by the yards. "This is the way things start, quiet and cold, as if there would never be any beginning."

"But what about tomorrow?" said something else. "What are you going to have to eat? What's going to happen then?"

Miss Fira and Miss Grusha had waited until now, until nine o'clock at night for their supper. When they heard Victoria's key in the lock Miss Fira came out of the ballroom with her lamb's wool on her shoulders and stood waiting in the hall. She was waiting when Victoria came in: the small, thin, bird-like woman holding her shawl at the neck with her frail, jewelled fingers, her hair licked up smooth from her forehead, her face sharply stricken with eagerness and the white-lipped smile she wore.

"Good evening," said Miss Fira uneasily. "I hope you will excuse me. My sister and I are from Petrograd. We knew the Romanoffs quite well."

28

She stood speaking, her hands moving nervously from shawl to skirt in haste, watching for some sign of gentleness in the tall girl's grave, unyielding face. "We had wished to ask you to tea," said Miss Fira, formally, "but we feared it might interfere with your day. It would be so pleasant if you would accept to dine."

Victoria took her cap off and put back her lock of hair. Miss Grusha came to the doorway of the room and took her place beside her sister. The same shy look of pride, and modesty, and fright was flickering quick as shallow water across their faces. Within her Victoria felt the movement of what had hardened in purpose and abstinence, shifting within its substance without alteration or advance.

"It's nice of you to want me," she said.

"Unfortunately," said Miss Grusha with a jerk of her head, "our cards are quite run out or we would have of course dropped them *chez vous* during the week. These French tradespeople!" she said, and she threw her hands up in a light gesture of despair. "I'm sure you'll find a difference in them too. At home things always went of their own accord, but here the tradesman who sees to our engraving has mislaid our plate! There's nothing we can do but just accept it."

Miss Fira turned her head sharply on her neck and fixed her sister in her quick, bead-like eye.

"As long as you told that," she said, "then I can tell about mother having tea with Oscar Wilde."

"You told about the Romanoffs," said Miss

Grusha faintly, putting her handkerchief against her fluttering lips. The two little women stood facing each other in the hallway, quivering in the cold.

"I thought you weren't going to be difficult any more?" said Miss Fira in soft aggrievement. "I haven't even mentioned Paderewski."

"But that's so short," said Miss Grusha. She spoke in a low, tremulous voice but her gaze did not fall before her sister's imperious eye. "He's nothing in comparison with the others."

"Remember, Grusha," said Miss Fira in rebuke, "you're speaking of one of father's greatest admirers." She dropped her hand open in appeal and turned to Victoria. "Do, please, come in," she said. Her eye turned sternly in rebuke upon her sister. "There's no reason to keep our guest waiting like this in the cold hall. Do come in. We're just ourselves this evening, so there is no necessity for you to change."

Victoria, with her cap in her hand, followed the two Russian women into the vast, fireless, lofty room.

"We're not allowed to cook here, of course," said Miss Fira with dignity, and Miss Grusha gave a scream of laughter.

"Oh, no, I should say not!" she cried. "Not a single thing!"

Miss Fira took Victoria's coat from her shoulders and, with no sign or look upon the shredded lining, laid it neatly down upon the bed. In the alcove to the back, Victoria saw the piano, up-

right, varnished yellow, with the score open across
its face. Miss Grusha had disappeared behind it,
and Miss Fira, holding her skirt up in one hand,
moved down the wide room towards it, conversing
with their guest and leading her by inference to the
alcove where the table was laid.

"Now do tell us what are your impressions of
Paris," she was saying, and they sat down a little
awkward in the uneased and seemingly unheeded
cold. Miss Grusha was humming in a vague high
singing-voice from where she was, and there came
as well from there the sound of dishes and the
smell of cooking food.

"Have you locked the door, Grusha?" said Miss
Fira, speaking in that kind, low, even tone the
gentry reserve for servants. Miss Grusha's voice
rose higher, wilder in song.

"I'll go and see," Victoria said. She stood up
quickly and went before she saw the look of anguish in Miss Fira's face.

"Oh, please, please, not our guest——" Miss
Fira said.

But Victoria had crossed the room, turned the
key in the lock of the ballroom doors and come
back to the table.

"It's a habit, you see," she said, smiling. "At
home I always did things for myself, and for other
people too because I was the youngest there."

"Oh, the Americans!" said Miss Fira, leaning
forward with her polite, quick laugh. "We've
seen so much of that, you know. Last year there
was a Spanish count upstairs, poor man. He had

once met some Americans and from them he had learned such useful things. He never had to ring for the servant to help him with his boots in the morning. It was quite a shock to us when he told us. In our country it is very improper for any one not a member of the family to speak before others of putting on or taking off an article of clothing."

"That isn't true," said Miss Grusha from behind the piano. "You'll have to forfeit."

An instant's conception of rebuke quivered on Miss Fira's face, and then she led the conversation off breathlessly again.

"The count was really delightful," she said. "It was such a comfort to meet some one of the same education, although he was quite penniless, poor man. You must never speak of him before the proprietress here. He was obliged to leave in the most distressing way. He had to climb out the window one night carrying his grip in his teeth ——"

"Like a St. Bernard," said Miss Grusha's voice.

"Of course, he hadn't paid his rent for months, and couldn't," said Miss Fira lightly. "So humiliating for him——"

"We haven't paid ours since last April," said Miss Grusha.

"We've often thought we'd like to make a change," Miss Fira added hastily, "but we've never quite made up our minds to it, and under the circumstances the proprietress wouldn't like to have us go." Suddenly Miss Fira leaned over the table, her eye lit with warning. "The servant's the one to watch," she said in a whisper. "She can see what's going on. The old woman hasn't seen for forty years."

"The last thing she saw struck her blind," said Miss Grusha, from behind the piano. "She saw Cécile Sorel in her mother's boudoir when she went in to kiss her father one morning."

Miss Fira began to quiver, in spite of herself, with laughter.

"Grusha made that up," she said. "It's amazing. She's read so much for her years that she doesn't remember what's really happened or what hasn't any more. Novels like *Madame Bovary*," said Miss Fira. "I don't think it's good for her. I tell Grusha that she's younger than me and it isn't the same thing. It might have some influence on her life."

There was a row of books across the mantelpiece.

"Now, there's Shaw," said Miss Fira, smiling politely. "He's just the wrong sort of writer for Grusha to read. Her mind is quite sharp enough as it is. Ladies, of course, lead a sheltered life at best and are not expected to take the same interest in economics as men. Are you a voracious reader, miss?"

"I prefer to ride horses," said Victoria. "Or to paint."

"Oh dear," said Miss Fira with an eager sigh, "we used to do so much painting when we were at home! We used to paint on china almost every

33   c

afternoon in the summer. Some time we'll have to open the boxes and show you the miniatures our mother did."

Miss Grusha came from behind the piano, bearing a small tray of dishes before her.

"There's very little," she said modestly. "In fact, there's scarcely anything. I hope you're not feeling exceptionally hungry. I did the best with what I had."

"It's a wonderful meal," said Victoria, standing up to help the shy, hesitant old lady set the dishes down. There were mashed potatoes, creamed cauliflower, a box of sardines with parsley laid like palms of homage on them, and one platter held the yellows of three fried eggs.

"Indeed, there was quite ample," said Miss Fira, rising quickly from her chair. "Unless something has happened to it."

"I've cooked it, that's all that's happened," said Miss Grusha, taking her place diffidently on the other side. "It always makes a difference."

"Grusha," said Miss Fira in cold, shaken outrage, "where are the whites of the eggs?"

Miss Grusha broke her bit of bread in two.

"These eggs came without them," she said.

"You see," said Miss Fira helplessly to Victoria, and she sat down suddenly in her chair.

"The eggs are good like this," said Victoria. "They're much better. I've known people who had to leave the table at the sight of the white of egg if it wasn't well done."

"It's very disconcerting," said Miss Fira in

34

chagrin, and she served Victoria to the vegetables.
"Of course, we always eat our most important
meal in the middle of the day."

"We each had an aspirin tablet and a glass of
water for lunch," said Miss Grusha, her eye on
Miss Fira helping herself to the sardines. Miss
Fira seized the dish of eggs and leaned politely
across the table to their guest.

"Are you interested in music, miss?" she said.

"You played Chopin the other night, the night
I came, didn't you?" said Victoria with the food
full in her mouth, and the colour ran up in Miss
Fira's face.

"Yes," she said in a whisper out of her throat.
A spasm of pain or despair or loneliness or love
suddenly screwed her face and passed. "Do you
—do you have to stay long here?" she said.

Food, said Victoria's blood, food chewed, swallowed, food diminishing on the plate, food taken
warm as liquor to the heart. She put her bread in
the egg and soaked the yellow up, eating, eating.
What's going to happen tomorrow, where will the
next meal be.

"I had a funny idea about Paris. I thought
people who spoke the language would find work
here," she said.

"My sister and I do work at times," said Miss
Fira, as if in understanding of the humility of it.
"Of course, it's not really work, for we wouldn't
dream of taking any recompense for it. We
address the notices for lectures and we fold the
programmes over. We have a great friend who is

35

quite a personality here. Perhaps you've heard of
Mr. Sorrel? He's an American too."

"Some people say he's an Arab," said Miss
Grusha, looking close at the plates for what there
might be left. "Whenever I've seen Americans
they always had their breeches on."

The plates went clean under their forks, and
Miss Fira said there was this difference, she said
Sorrel was an artist. She said he was a dancer, a
painter, a light shining somewhere in a window on
the other side of the trees. She said Sorrel's door
is never locked and anyone can go in and sit down
at the table. The hungry, the ill, the unhappy,
even the poor, poor things. He is always arrayed
in the cleanest, purest robes. He wears sandals in
every kind of weather, and still his feet are spot-
less. He upholds a tradition in his bearing. His
long white hair is kept as beautiful as silk. He is
so good that he smiles even when he sprains his
ankle. He says that in children there is the endless
recreation of the world.

"He took us to the cinema last summer," said
Miss Grusha. "We saw 'Shanghai Express'."
She stood up and stacked the plates one inside the
other. "He gave us ice-cream afterwards, too,"
she said, with her eyes bright. "Strawberry and
chocolate."

"He'll give you anything he has," said Miss
Fira, her lifted face saying rapture, rapture. "He
puts his arms around you like a shepherd when you
have gone a lifetime without the feel of it before."

"When we go there to work he gives us things

to eat sometimes," said Miss Grusha from behind
the piano. "He gave us chestnuts last week."

"Sorrel helps every one," said Miss Fira, speaking shyly to Victoria, as if fearing the implication.
"He helps them by giving work to them."

Victoria uncrossed her legs and reached into the
pocket of her jacket.

"Do you think Mr. Sorrel would have any work
for me?" she said. The words did not come easy
to her and she was smiling faint and high. "I had
an idea things would be cheaper here, food and
the rest of it." She took her hand from her pocket
and put two francs on the table. "I've got that
much left," she said.

CHAPTER FOUR

The house had been given them, given for a little while as things were given to the Sorrels: fame or followers or money or hard times. Nothing lasted, nothing endured too long or quite long enough for them. Whatever they had passed on and was forgotten in the life of the other thing that came to take its place. Even from the street, the house had its own disordered, improvident air. There were pieces of board and box and discarded pottery cast out on the winter stubble in the garden, and in the windows of the porch the blocked and painted stuffs were hanging as if nailed over provisionally against the weather. Even from the outside it could be seen that the house and its respect were making shift for the moment with the people who had settled in it, standing in cold and vacant confusion, a dismantled, disreputable caricature of what it once had been.

Miss Fira and Miss Grusha took Victoria in, leading her audaciously the way they knew so well. At the door they stopped, breathless with the sense of their possession of the right to open it and enter, glancing quickly at her face for the respect there

must be in it for their familiarity with Sorrel and
his ways.

"Perhaps I had better wait," Victoria began.
"Perhaps you had better speak of me first before
I go——"

But Miss Fira shook her head and smiled, and
the wrinkles ran up in her delicate skin.

"Come," she said in a whisper. She touched
Victoria's arm. "Come in," she said. "You will
see."

In the long, low, scarcely-lighted room, Sorrel
was leading the others in the dance, taking them
down the length of it from act to act in the physical
image of how a man who labours must, in deference to his muscle and bone, strike or fell or sow.
There was an endless weave of movement in the
room, a turning and leaping of many bodies in the
afternoon, but the only voice that spoke was Sorrel's, twanging thin and sharp through the beak
of his nasal arch.

"One, two, and—three!" said Sorrel, and the
young women, some with glasses on their noses
and some with their coloured beads forgotten on
their necks, and the bare-limbed, thin young men
in their tunics leapt in confusion in the dim, un-
carpeted room. At the far end stood a glass-house
built, in the tenancy of other people, for the win-
tertime of plants, but now it held the frames on
which the colony wove and painted cloth. The
walls of the room were hung with Sorrel's posters,
bold in a few strong colours: the bodies of
men with sinews and dark-burned limbs planting

the earth or hewing trees or breaking fallow ground.

"One, two, and—three!" said the brassy, high, mid-western twang. Wearing a white tunic that came to his knees, Sorrel leapt agilely from one movement to the next. His hands and feet were small and finely made, certain and clean, and his pure hair was turned up from the neck and bound with a white cord across his brow. The sinew ran thin and knotted under his skin as he danced alive and separate from the others, as a farmer might leap human and lean through rows of man-high corn.

"One, two, and—three!" cried the voice of Sorrel in the voice of a farmer starved strident and wild in the west, leaping bewitched through his wind-crazed, monstrous crops.

Some of the women had left their jewellery on despite their Grecian tunics, and some of the men had no hair on their heads and watches on their wrists. Only in Sorrel's body was there a frenzy and delight, a knowing, scribe-like set of face and neck unshaken as he led the others down the room. A woman in a long grey robe stood by a gong at the door and struck the time with a hammer. A white cloth was laid over her head and pinned close around her full, pink cheeks, like the head-gear of a nun. Behind it fell to the corded girdle, seemingly concealing the lengths of her undone hair.

So the gong struck in keeping with Sorrel's voice, and he danced with a faint, thin smile on his face, an exaltation which gave him the look of a

divine. He might have been a preacher exhorting
his people, calling in this way on them because the
ways of speech had failed; and so might this place
have been the temple to which he drew them, wilfully blind to their shortcomings, wilfully deaf to
what they spoke in sin. There was no impatience
in his eye, for he did not seem to see them. He
made the design of action in precision before
them, without rebuke, and they cast about behind
in chaos for the grace and fervour to subdue their
unexpected limbs.

"One, two, and—three!" said Sorrel, and the
others sprang and turned in their uncouth, scare-
crow dance.

There were thirty people or more moving in the
room, men and women whoever they were, followers in tunics or office-workers come there on Sunday afternoon for the sight of his exaltation and the
different sound of what he would say. All week
they had enough of what they did, come out of
shops or factories for a taste of what was high and
clear as mountain air, of what was art and of what
was expression of the uncompromising, uncorrupted soul.

There was one among them who danced in his
short rose tunic, his limbs as thick and muscular as
boughs, his hair spread out on his head like a bush
stripped bare of leaf or promise. His neck sat short
and wide on his naked shoulders, rooted close in
the flesh of them, and the head of dry, wild curls
stood wide from his little face. Perhaps he had
been intended for height, but he had grown

dwarfed from his own great physical might. His
soft brown eyes as he skipped were fixed on the
women dancing, but he himself could hardly move
for the muscles that cramped his legs and arms.
He was so narrow he could have been put in a
Christmas stocking with his head left sticking
out the top; he had such a small, evil face with the
soft eyes lolling in it that he would have frightened
even the saints of that time of year away.

"That is Peri, the Greek man," whispered Miss
Fira.

"Come in, come in!" Sorrel called out to them
when he saw them in the door. But in his eagerness for something else, for the sermon he was
stepping out or the vision of where this dance
would take them, he looked through and beyond
the sight of any people. With all the room in action about him, he seemed to dance alone, remote
as a smiling, pure eagle perched high in his belief
in rock and air and sky.

"Come in, come in!" he called through his eagle-
beak, and behind him the congregation danced
like people drunk or dazed. And now the woman
in the long grey dress left the gong she was striking and came into the dance. As if she could bear
no longer the unsightly leaping of the shapeless
men and women, she undid the white cloth from
her hair, unloosed her girdle, and came into the
measure of Sorrel's voice.

"Dance, dance, and—dance!" she cried in time
with him. "Watch Sorrel, *tout le monde*! Try to do
that way!"

"That is Matilde, the witch," said Miss Fira behind her muff, and the two little Russian women made sour mouths at each other.

It was then that the children of the place came and stood silent in the other doorway, stood in their shaggy tunics watching the sombre, dark-eyed, dark-legged men jumping to the count of Sorrel's voice, and the lean, the fat, bespectacled women with bracelets on their arms or beads around their necks, their hair in artificial waves or not, their limbs tied fast with veins, their tunics long or short on their bare legs, dancing, losing the way again and again and turning in confusion, dancing, slipping, seeking the way to go. The tallest little girl had straight hair to her shoulders; her face was Matilde's or was not, and she, like Sorrel, was elegantly made. She wore on her mouth a faint perhaps Sorrel-seeming grin of youth and hardihood, and her bones were neatly set together. There was her face, impish and without illumination, watching with no tremor, no sign of trepidation or reflection, no mark of thought or thinking, like a wild cub's face set handsomely with jauntiness and greed.

The children too came into the dance, into the straight, queer, leaping movement in the room. Their faces were as poor and thin as old men's faces, their hair, the boys and girls alike, smacking in long, darkish braids on their backs, their thin legs making no sense of the direction. The four small children jumped on their bare, soiled feet among the others dancing in the cold; they did not laugh, having survived without it, but took their places gravely in the gigantic ritual of despair. The tall little girl closed her eyes tight, and her joints went loose and limber as she danced, her arms hung down, swinging brown and lean between her naked legs. Her feet in their sandals stepped, not Sorrel's dance, paying no heed to it nor to the time he counted, but shook the Charleston out from one knee to the other, fast and wild.

"Talanger!" said Matilde, the witch, pink-cheeked in her undone gown. "Talanger, do it, do it as Sorrel does it! Come here beside me! One, two, and—three!"

Into the room from the other side danced Mistinguette, or who might have been, her hair yellow and curled from the top of her head, her short nose white, her legs high-calved and delicate lifted on patent-leather heels, her mouth red, her nails varnished, dancing with the skirt of her dress held out and her silk knees coming out from under. She wore diamonds on her fingers and in her ears, the tops of her breasts said *bon soir* to the place. Her eyes were fast on her high-heeled feet below her, moving quick, moving fast, her eyes down under her lids with a row of artificial lash planted like pine-trees black across them, dancing in and out through the tunics, in and out, her upper lip humorous enough for a white moustache of powder to lie along it, out and in, her legs like a girl's in beauty, her bosom swelling towards forty, her flesh white and farded, rich with the opaque surface and smell that is borne away from the stage.

44

After her out from the hall came a fat man dancing, patent-leather shoes on his suave, quick feet,
a watch-chain over his stomach, apoplexy blooming in his cheeks; he was wearing a small greying
cap of neatly-brushed and well-oiled hair. His
cuffs were clean in his good, grey sleeves, his collar
white, his cuff-links emerald. Out over the boards
he came, dancing, dancing, moving his well-kept
hands in his cuffs, his feet slipping shiny, supple
and long. He had a gold-linked bracelet hanging
loose around one hairy wrist.

"Edmond!" called out Mistinguette, richly,
sweetly, watching her silk knees moving to the
sound of Sorrel's and the sound of Matilde's voice.

"Estelle!" called out the Frenchman, dancing
quickly through the dancers. The blood was high
in his face, his neck was full to bursting with it.
He was smiling, a gold tooth showing on each side
under his greying, clipped moustache. She was
dancing now in front of Sorrel, her legs in their
close, light silk kicking, and Edmond wove swiftly
through the others, through the office-workers,
the children, the shop-girls in their tunics, his
paunch like a dove's breast out before him, dancing to where she was.

"One, two, and—three!" Matilde cried out as
if in protest to the others, and the men and the
women in their tunics flung themselves forward
and cast their invisible discs away.

"One, two, and—three!" said Sorrel, his thin-
lipped smile given to Estelle and Edmond who
came from two sides on him and took him by the

hands. Around they went with him, with Estelle's laughter held and shaken clear as water on her tongue. Around they went, with Sorrel crying soft, breathless yipes of laughter, his short skirt flying, and the Frenchman's jowls went dark with the pleasure of his blood.

"One, two, and—three!" cried Matilde, having no time for them, and the room in movement quivered and reared with broken steps and sound. The laughter shook so fast from the Frenchwoman's mouth that Miss Fira and Miss Grusha put the curls of their little black muffs to their faces to hide their gaping jubilance lest it should betray too much of them.

"Come in, come in!" cried Sorrel, gasped Sorrel, blew Sorrel in the high wind of their passing. He seized Victoria's hand as they spun by. The Frenchman opened his round, voluptuous hand and gathered Miss Grusha in, and Estelle's jewelled fingers closed on the short, black cotton glove that covered Miss Fira's hand. The black muffs went flying captive on the cords around their necks, their boas rode across their shoulders, and the pins fell singly from their neatly fastened hair. There was no breath left to them, only a fluttering sense of life that might have been ravishment and might have been protest for the dignity they bore.

In a moment, Sorrel broke away and fell back, shaking his head in exhaustion, and wiping the tears of laughter from his eyes. He had eyes like a woman's, green and wondrously lashed, and the care of himself was loving and dramatic, like a woman's care. He had a fresh blooming skin and his hair was undisturbed, still bound as smooth as milk around his head.

"Oh dear, oh dear, oh dear," he said with a deep sigh of laughter. He still held Victoria's hand in his and the callouses were set like medals in the cushions of his palm.

The whole room had stopped its movement now, and the people sat at rest on the dark wood benches or on the rugs rolled up against the walls. Estelle had lifted her good, silk dress and was fanning her neck and her face with its skirt, and Edmond was mopping his forehead dry. Only the look of censure and question stood in Matilde's face, on the flat Slavic cheeks, in the untended, hanging hair; the broad mouth ready to say it to Victoria before Miss Fira said:

"Oh, Mr. Sorrel, do excuse me. This is Victoria John."

The half-naked, laughing old man took both Victoria's hands and shook them.

"You know, it's very nice of you to come," he said. His green and miraculously lashed eyes were level with her own, looking in some kind of tenderness and helplessness upon her, but remotely, impersonally looking, as if into the memory of what had once happened somewhere else or beyond it into the vision of what might be.

"If you will help me make the fire, Victoria," he said. "Then we can all sit down and Matilde will let us have some cake and tea."

CHAPTER FIVE

Sorrel was talking, speaking out of other things that had taken place elsewhere, looking into the last of the fire in the evening and speaking, not of the colony, but of mountains in America, wildernesses he had gone through, red-beaked, his cheeks weathered. He did not say any names she knew: not Matilde, nor Talanger, nor Estelle, as if they had come a long time after and were only what was left to him, and these others were the people of his blood.

They had gone on small, wild Indian horses, and the sound and smell of these horses was there but not the sound of any one sleeping in the Neuilly house. They had gone back, seeking a river's source, and from them he had learned the weave of their cloth, and the language, and the rain and the crop dances, and the festivals of fire at night. Knowing that people of identical will take of themselves identical direction, he had no word to mar them, not colony, or group, or tribe, speaking of their ways until what they were opened into the deep-throated thunder of woods and wind in the autumn, the copper and yellow seen and the crab-apples, and the winds blaring out a silence as rich as late October clouds.

She could see the history well when he talked, for they had come from the same country and the words they used were the same. He might have been saying: do not see this house, do not see the people in it, but he used other words to say it. Rooms aren't any good to you, he said, because there have been too many people in them, but there are other places. He sat warming his bare feet at what was left of the fire, speaking of the way he had gone with the Indians last night or the night before, as if implicating her in some way with what had passed. He spoke of the Indian skins and the hard bread made, but he was saying other things entirely, looking straight into the little light of the fire with his empty cheek seen and the granite jut of his nose. He was saying: believe in me, not because of the things I have now but for the things I had before, believe in me. He did not ask this, but in his speech he was resurrecting it for her, scarcely knowing that he was speaking perhaps or knowing to whom he spoke.

The rugs in the house and the press and the block-prints even had all been made in other countries. They belonged to islands or to hills and to a different temper, for all of them had been made in the time of his youth. And now he was casting back to the time that had shaped him lean, swift, wiry, quick as a cat on the balls of his feet. His voice was strong as a young man's voice still, and his limbs were firm and bare and filled with blood in the cold. But there was another thing, like a veil of gentleness drawn about him, and this must not have masked his will when he was young.

For awhile he had lived in Cyprus, and his wife danced there at night, and the people came and learned their dances. The rocks that went down to the water were grey, and the maquis grey on the island, and the leaves of the olive-trees grey with a wash of life rippling over them like a tide. He had taken the oil from the olives, working day after day with the people, bringing the restlessness he had to the wide, unhastening, almost-halted stream of their advance. He had the sharp, hard bones of north-Indian people, and he moved quickly. The sun of that island and the goat-milk and oil laid rich, golden flesh over the natives' bones, but it gutted him empty. It drew his skin tight from joint to joint and dried coarse as a horse's tail the long, unbound black hair. When he left the place, he took nothing at all of it with him. He might have been coming back from Arizona for all the twang of his voice or the way he walked had changed.

But what of now, here, now, Paris, the people who go soft as moths through the rooms, and this house held together by the sound of your talking, Sorrel? Whether she said this or whether the quality of her listening altered, the old man looked around suddenly, startled out of the place where he had been. *Now?* If she had spoken it would have been like a blow to him. Now was the time that he did not want to remember. He had ceased talking, but something like a hand was lifted in defence in him, as if to stave off what questions she might think or say. He sat in dignity before the almost-extinguished ash, his arms at rest, the veins in his bare arms outstanding in relief, his toes bound to the leather soles laid straight and even on the unswept hearth. Because of all he had said, the blood and the identity were drained from the people who slept at night in his house; for him they were not the living, and in a little while they no longer lived for the one who listened to the long, fervently-told and quietly-told history that was less the story of one man than the tracing backwards of a people, following them through the poverty of houses, streets, towns, settlements, the unfertility of lands, the wilderness, in search of what came singly from a source of stern and uncorrupted race.

He faced her a moment in perplexity, suddenly stricken it might have been by the suspicion that she had not listened artlessly to him. As if for the first time it seemed to come to him that she was only a stranger brought in by the Russian sisters one afternoon. She had helped him build the fire, sat down to supper with them, and stayed on through the evening, but in a little while she might get up and put her coat on and go, bearing with her the silence of disparagement and ridicule because he had talked to her in words of the dead, out of the death of his own youth and love for places he had moulded with his hand.

But Victoria heard her own voice speaking.

"If you would like to have me here, Sorrel," she said, "what kind of work could I do?"

"You don't know yet whether you'd fit here," he said in a minute. He looked back in the ashes. "Things like food to be cooked, dishes to wash." The tall trees of America were no longer there, but he wanted to speak the truth to her. "There's a shop in town where we sell our sandals and tunics," he said, smiling a little grievously at the thought of himself a commercial man now after what he had been. "We have to work every day of the year, you see."

His face was thin, Indian-boned, rugged, and suddenly his mouth turned up in it, stretched crescent-like in his cheeks as if he were chewing back the tears in his jaw. But he wanted nothing given in haste and then taken back again. There had been too many ready, too much offered by others, and taken away again as quickly if the food got scarce or the weather turned too cold.

"The door into the street there," said Sorrel, "is always open. Whoever wants can come right in and sit down with us, like you sat down tonight at the table. Whoever works here, we don't judge and we don't deny them."

But there was another thing: he had seen so many of them, girls giving their good clothes away and coming here to wear tunics and sandals, young girls like this one, believing in another name for it than what it was.

"We work," he said again, and suddenly he reached out and took Victoria's hand hard and quick in his fingers. The tears had come out on his lashes and were hanging perilous there. "Doing it day after day seems to take the art right out of it for most," he said, and his Adam's apple rode up and down in his neck. "It's only afterwards you can see what we're doing has any beauty and creation."

They heard the soft passage of a woman's feet on the stairs, and Sorrel let drop Victoria's hand and sat back on his bench and wiped his eyes in the edge of his robe. When Matilde came into the room, he looked around at her, smiling.

"Victoria wants to come and work with us," he said.

"Work with us?" said Matilde. She sat down with them, her feet unclean and bare, her cheeks rosy; she was eating apricots, the dried, leathery bits of them, out of a paper-bag in her hand. "You have to be prepared," she said, speaking her English with an accent. A small, askant, almost contemptuous smile was on her mouth as she chewed. "You haven't read Sorrel's books yet or heard him lecture. When you come here it's just as serious as taking the veil," she said. She looked at Victoria sitting across from her in the lamplight. "There's nothing like high heels or lipstick here," she said, and Victoria thought of Estelle for an instant, and put it aside in silence again. "We don't eat meat or drink alcohol." Matilde put another apricot in her mouth. "You might think yourself too fine to do the kind of work we do."

Her eyes were round and blameless, and she

seemed to be speaking only in guidance to Victoria; but still it was there, unmistakable, a contempt and a belligerence in the chew of her obstinate, full face.

"Too fine!" said Victoria. She took out her handkerchief and drew it across her mouth. "Look," she said. "Lipstick comes off. It's just that I feel —I feel I've lived like a coward when I hear the things Sorrel has done."

The wide, plump woman sat ungirdled in her gown, chewing slowly, ruminating, her bland eyes slowly examining Victoria: Matilde, the woman of the house, seeing at once the whole landscape of what had happened in other years, the history of betrayals, thefts, disloyalties. It was there in her face that she wanted no more followers for that; her blood moved savage and slow and dumb in her to protect him from what they could do. The sweet, fresh faces of young girls and all their eagerness and instability promised, she had seen enough of them; they came under the roof in the name of romance and they destroyed whatever else there was because they could not recognize it there.

"I've always worked hard," said Victoria. "I'm not afraid of that. I can paint, and type, and do my share of everything that has to be done."

"There's the shop," said Matilde, slowly, bitterly ruminating in her flesh. "You could work there, and we could give you your meals and a little money besides. But not to sleep here," she said firmly, closing the paper-bag over. "Not at once, anyway, until you were certain and until you could accept the philosophy of life that the others do."

Sorrel did not speak again, but when he turned his head and looked at Victoria there was a shyness in his face, an uneasiness that she had recognized the utter speechlessness of the rôle he was now made to play. His eyes were clear as lakes, and beauteously fringed, but loneliness or hopelessness or fright twisted his face into a small voice crying out in silence: Victoria, I am an old man lost among peasants, French shop-girls, vaudeville artists, Greeks come out of their own country kicking their heels up in a strange land. Nobody that was there is here now, or knows the tune of Waal I'll be switched the hay ain't pitched or the sound of thunder in the Alleghenies. Victoria, Victoria, said the sound of his face over and over until she got up to go.

She did not look again at Matilde when she shook her hand, but to Sorrel she said:

"I will come, if you want me, and I'll stay as long—as long as we believe in each other."

She put her cap on and shook hands with them, and she went back across the road in the dark to the house where her room was. There was no light in any window, but from her bed she could hear the little Russian women crying out with the dreams that pursued them even in their sleep.

CHAPTER SIX

It was the custom from the beginning that one of the children, one of the small four children or the tall girl, Talanger, should go with the shopkeeper to the city in the Mètro every morning and help mind the shop all day. This gave them young a sense of the opposition and repugnance of life, Matilde said; it gave them the sight of butcher-shops with the meat hanging in them, and women in the streets wearing fur coats on their backs. Matilde pointed out the fresh meat on the hooks, saying: "Look, children, there are people who eat dead animals!" "Like scavengers!" said Talanger in derision. But they were hungry after every meal they had, and they used to sit on the bench by the shop-window sucking their long braids and watching the well-dressed people pass.

There was no explanation made of the children's being, of how they had come to the colony or why they were growing up there. There was no centre from which they moved or to which they returned in the evening: Hippolytus, Prosperine, Athenia, and Bishinka did not lift their voices but lived as if with a weight of inexistence on them, like unbe-

gotten children, living in the abyss of still unbroken sleep. The words mother and father were
never used in Sorrel's house, and only at night
when the children returned tired did they go near
to the two women who slept in the room beside
them, the two be-tunicked women, the one French,
the other Italian, who painted the colours on the
scarves all day. Only if the dinner were late, or
they felt the cold, did the children go into the
glass-house where the women worked and stand
by the high stools, waiting there in patience as if
some acknowledgement would come, as if some
comfort must be given. Or they went quietly and
stood by Peri as he cut the shape of sandals from
the broad, tough sheets of leather; standing quiet
by Peri whom they did not call father, and by
Gabrielle and Cina who had as mothers perhaps
shared the Greek man's substance between them
year by year.

There is nothing left of the stairway up to the
loft in back, nor the beams, nor the bell that rang
upstairs whenever the door opened in from the
street below. People walked close to the shop-
window's glass, handsomely dressed because of
the quarter, and the traffic passed one way in endless dignity and hush because of the embassy on
the other side. But behind in the alley, set in green
stone and slime as rich as a jungle pool's, stood
the depths of the beauteous cabinay. Once in a
while a wagon drove down the street in the early
morning, and the boa-constrictor it carried was
uncoiled to suck out the mysteries of that dark,

unfathomed cave. But whatever happened in the rear of the place, still the clothed and the fed went stepping by at the front, looking for idle things in the windows.

The sight of Miss Fira and Miss Grusha running quickly along as if in fright was a strange thing among the furs and the limousines and the slow-stepping people on a winter afternoon. It was marked in terror on their faces that they scarcely expected to get safely back to Neuilly again that night. Talanger opened the door for them, humming lackadaisical, moving her brown, lean legs to the weary singing sound.

They took off their coats in the shop at once and shook them out as if they had come a long way in bad weather, in an open sleigh with a white bear robe over their knees, maybe, in the teeth of a blinding storm. They did not come singly in, for all of their ancestors came breathless into the place with them, lace handkerchiefs out at their cuffs and brooches pinned on their bosoms: all the ladies in high-necked shirtwaists and pompadours and ostrich feathers in their hats who had sat down to tea with Father Rasputin of an afternoon in Moscow; ladies who had never believed in the plague, or in carcasses of cattle lying, dry as parchment, for miles across a drought-desiccated land.

Now they were safe behind the plate-glass window, the lot of them, greeting Victoria in a little flurry of conversation, touching Talanger under her impudent chin or the locks of her straight, untangled hair. Victoria had made tea on the gas-ring in the loft, and buttered bread for them, and they sat down on the poets' benches, their eyes sharp, for all the delicacy of Miss Fira's conversation, on the number of slices each one might have.

"Of course, *she*," said Miss Fira, speaking in English with a slight gesture of her head towards Talanger soaking her bread in her cup, "belongs to the witch woman. I don't want to mention any names."

"There was quite a scandal," said Miss Grusha, picking the crumbs up from her plate on the ends of her fingers and putting them between her teeth.

"The man you've seen wearing the hair helmet," said Miss Fira, avoiding the sound of the disciple's name. "I'm sure you know whom I'm referring to. He and the witch-woman were man and wife in Poland. *Peasants*. Estelle and Edmond heard the whole story from him."

Talanger reached for the platter of bread and butter, but Miss Grusha was the quicker.

"Our father, *à propos*," said Miss Fira, lightly stirring the sugar in her cup, "never approved of what Nijinsky did to dancing."

"He had a screw loose," said Miss Grusha with her mouth full.

"Not father," said Miss Fira in rebuke. She turned with her smile to Victoria again. "I was referring to the Tartar. He took the jump right out of St. Petersburg. Our father used to say he did it as propaganda. It gave every capital in the world the most garbled view of Russia. All the peasants began putting on airs about it, the way your negroes began acting once they had the vote. The man," said Miss Fira, lowering her voice suggestively, "in the hair helmet came of a Russian family. He and his wife," she said, and she cleared her throat, "left Poland for the sake of 'The Dance'."

"Sorrel's wife used to trip them up if she ever caught them dancing," said Miss Grusha with a cry of laughter.

"She didn't get on with the witch," said Miss Fira, leaning towards Victoria over her cup of tea. "The two of them joined the colony and Sorrel's wife soon saw which way the wind was blowing. No woman had ever come between them before. The man in the hair helmet went to Russia for a year, and the witch took a new place in the house. She began giving orders to every one else, it seemed, because she and Sorrel were going to have a child. *This*," said Miss Fira, with a jerk of her head, "was the one." Talanger, her long, slim, hairless legs crossed over, was eating bread and butter and reading the *Catholic World*.

"Sorrel's wife turned the lot of them out," said Miss Grusha, rocking her black silk elbows in her hands. "She'd had enough by that time."

"The house was hers," said Miss Fira, firmly. "Given her by a duke."

"When they left," said Miss Grusha, "they took the bathtub with them."

In her eagerness to say it first, Miss Fira could not say it all at once. Her bright, fanatic eye rolled wildly at Miss Grusha.

"Sorrel's wife was having lunch with the President of the Republic," Miss Fira said.

"She was his mistress," said Miss Grusha.

"Grusha just made that up," Miss Fira whispered, wild and shrill. She could have struck the other one in her distraction. "She was a great artist. She never mixed in politics. My sister's thinking of Kshessinskaya."

"I'm thinking of the chocolate éclairs Sorrel gives the women for tea on Wednesdays," Miss Grusha said.

"There's more bread and butter in the loft," Victoria said. "Sit still, little ones, and I'll bring it down."

In the room over the shop were the dark benches along the rafters, and the gas-ring waiting, and the folded wool-hides dyed black or orange, worn and unclean from the exhaustion of people who had lain down on them at night here or in other countries; there was the mirror with the tall, young girl facing her in it, the box of paints and the easel by the low window, there was the bread to be cut and the butter in its paper, and the question lying like a ring of breath on the tall glass, asking what am I here for, what am I doing here? It was sharp as the bite of the paints laid scarce and neat in the paint-box and the painting itself set up on the easel, asked not in panic but in warning to dereliction or evasion. Then she cut the bread thin and spread the butter on it, and went down the spiral stairs again, feeling her way in the dark.

"Sorrel's wife was too good," said Miss Fira, wiping the tea from her lip. "Every one who saw her dance left the theatre crying, and she had a heart of gold."

"The witch would have cut that out of her too if she'd had the chance," said Miss Grusha. "As it was, she went away and died."

"She went away and gave them a day to clear out of the house," said Miss Fira. "So the witch went through every room and took the things she wanted. They took the tub out of the bathroom and they didn't turn the water off so the place was flooded and the ceiling fell in the salon when she came home in the evening."

"They've got the tub out in the backyard now in Neuilly," Miss Grusha said. "Sorrel wanted it to grow corn on the cob in. He said they ate it in America. And the witch wanted it to dye the scarves in."

"She gets whatever she wants in the end," said Miss Fira, her voice almost extinguished by the fear of whoever might be listening, her eyes sharp for the sight of whoever might be spying into the be-draped, quiet room. Behind them was the plate-glass window and the wintry look of people going by in the twilit street. "No one else has any say about it. Not even Sorrel. In a few months she got the man in the hair helmet back, had him come running back from Russia to save any look of scandal when the baby was born."

"He came back twelve years ago, that was," said Miss Grusha, eating. "And he's never opened his mouth to the witch or to Sorrel."

"He doesn't believe in a communal life," said Miss Fira. "He believes in individualism."

"Anyway, he won't clean out the water clo," said Miss Grusha with a snort of triumph. "That's one thing the witch can't make him do."

The furtive duet of their telling had ceased now, and these things Victoria heard as if they had been spoken not for the explanation of people they sought to make, but only for the lifting of two voices that had waited a long time in silence to perform. Whatever they said of Sorrel was a defence of love they made to save for themselves his purity. Out of their own virgin infatuation for his sainthood there came a delirium of blame on the woman who was close to him as they could never be. If there was truth in everything they told, there was truth too in their poverty: only the wealth of Sorrel's voice or the majesty of his presence, barebrowed, slightly bewildered in his white dress in a room, restored them to promise and impunity.

"When Sorrel's wife was alive," said Miss Fira in a moment, "there was always real linen on the table and her family silver. Everything was neat and clean as a pin."

Talanger stood up and closed the Catholic paper and slipped it under the sheep's hide rug that lay on the poets' bench. Matilde came into the shop sometimes toward evening, and she must not see it. Talanger stood stretching before the long mirror on the wall, her bare, slim arms out, her tunic lifted above her small, child knees, her mouth open in a yawn. She was all of one colour, pure and smooth and straight, as if whittled out of a single end of ash.

"Oh, my lovely one," she said softly, carelessly to the glass, speaking in French but with the accent that Matilde's language had given her. "Oh, child of Jesus, exquisite beyond all things, the spirit of the divine Father is in thy face."

Slowly, with her arms hanging lifeless, her shoulders drooping, she began to dance before the length of the mirror. Her eyes were half-closed in her short, golden face, as if she were near to swooning; her bare feet moved languidly in their sandals on the floor. Slowly she began, but her feet moved faster, her head hung lower, the hair swinging thick and straight from side to side. Her thin legs bent at the knee, went loose with it, her lips parted, and out from under the soles of her feet the Charleston went flying, faster and faster. The blood came into her Mongol face and stood high on her cheek-bones, burning.

"I'm hungry," she said. She stopped and looked at Victoria. "Is there any cheese left upstairs?"

Miss Fira had risen and was putting her black coat on. She tied the boa at her neck, straightened the veil under her chin; bridling with preparation, she pulled her black cotton gloves to her wrists and snapped them fast.

"We've such a way before us," she said, with an artificial little flight of laughter, "I do think we'd better be starting."

As if they would not sleep in the same house that night with only a wall between them, Victoria shook their hands and said :

"You must come and see me again very soon."

"That's very kind of you," said Miss Fira, " but we do feel it's an intrusion on you. There's so little respect left now in the world for the work-ing-hours of an artist. New régimes," she said significantly, and she sighed.

"I wasn't painting when you came," Victoria said. She went to the door with them. "The light goes so early now."

"Oh, dear me, of course!" laughed Miss Fira. Suddenly her teeth struck together as the blast of air from the street smote her face. "Good-bye, good-bye," she cried, shaking, "don't stand here and catch cold, my child! Do run in quickly! Come, Grusha!" she said.

Miss Grusha followed her sister slowly out into the winter evening. Her gloved hand, trembling, held the black boa closed at her throat. She looked in timorous, wild hope at Victoria.

"There wasn't any cheese left, was there?" she said.

CHAPTER SEVEN

Sorrel's room stood at the top of the house in the sun, if there would ever again be sun, and he had white-washed the walls fresh and set down on the clean floor-boards the rugs in rich-coloured wools that he had woven in Cyprus. His paintings stood against the walls, still with some unpainted portions in them, as if he were almost ready to get to work at them again, next week perhaps, or when the spring came, or at some other time. He slept on a black wood bench at night with a cover of sheepskins stitched together laid over him. His silk tunics and those of finer wool were laid away in a chest.

Matilde's room was across the landing, but her door was kept closed on whatever the wintry light might show. When she came out from her room, she came in haste on her sandalled feet and shut the door at once behind her on the slice visible of nameless, articled confusion. Orange-skins, soiled tunics, paper-bags of dried fruit, old newspapers from Poland and Russia piled in the same stained disorder as lay beneath her hair-kerchief and hair and hung in the long, impure-seeming, greyish tunics which darkened at the hem.

66

On the second floor, Talanger and the four small children slept on sheepskins that were laid down at night upon the unswept boards; Cina and Gabrielle shared the small room next to it, sleeping on the box-springs of a double bed, covered with blankets Sorrel had brought back from Mexico. Only in Sorrel's room had any effort at cleanliness and order been made. Everywhere else there was the bleak and absolute confusion of what unfurnished, unheated, untended refuge nomads might have stopped in for a time. The two men of the colony, Peri, the Greek, and Arthur, with his helmet woven of coarse, auburn hair, slept in the glass-house room on poets' benches, their locks long, their eyes sharp, like dogs asleep but still alert for love or danger, lying prostrate under their sheep's wool at night.

By the door into the glass-house a photograph was hung: it was the picture of a strong, full-fleshed woman in a Grecian tunic. Her head was small above her flesh, gentle and neatly done, and her round, bare arms were open. She stood tall and lovely with her arms stretched out from the picture, and under it her own hand had written: "I would teach the whole world to dance!"

Victoria stood a long time on Sunday morning looking at the photograph of Sorrel's dead wife. Whatever they were, they had been that thing together, and when she was dead it left room for the other things to come: the cobwebs across the corners, and the dishes piled up in their filth and waste in the kitchen; the cold slipping ice-white under the doors, marching strong as an army through the windows to the flesh and bone and marrow that survived in squalor there.

Sorrel came running downstairs, running quick and silent on his sandals. He was wearing a long brown dress, like a monk's frock, and a dusting of black lay all over his dress and flesh. He had tied a cloth over his hair to save it from the soot, and his teeth were white in his face when he smiled.

"Hello, darling," he said, and he held his hands up and away to show her the black dust of coal that was on them. "You see, I've been cleaning the stove-pipe out," he said with a laugh. The sweet, guileless clarity of exaltation was shining in his eyes. He was careful to touch nothing in the long Sunday dancing-room, keeping himself in his frock and his cloth from the draperies and posters, from the benches, or from coming too close to Victoria. He moved delicately, as if to soil nothing with his dust, but the corners were piled high with the dust of months of dancing, and plates from dinner the night before stood still among the blocks and papers. But as if he did not see these things were so and must spare the immaculate room, he went directly to the chimney, the laughter never quite ended in his throat, his Adam's apple dancing with it, and entered the ashes of the fireplace on his hands and knees.

"No one," he said in his brief, dry voice from the darkness where he was, "is willing to go into things right from the ground up. I'm one of these guys who likes to see the innards of things." His feet in their sandals came out backwards across the hearth. "There isn't a mite of reason," he said as he sat down in the grate, "why my stove upstairs shouldn't be pulling like a house a-fire. My pipe goes up this chimney. There isn't anything to hinder."

He clasped his hands around his knees in his dress and sat there in bewilderment a moment, his head-cloth over his hair, his beak knife-thin over his smile.

"I don't know anything about Timbuctoo," he said, "and I don't know a darned thing about heaven. I've never been to either of them. That's what I tell 'em," he said to Victoria, or to the room, or to the vision of his own self in the direction he was going. "People come here," he said, and the chuckle began to shake in his lean neck again, "leave their families or their businesses or their husbands or their wives, and then the truth comes out! They've come here looking for God! That's what they come to me for! My dear, dear children, I say to them, I don't know anything about the poor old fellow. God, I say to them, why, there's more God in a dish of stewed prunes than in any book that's ever been written about him. But people, you see, my dear girl, they don't want stewed prunes instead of God. They've had stewed prunes ever since they were born, so when they grow up they want something new."

In the cold room Victoria kept her coat but-

69

toned over, but Sorrel sat scarcely clothed on the hearth, his bare arms clasping his knees in his loose, woollen dress, his face dark as a turtle's with soot, with no thought for the cold.

"Because I'm happy," he said, grinning tight and thin, "people think I must have something new. That's why they come here," he said, and before her his green, womanly eyes were swimming away in fear. Coming after me when I'm old, picking at what I've got, asking me questions. Nobody bringing anything, but coming for what they can take away. "And after a while they go off again, angry with me, oh yes, darling, mad as hatters with me because I didn't give them what they came for!" He shook his head back and forth under the cloth and the laughter sighed out of his lean, lipless mouth. "Oh dear, how angry they get with me!" he laughed. "Why, one young woman went flouncing off because I wouldn't take the time to talk my philosophy to her for fifteen minutes a day! Philosophy? I told the poor dear, why, just look around the room here. Look at those panels over there!" Sorrel turned on the hearth and threw one hand out towards his paintings unrolled monstrous on the walls. "Do you think Donatello took the time off to explain how one bone meets another, how the shoulder's made for carrying, and the hand's made for giving shape to things?" He lifted his eager, exalted face towards Victoria. "Oh dear," he said, "it's so tiresome! Every one blind and every one idle. One young man I told to get inside the chimney. You just keep looking up long enough, I told him, and you're sure to see God peeking down over the top at you!" His voice rose with his laughter in delight. "Oh, they don't know what they want," he said. "They don't know what they want."

Beyond in the kitchen the stove was standing black and burdened in the corner, piled up with the dishes left from two meals, and wigged with long black curls of grease. Out to the front of the house where the hand-press stood on the covered porch, the tables were lost under the litter of blocks and lead and the scattered alphabet and the red and yellow posters they had made too many of and cast aside. Except for the children running overhead, there was no sign of life or movement in the house.

"What about lunch?" said Victoria. "I might wash a few dishes as long as nobody else is."

Sorrel looked up at her, startled, drawing the veil of soft bright bewilderment and pain across his eyes.

"Dishes?" he said vaguely. He looked towards the kitchen. "Oh, it must be somebody's day for it," he said. "It's always somebody's day in the kitchen. Matilde will have to tell you about it. I don't keep account."

He wanted the mood he was in, he wanted to return to it and be lost, unseeing, in the things he was saying to Victoria or to any one there was. He did not want the other things, for they were not his language and sight to him. For a moment

71

he did not even want the sound of the high heels
coming downstairs behind them.

"You see," he had begun again, "disciples are
not very often willing to be disciples——" and
then Estelle on her high black heels came into
the room. She was very well painted, in preparation for Sunday, and her eyes were hard and
round, boldly, theatrically blue. She saw the old
man sitting on the hearth and her upper lip rose,
as a curtain might, upon the spectacle and sound
of her white teeth and her half-sung words.

"Sorrel," she said, her throat softening as it
took his name, *"tu es complétement fou."*

Sorrel stood up on his limber legs, and the
cords in his neck stretched thin as wire as he threw
back his head and laughed. He would have gone
closer to her had his dress and his hands been
clean, but her skin and her fair shining hair and
the silk of her legs and skirt were enough in themselves to keep him away.

"You and me," he said, "you and me are the
only ones who never doubted it. But you won't
tell."

His long, unlipped mouth was turned up in his
face, and his voice was worn thin with the rusty
laughter that tightened down like a screw within;
there they stood speaking, their eyes filled up with
the indulgence and intimacy they had for each
other's ways. The flat, back-country voice of
Sorrel as he talked shaped in some likeness of
himself and his country the scarcely recognizable
pieces of foreign sounds, and the warm, round,

breast-deep trills of Estelle's talking betongued
with music the cold, the squalor, berated the
shiftlessness of every other woman in the
house.

"You can thank the *bon Dieu*, my poor Sorrel,"
she said when she had enough of saying other
things for awhile, "that I'm still able to get
dressed for Mass on Sunday and pray at least once
a week that the lot of them will die like rats from
poison and leave you in peace."

She looked at Victoria with her coat on in the
cold and the hard, high, mistrustful eye remained;
but as if remembering that the curtain had risen
and the audience was there, Estelle opened her
square, red-lipped smile.

"Disciples," she said, smiling. "Nibble, nibble." She made the soft, white, quivering nose of
a rabbit at lettuce. "Nibble, nibble, little Sorrel.
I'd like to see them all nibbling poison and
dying in their own dirt." The calves of her legs
and her bosoms swelled with it. "The biggest
dose for Peri and a special cramp in the guts for
Gabrielle."

"Hush, hush," said Sorrel, but he was smiling
at her in devotion.

She made a rich kiss of her mouth and laid it
softly in his empty cheek. It left a place as red as
blood where the chimney soot had been.

"Oh, my *chérie*," sighed the old man in peace,
"I think I'll take a bath."

"Your lunch will be ready in half an hour,"
said Estelle, turning again and touching with her

painted nails the dark roots of her yellow hair.
"God alone knows when the others will eat. It's
Peri's day, so none of the dishes are done."

She stepped high and elegant into the kitchen
and put a lace apron on over her half-bare bosoms
and her Sunday dress. On the shelf over the sink
she set her diamond rings. Victoria had taken her
jacket off and rolled up her sleeves and was filling
the dish-pan up. For the look of distaste on
Estelle's mouth for all that was cast about in
cold, habitual filth, Victoria spoke out in comfort
to her.

"It won't take us long to get the dishes washed,"
she said.

Estelle stopped still with the bunch of small
young carrots in her hand and stared. With the
tenderness for Sorrel gone out of her face, there
was nothing left but the powdered, the Mis-
tinguette-featured, impudent dry mask. She stood
there motionless on the unwashed kitchen-tiles,
short-waisted, Mistinguette-limbed, with a scru-
tiny of hard blue glass.

"Dishes?" she said, having taken Victoria's
measure in contempt. "I wouldn't touch their
dishes if they came on their knees asking for it."

She struck her enamelled lighter and savagely
opened wide the gas. She set a saucepan of water
down hard on the blazing ring and began scraping
her carrots with the blade of a silver penknife in
her corner. Her hands were almost ready to be
old, and stripped of their rings they had a look of
patience and of nervous, outraged vanity.

74

"Do you think I belong here? Do you think I belong to the colony?" she said.

Victoria watched the wide opals of grease floating over the cold, quivering surface of the water in the pan.

"I thought you lived here," she said.

"Of course I live here," said Estelle. "My husband and I live here." She dropped the fresh young carrots through her fingers into the water on the gas. Her cold, her absolute, blue eye was turned on Victoria as she wiped her hands. "We were here before anybody else and we'll be here after everybody goes," she said, belligerent and invulnerable in pride. She made a sign of a key turning in a lock. "We have our own room," she said, "and we keep it locked. There's no way of knowing who the people are who come and go."

CHAPTER EIGHT

To be young is to be filled with mercy and patience, having lost nothing yet nor knowing even of the bereavement there can be without death coming, nor knowing that to be young is to see mercifully. Or in the morning it is to hold the hand up to the light and see the endowed blood running in it, and to be ready: I am ready to take each act of my life as a stone in my hands, never to be denied, and my words will be like stones to myself, as hard and irrevocable. Now I have ten francs a day in my pocket and people to go back to at night I can look at the days ahead or behind me and think of what they will make in the end.

When the bell rang upstairs in the loft it meant the door from the street had opened into the shop below and any one might be waiting there, voiceless below. It meant laying down the painting-brushes and hurrying over the loft floor to the steps that cornucopiaed up from darkness, knowing with eloquence in the heart that to be young is to be ready for whatever there is. Either for Matilde's face under the soiled headcloth and the cheeks smiling, coming in with a tomato and a cup of goat-cheese to share lunch, or for Sorrel, his toga soft as a swan's breast across his neck, his lifted, hawk-like face stamped thin with winter; or for whatever stranger there was, descending the tower-like stairs in the dark to him, asking without words: why does it shake like the cold inside me, what am I ready for, what do I want to be there?

"Why do you always paint pictures of old men with beards?" Hippolytus asked on the uncaring stream of voice whereon the French words drifted, petal-like, scarcely uttered. It was cold in the loft, it was December, and he sat chewing his long braid of unwashed hair against the low window's winter light.

"If I paint strong old men enough," Victoria said, "perhaps something will happen to my own face. It's too small. It doesn't say anything."

Under Hippolytus's sallow skin his spine was there, white and fragile as the bone of a fish, curved feathery by the burden of non-being he floated under. So they were caught, quick as minnows out of the still water of sleep, Hippolytus, Athenia, Prosperine, Bishinka, hooked through the gills in separate moments when two people lay awake at night. It had never been said who had given the children life, but Peri the Greek sat soaking his feet clean in a basin of water in the loft, watching the brush move over the canvas, listening to what the voice of Victoria and the faint voice of Hippolytus said.

"Why do you have your hair cut off like the

men who eat meat?" said Hippolytus, muted because he had never called out loud or sung. "Why do you go to another house at night to sleep in a bed the way the meat-eaters do?"

"Because there will be something else some time," Victoria said. "All the books I've read say something happens in the end."

"Why are the men all old in your pictures?" Hippolytus said.

"I'm painting the lives of the saints," said Victoria, painting. "One after the other because they were angry, good, old men."

"I used to paint too," Peri the Greek said suddenly. He took his feet out of the water and began drying them slowly on an end of rag. He had been out all night in the cold with Sorrel, the two men driving in Sorrel's car throughout the city with posters for the next lecture rolled up in the back seat, going from billboard to wall with their bucket of paste and their brushes to flap the fresh-printed, hand-blocked posters up along the boulevards. The hem of his dress was black from the gutters he had splashed through at night and his hair was curled tight on his head like a great coarse wig, still wet from the lot of sleet that had fallen on it. He did not lift his eyes to her, but smiled uneasily to himself as he dried between his toes.

"I used to paint when we were in the country," he said, smiling and turning his short, dwarfed face away. "I had time for it in the country. Now I haven't time for it with the kind of life I have to lead."

He dried his thick, yellowing feet in the rag, his head hung down, his smile shaking.

"I don't get much time for myself," he said. "I used to be free to sit down and write poetry when I wanted."

Victoria squeezed out a brilliant worm of blue on the palette.

"I'm young," he said. "I'm twenty-seven. It's one of the good ages for a man." His bush of hair stood out from his skull and his smile hung, shame-faced, under it. "There's the way a man feels about women too," he said.

The bell rang in the loft and Victoria went down the stairs and into the shop to whomever would be there. She did not think it would be a face like any face she knew; it would come quick, lean through the door, it would roll rich as an Italian face, warming like the sun, it would open its throat wide and roar with laughing. The saints, oh, for crying out loud, dear girl, the saints! Here's sin as rich as butter, olive-skinned, mouth wild as wine. It would come straight through the glass saying: eskimos have ice instead of silverware, stripling. The South Pole is no farther if you can bear the wind than the rue de la Paix.

But it was Matilde who came into the place and sat down on the poets' bench with her knees spread.

"The show-window looks very well," said Matilde, smiling. She had a little paper of dates and a bag of dried prunes in her hand. "You've put the tunics and scarves out nicely."

Victoria could hear the voices of the children, remembering the indescribably slow chain of speech that passed word by word from them binding them almost imperceptibly to consciousness. "Why do you wear clothes like the women who eat meat?" she could hear Athenia saying. She had soft, doe-dappled skin and her eyes were dark in her face. "Why do you burn paper in your mouth like the men who eat meat?" asked Prosperine, scarcely aloud, the words set out like dry leaves, one by one, on the stream of living that went past. When the words were gone, Prosperine did not remember what she had said any more, but her eyes remained fixed on the ripples left behind. "Why do you wear dresses like the women who eat meat?" asked Bishinka. He touched the blue cloth of her dress because it was hanging down beside him. In his eyes there were yellow seeds of sleep and the scrolls of dirt in his ears showed under the stiff short braids.

"In the summer time," Matilde said, smiling, "if you still want to work with us then, you can put tunics on the way we do. Not now when it's so cold," she said. She ate the dates steadily, filling her smooth marble cheeks and with her fingers laying the hard bits out of her mouth aside. So she sat, plump, soiled, nun-like under her head-dress, speaking. "We make a fire in the garden and everything you've worn before goes into it. There's always something the new disciple can't bring himself to let go into the fire. Sometimes a few things even, but always one thing. Perhaps a fur coat or a pair of evening slippers. But everything has to go in so the past will be destroyed."

She spat a prune-stone out and added it to the other bits on the edge of the bench.

"I'd hate to see my blue cloak burning," Victoria said.

"Ah ha!" said Matilde. "You see!" and she passed the dates to her, laughing. But gravity came back at once to her, as a Mother Superior instructing a novice might suddenly remember her beads. "Now when it's so cold there's no point in your changing," she said. "But later we will all go south and spend the summer working in the country. There is a big place, near the sea, where every one swims. We sleep under the trees at night when the weather is good. People we know drive from other cities and there we all meet and spend a few weeks together. We weave there, we do all the weaving for the winter, and Gabrielle and Cina go on with the painting, and Peri and Arthur go on with the sandals and printing, and Sorrel prepares his lectures and poetry for the winter."

It all had a shape and a pulse of its own in Matilde's mind: the winter months were the time of endeavour in a bitter, relentless world, but in the summer this could be cast aside and never believed in till the cold set in. In the warmth and water of some other place but here, the spirit of why they had come together at all must be revealed purely and serenely to them.

"Matilde," Victoria suddenly said, watching the prunes in the Polish woman's mouth, "what do you think it is that has made them all come together?"

Matilde stopped chewing for a moment. Under her nun's veil, she glanced up, startled. Then she began to turn the prunes, slowly, ruminating in her mouth.

"Why do you ask that?" she said. She spoke as if in banter, smiling, with an imp's look, a look of Talanger in her bright, suspicious eye. "Don't you know what it is that made you yourself come to us?"

There was nothing in the shop-room now except the remembrance of Talanger dancing the Charleston before the mirror. There was no sound or sight of Matilde, but there was Talanger whispering to the glass: "Oh, child of Jesus, oh, my beautiful, the spirit of God is in thy face!" Her little girl arms hanging lifeless, her shoulders perishable in her tunic, she was dancing the length of the mirror, whispering: "Victoria, if I didn't tell any one would you give me a crucifix to wear?"

"I do not think I am very much, Matilde," Victoria said. "But if I work well in some way, perhaps I will find out clearly what there is to do. I am waiting to know why I am here. I do not know."

"I am waiting for Jesus," said the memory of Talanger's voice. She was dancing in front of the mirror and waiting on Thursday for the Brides of Heaven in their white veils to go by.

It was December and the boards scrubbed clean enough to kiss in the loft, the oil-cloth under the gas-ring clean as skin. St. John was still in the wilderness on the canvas, ready to die young, and the bell rang out and the door opened and closed in the shop below. The breath went out of Victoria's mouth and she went down, shaking, in the dark; this time the face and the voice would be something else; would be eyefuls of wisdom, would be laughter snorting, would be a mistake come into the place, an accident, a sound like Caruso sweetening the rafters, a jig like Bach moving deeply as organ throats, would be something not photographed or remembered, not the two dead women and the live one off the mantel-piece in Neuilly, but blood rich and strange and new enough that could not be denied.

On the other side of the curtain the figure could be seen, a stranger come in from the street outside and waiting, and Victoria stopped in fright and put back the lock of hair from her face. It was cold in the pit of the stairs and the words began to shiver in her heart: what will it be when it comes, what are you waiting for?

This time it was a lady who had come into the shop, dressed well in broadcloth and silver-fox with her face painted up and pinned like a rag under the brim of her hat.

"Do you speak English?" she said in complaint. "I thought I'd just come in and have a look at what you have." Her strained, haggard eyes moved over Victoria. "I was here last year," she said.

83

"Only you're not the one. The other one was dressed up like Mr. Sorrel. I always wonder what kind of underwear he wears."

Victoria brought out the scarves, the tunics; parted the soft whispering papers before her and spread the painted and hand-woven silks across the table.

"That's effective, isn't it?" said the woman vaguely. She lifted the colour of one and held it before the mirror against the destruction of her face. "When I got the things home last year," she said in blame, "I never heard the end of it. Nobody was satisfied because every one wanted the design the other one had."

"But it's just as though you came in to buy a painting, or a book, you see," said Victoria. "It's really *your* choice that matters. . . ."

The lady looked uncertainly at her.

"Yes," she said, unconvinced. "I suppose it's what *I* like, isn't it?"

Poverty, describing the pure arc of defeat, is the time of life when the sight goes dim in the eye and days abandon sequence, having become contrivances for deluding one appetite or the next. The lady paid the bills out on the table, loath to leave this place of beauty.

"Do come in for a cup of tea with Mr. Sorrel on Wednesday," said Victoria. "He receives at five once a week. He would be so pleased by your appreciation."

"Tea with Mr. Sorrel!" cried the American lady in delight. "Why, I'd just love it! That's what I don't find over here at all. I don't find that same appreciation of the artistic the way we have it at home. Why, take our local galleries over there!"

The draped walls rippled with the blast of the closed door across them when she left. Hippolytus, Athenia, Prosperine, Bishinka, said the silence, ask questions of me until the answer begins.

CHAPTER NINE

When Estelle opened the door of their room in the colony's house and stood there in her black lace brassiere and short silk drawers, there was no mistaking it: the slightly purplish powder stood on the dressing-table in a bowl as big as a chamber-pot, the suede coffer for her jewels was open on the mantelpiece, net stockings, ready to dissolve at the sight of water, were heaped on the back of that singular and outlawed object in this house—a chair. The place was the dressing-room, back-stage, of any music-hall star, with the cigarette stubs of all the men who came there in the ashtrays still and the smoke from their mouths hanging motionless in wreaths upon the unbroken atmosphere.

The bed was a divan with four wooden feet showing under the pale, faded velvet cover, wide as the room and banked with gold-laced and wooden-beaded cushions. A pair of black satin corsets had been taken off and laid down there, and the Pomeranian had gone to sleep upon the rosebuds of them.

"Come in and have a drink with us, Victoria," Estelle said. Victoria paused a moment in the

hall. "Sunday's as quiet as the rush hour in the
Métro in this house with the charging cavalry
downstairs. Edmond's gone out for a bottle of
Pernod. Come in."

The sound of the gong struck by Matilde beat
the time below, and the house shook slightly,
sprung from the impact of the bodies that leaped
in Sorrel's rural wild ballet, and for the first time
Victoria crossed the threshold of Estelle's and
Edmond's locked and private place. Estelle picked
the yellow satin underwear off the other chair in
the room and hung it with Edmond's string of
neckties on the door.

"Sit down, Victoria," she said.

There were no curtains either at the windows of
this room, but Estelle had fastened a square of
pink silk over the glass of one, and a piece of green
baize from a card-table was tacked across the other
so that the people passing in the street or the
neighbours could not see inside if ever they had
wished to lift their heads and see. But there were
such respectable people in the other houses and
such quiet ones who passed by in their good
clothes under the trees, that surely they must all
have looked the other way to avoid facing the
shame of this one unworthy place. The half-
naked, be-tunicked tribe that had moved into this
house had given another reputation to the neighbourhood: they had destroyed the grass, let the
wood go unpainted year after year, let the shutters
fall out of repair and cry all night on their hinges.
When the slates blew from the roof, the slovenly

men and women in their robes let them lie un-
noticed, it seemed, in the cluttered garden. The
disgrace of pink silk over one upper window and
green baize across the next only advanced the
widening of that impassable breach which stood
between the demented and the sane.

Victoria sat down shyly on the chair by the
dressing-table and looked at the faces of the actors
pinned around the walls.

"I'll go on dressing," Estelle said. "Our
act goes on at eight. We always eat in town
before."

Whether for economy or display, everything in
Estelle's and Edmond's room was larger than
things in other places: the bottles of eau de
Cologne and mouthwash as big as magnums, the
mauve powder-puff soft and deep enough to stroke
like a bird's full breast, the hand-glass long-necked
and elaborate in which the faces of two people, if
placed cheek to cheek, could easily be seen. Even
the photographs of other people from the stage,
larger than life, were monstrously lashed and
pored. The lower story of Chevalier's mouth
supported, as it might a cigarette, the words his
mouth was singing and his lip; the straw hat on
his eye was big enough to hold the family wash,
gigantically detailed and lustrous in its weave.

"We have to have our meat once in the day,"
Estelle said, and the house shook like a warning
from below.

"There're at least thirty dancing this afternoon," Victoria said. Estelle lit the little alcoholic

flame on the mantelpiece and set her curling-irons across it.

"*Dancing*, my poor friend?" she said. "You call *that* dancing?" She stood, high-calved, white-fleshed in her brassiere and a pair of salmon drawers. "Sales' girls," she said in contempt. "Do you know what most of them do all week? Sell bidets or soup-strainers in the Galeries Lafayette. Not even girls from the perfume and toilet articles department where they pick them for their complexions and their legs." She tried the irons on a piece of toilet paper and watched the smoke hang upright on the bedroom air. "God knows where the men crawl in from!" she said. "Chzecs, Poles. You wouldn't find a Frenchman taking his pants off and skipping around in public in a *courant d'air*."

She put the irons in under her brass waves and turned to the glass again, talking to the sight of Victoria reflected, young, boy-like, listening on the chair.

"The idea of the door standing open to any one who comes along and takes off his woollen underwear if he feels that way and starts hopping around on his corns and bunions! Sorrel," she said bitterly, but suddenly it was there again, the tenderness and the care for him, for what he put inside him and for what he wore. "Sorrel is a dancer," she said. "It's born in him. You can see he's a gentleman and a genius even when he hasn't a stitch on. But do you think any one in this place cares for Sorrel? I've seen him sometimes tired

enough to cry after dancing all afternoon or standing up printing his programmes, and then having
to do his hair and go down town and lecture to
the gaping lot of them. He's not a young man,
you know. They ought to leave him alone."

Mistinguette, in ostrich plumes, her shoulders
bare, was pinned against the paper by the glass.
The lifted head, the short and childlike throat
were not old nor had they anything to do with
frailty, but in them was borne a perfectly concealed despair, an impudence so flaunted that any
one who saw must tremble for it: she had carried
it this far so well but there was no telling for how
much longer it might be.

"He can't even eat the food in the place," Estelle
said. "Five years I've seen he has a lunch he can
eat, anyway." She held the little mascara box in
her hand and brushed her lashes upward, facing
herself, her soft back bare, the buttons of her brassiere fastened between her full white shoulder-
blades. "When I had my house in town," she said,
"I used to send the limousine and chauffeur for
Sorrel every day. Every day he had lunch with
us." The smell of hot brilliantine and scorched
paper was sweet and artificial on the air. Downstairs the show was in progress, the ballet leaping
in individual directions, and here were the pre-
parations being made in grease-paint for the thing
to take place on another stage somewhere. "Edmond and I came here to live when the *crise*
began," she said. "But we can still afford to eat
a decent meal. You'll notice one of these colony

offerings is enough, even for the starving. Did
you ever see any one coming back a second time
for a meal here?" she said.

"I came back," said Victoria.

"Well, you——" said Estelle. She brushed her
lashes up. "You'll get over it."

"I don't know," said Victoria. She did not look
at the other woman, but she said: "I came for
something else." As if it was pride that stopped
her she did not say any more.

"Oh, for the love of God," said Estelle, wearily.
"Edmond and I said it was because you were
broke."

"I am," said Victoria.

Estelle turned around, her bosom arching in
contempt.

"What do you think you'll get out of selling
things at the shop?" she said.

She had said this when Edmond came in
through the bedroom door with the bottle wrapped
up in paper under his arm. His vest was buttoned
close over his belly and his watch-chain lay across
it, he was wearing rings on his dark-haired fingers,
his diamond stick-pin was in his cravat, the blood
was ruddy in his jowls and his hair lay back like
a young man's hair, thinning and smooth under
the scented oil.

"How's the circus?" said Estelle. "Who's getting the biggest laughs downstairs, Peri or
Arthur?"

"I came in through the back so that Matilde
shouldn't notice," Edmond said. He smiled at

them, a small ruby-lipped smile under his greying, clipped moustache. The string of neckties and the hung underwear swung out and in with the door as he closed it quietly behind him, and the Pomeranian stood up on the corsets in greeting, the light side of her tail laid over her copper back.

They did not know when they had first set foot on the stage; it had begun, as do the final things in life, without beginning. They were the first generation of it, they said, but they talked of it with assurance as they drank, glibly and boldly secure, sharing the same secrets of its glamour, the special adventure of its tradition which could not be communicated by sight or word but only through the living of it. They sat on either side of the square bed, preserved in stays, silk hose, immaculate slippers, their nails and hair tended, their voices succulent, playing as Stavisky must have played at ease and security, handsomely, unsparingly and with the gift of eloquence. Even when their tongues began to run free with Pernod, they did not behave as if the audience had left the place, speaking of their house closed up in Paris, of their ornaments, their chauffeur and their limousine, as things that had slipped out of hand five years ago through unforeseen movements of the Bourse and stage-managers and theatres closing down. Whatever had happened, or would, Estelle kept the make-up of impudence and scorn, the subterfuge laid expert under the blue glass eyes so that no one might make out the childhood freckles scattered pale across the delicate, achromatic skin.

Any one not of the stage was uninitiate; but in Edmond there was an added thing: his brother had painted and his mother had written poetry and he had a reverence he brought to any kind of art. With a deference that is a part of a shrewd national respect for style, he understood the signs as they were given. Sorrel, for the life he led, was a noble and spiritual man to him, and because Victoria put paint on canvas Edmond spoke softly to her, heeded her presence and her voice in courtesy. They were sorry for any one who had not good clothes to cover them, or for any one whom the appetites had left alone. But for him, he knew these things came after to an artist; he had seen it in his brother's life, he said.

They sat on the two ends of the divan-bed, drinking their glasses of powerful milky-green. Estelle was laughing, her teeth white, the sound secretive and high, because of the things they knew Victoria had not grown up to yet. Good wines, spiced dishes, women, even, were things his brother could have done without and never thought of them again. "But you're young enough to get over virtue, Victoria," Estelle said.

Rich food, thick wines, the tastes aroused, unsuspected still in her quiet, slender bones; the wings of the heart lifting in actual, physical delight not only for the weather or for music but for the relish of a personal thing. She sat drinking the

Pernod with them, thinking that to be American is to be puritan, to be American is to stand outside and watch, or else to abandon oneself for ever to whatever is. Words out of a book, like whisky taken, or a painting seen with anguish, the love of these so pure that the moment comes close and falls like fruit upon the mouth.

"If you are American, you are puritan," said Victoria, holding to the small young face in the dressing-table mirror, the hair weaving, the eyes that appeared and disappeared in the glass.

"Hi, hi!" laughed Estelle, stretched out with laughter on the gilt-lace cushions, and Edmond's laughing shook in his stomach. The warmth of their intemperance, of Estelle's white-bosomed, suave-legged laughter, of the tides of Edmond's red-lipped, reverent love for the youth and the shape of any woman was flowing sweet and possessive over the floor-boards, over the smoke-wreaths to her.

"Tell that to Sorrel, Victoria, tell that to Sorrel!" cried Edmond's laughter.

"Tell it to Matilde!" cried Estelle.

The divan on which they shook was floating in deep undulation, was falling and rising wild on the high seas of their knowing, dipping under their flags, the colour high in their faces, drifting, drifting out beyond, the two French people seasick with laughing, ebbing in derision from Victoria and ignorance and virginity.

"It used to keep him busy!" Edmond called back to her, the tears of laughter shining.

"It used to keep Matilde busier finding out and sending the girls off!" cried Estelle.

Edmond brought out his long silk handkerchief with a flourish and blew his nose in it; the scent he used drifted back across the flooded room to her and the handkerchief waved slowly, slowly towards the shore.

"The two of them Matilde lets stay are ugly enough to scare even Sorrel," Edmond called back. "He leaves Cina and Gabrielle alone!"

"Phew!" cried Estelle, and she pinched her nostrils closed in her bloody nails. "They smell!"

Victoria put her hand through her hair, and it was shaking. She set the glass down empty on the tray of pins.

"I don't understand what you're saying," she said, and when she stood up the chair fell over backwards.

"Don't understand!" jeered Estelle across the water. Her voice was full and warbling, rich as a mother's, but ready then for obscenity or insult.

"She doesn't understand," Edmond said quickly, and suddenly she felt his arm around her, holding her up, the clean, sweet smell of the pomade on his hair fragrant as a coiffeur's head, the silky-threaded plumpness of his hands holding her firm against his watch-chain and his paunch. "Quiet, quiet, *ma petite*, you mustn't cry," he said. "Hush, now."

"Listen, Edmond," Victoria whispered, "listen, I'm laughing."

95

"The poor kid's drunk," said Estelle. "Drunk on a Pernod."

The soft silk handkerchief held in his hand was stroking slowly, wondrously in tenderness over Victoria's face, and she felt the grin stretched on her mouth and the tears falling. His breath, the licorice, honey-suckle smell of drinking taken in and out was blurring her eyesight as if he had breathed on glass.

Part Two

ANTONY

CHAPTER TEN

Antony walked in through the glass door one afternoon in January and the mirrors came to life at once and filled the shop with several lightish, quick-eyed young men.

"How are y'?" he said with a nod. "I'd like to see a scarf for my wife." He was carrying *The Degradation of the Democratic Dogma* under his arm.

If it had not been Victoria sitting behind the table adding numbers, it would have been somebody else and the conversation might have altered here and there, but not enough to make it something in recognition of the other person sitting there. He had come into a shop to say a few things to any one he found there, his limbs run scant from opposition, his bones stretched out for whatever he was after, his eye peeled quick for nook or cranny where the spider might weave a web over after he had passed, or where the moss was soft enough to leave no print behind.

"I saw you from the street," he said. "I don't want to buy any of these things unless you want me to."

When he stopped talking he looked quickly,

curiously, up and down and back and forth, running fast from the face opposite, scarcely pausing for breath in the shade of whatever features happened to be there. He took off his gloves and laid them down, stripped of the shape of his hands, empty, on the table between them.

"I'm out," he said, quietly, "after a straight back and shoulders. I followed something from the Madeleine, but when I caught up with it it wouldn't do. My wife," he said, and he sat down, "makes things out of clay. She needs long legs and a queer face, either a man or a woman's. I think," he said, but he did not finish it. He said they had just come back from Egypt, and he turned out his pockets to show her the corners of sand still left in them.

"That's enough to bring back of a place," he said. The grains of it came out with his handkerchief and said hush across the papers on the table. "It gives you the split hoof of a camel or whatever you want to remember. It's the first time I've walked up this side of the street. I always take the other. I believe in embassies, and always in the emissary of the soul. The patterns on these walls take the sight right out of the eye like an operation. My name's Antony," he said, his eyes escaping. "I believe in bone."

Suddenly Antony unbuttoned his tan coat and put his arms out on the table. His hands lay there bleached and narrow, with no flesh on them, lay side by side like sleeping women. His eyes went up and down the walls where the draperies and

scarves were hanging, fleeing from thoughts that
seemingly would split with laughter if he spoke
them out.

"If you would like me to show you the things,"
said Victoria, and she saw the set of her own face
in the glass, stern and dispraising, with the gaze
held hard in her eye. "You'll see they're simple
enough. They're made by Sorrel and his people."

Antony sat smiling his long-lipped, isolate grin.

"Do you have to work here?" he said.

There has been so much said for poverty, for it
and against it: that music can come from it, and
divinity, but the thought of it imposes an objec-
tion, like a uniform worn, and Victoria saw her
own in the glass. Antony had seen it standing on
street-corners, maybe, with its hat out for mercy,
but if he turned around suddenly and faced a mirror he would never find it there. Nor could it be
waiting at home for him, immeasurable in solitude
like a statue hewn in the room from the cold.
Perhaps he had read in books about it for the
unaltered taste of desperation, but he could speak
aloud of it, not as the poor might speak, but as of
a thing that could be annihilated as completely
as it might annihilate. On one side he saw good
luck and on the other bad, and the features of his
face had seemingly entered the conflict: his eyes
divided, his mouth wide, clean-teethed as a boy's
mouth, his nose short, his lip long, his skin with
no sign of weather on it.

"I like working here," Victoria said. "Would
you like to look at a scarf for your wife?"

"She never wears them," Antony said. "Never carries a handbag, never wears gloves, never gets her hair curled. She hasn't any memory for objects. Neither have I. We eliminate everything we might forget or leave behind. I've left my hat everywhere for ten years. Now I never wear one. I'll probably leave my gloves here when I go so that I can come back after them. We never make appointments because we can't remember where we said to meet."

"She might like a tunic," Victoria said.

Antony shook his head.

"Everything we like," he said, "has two legs or four, so it can run after us when we forget it. She breeds white wolf-hounds. I keep horses. We like people," he said. "We like people more than anything else in life."

He was sitting there below her, his eyes empty as a statue's, his legs crossed long and elegant, his flesh motionless as stone. Outside the cars passed ceremoniously, in deference to the long-stalked flags that clustered over the embassy archway.

"What do you do with the quiet here?" said Antony. A shiver of ice went down his back and he turned his head as if some one were standing behind him. "What do you do when you're left here alone?"

"Upstairs there's a place," Victoria said, "where I can paint my pictures."

"What kind of paintings?" said Antony quickly. Whatever he was was lost at once in the wonder for the thing somebody else might be.

"I do still-lifes some," said Victoria. She felt the colour run into her face. "Sometimes I paint my lunch before I eat it."

"In oils or water?" Antony said.

"In water-colours now, because they're cheaper," Victoria said. "I'm doing the lives of the saints— I've been doing them a long time."

"I can bring you a lot of oils," Antony said. "I've given up painting. I can bring you a green glass palette shaped like a heart. You don't have to tell me your name, you know."

The silence and dark in the stairway behind was deep enough to echo the voices heard in her life before: the voices at school, and her mother's voice, and Lacey's voice speaking. The family said the name in grief and blame to her because she had been only a little while with them out of pride, as a stranger without money might have stayed; and the girls in school said it curiously, in mistrust or in derision; and Lacey called it out at night, ringing and high, like a mare gone wild in clover. She could see it upholstered in white, woven into the cushion, the gilt-carved legs of the name standing in the sun under the bird-cage in the family's house.

"My mother's name was Victoria," she said. "It's mine too."

"Yes," said Antony. "That's how things happen. I had a grandmother called Fly-Fornication Adams. It was given her to use with the dignity of the Adams' boys fireplaces. Any of the things with names," he said, "friendship or what, have no meaning until they're put to use. Victoria is as chaste as silver. It has nothing to do with the heart. You must meet my wife," he said.

"We spent last Sunday writing the poetry of D. H. Lawrence over the walls of the way we go into our house in the country," he said. "It looks like the shadow of somebody standing there. Because he is dead now it is like walking into the tomb of the Pharaohs every time we go home. What do you think of Death?" he said. "It begins with a capital. Victoria. The life of the saints. I think I'm afraid of you. You look very nice when you smile."

The gas-heater in the corner had a border of blue and orange flame growing across it, and Antony went to it and held out his hands to the heat.

"My wife," he said, "is making a frieze for a swimming-pool. That's what I came in to ask you. I promised her the back and shoulders. Couldn't you lock the door here and come home and meet her?" he said.

"No," Victoria said. "I work here till seven. Then there are things to do at the colony when I go back."

But Antony had forgotten. He said: "I'd give anything I have for a glimmer of Donatello's John in from the wilderness to carry around in my own eye. You'd like my wife," he said. "Being so many people at the same time, she interrupts me all the time," he said. "Even here. Whatever I'm doing, the way she looked at lunch today or how she'll look tomorrow has more reality to it than anything else I see."

He spoke very fast saying, school was sitting
in a room for me with bodies I'd go mad looking
at if ever I'd looked. There's nothing worse, he
said, there's nothing worse than being young. I
saw everything else in the schoolrooms and it
didn't matter, any kind of wood or chalk on the
board or things going on outside the window.
But if my eyes came to a boy's face I did that
trick, I can still do it, I can do it in the mirror to
myself, I can look so clear and hard at a thing
that it's wiped out by sight, I can wipe the mirror
clean by looking hard at it. It gives you a jolt
when you're in a room alone. It's as if my eyes
turned inside me and looked down into what lay
at the bottom. The clock in the classroom was a
face with features to it and it marked the time
exactly with the pulse ticking in my wrist. I never
took my first two fingers off the heart-beats in my
other arm, watching the clock's hand marking it
exactly. When the teacher's voice said Antony
Lister nothing moved inside me, nothing stirred.
Lister she used to say louder and looking at the
clock something in me remembered my father
coming home at night and the white fur rug on
the floor in front of the gas-logs and the man
bringing him his letters on a plate, and the name
Lister written on his mail, and his kid slippers
brought into him, and our names were the same,
the same as the ancestors who stepped out, fault-
finding and censorious at Plymouth. That was
the only connexion we had. Antony Lister was a
sound that came up from inside and broke even,

the way I heard it. But I never saw the teacher's face when she said it. I had wiped it out blank. One day the clock in the classroom stopped and I couldn't tell the difference between the two things, I didn't know if my pulse had stopped ticking or the clock. I was left holding on to nothing in my wrist and the face of the clock was wiped right out from looking at it. I fainted, and I couldn't go back to school that term, and then I couldn't go back to that school, and that was a kind of a death. Death with a capital D, he said. He was squatting down before the gas-heater, warming his white open hands.

"You must meet my wife," he said.

Victoria lifted her hand and put the short lock off her forehead. This is the way people speak, she thought, when love is not a name any more but has been recognized alive in somebody else's flesh. Because of her he walks into strange places, stops people in the street, carries books under his arm to implicate strangers into what they are together.

"Why do you want it intruded on?" Victoria said shyly.

Antony sat still, squatting on his legs, and looked at his hands before him.

"Intrude?" he said. "Intrude on what?"

Victoria's blood was warm with shyness, and she felt her voice shaking for courage in her mouth.

"On you, on you two," she said.

He lifted his face, still as if he could not understand this, and everything else was taken from him for a minute, the hasty-flowing waters of his conflict washed past and left him slight and young. His face was turned to her, stranded, the eyes pale as violets, the mouth wide and wounded like a child's.

"As for that," he said, "nothing intrudes, you know."

Suddenly he stood up straight, and gathered his gloves up, without thought as though his fingers had remembered them there. He leaned back against the long mirror, his gaunt, almost callow, almost heroic face held up.

"I want to ask you a question," he said. "I don't know what you can do with it. Victoria," he said, "how many lovers have you had?"

Victoria stood unmoving, holding what might stir or waver quiet in her, her lids unflicking; but inside the laughter began, the great swells of laughter rising beyond restraint, beyond endurance, the shaking substance of silent, awful laughter quivering in possession. Never having given a name to what might come in through the door or seen it clearly, plattered spaghetti with the red sauce heaped hot on it, or opportunity cold as a slice of an astral body, nor foreseen anything except the door opening and the bell ringing upstairs in the loft, she put what he might be aside for a little while longer.

"You don't know anything about me," she said, with the hilarity shaking unseen inside her. "I— I am a puritan. I live by myself. I'm of no importance at all."

CHAPTER ELEVEN

The house in the trees with the gravel walk up to it, the landlady sitting blind in the room above them, her hands on her cane, not knowing night from day but harking for the stealth of her boarders, these were the total of Miss Fira's and Miss Grusha's nights and days. Victoria came back to sleep in the house in the dark and went off in the early morning from it, but for the Russian women there was only one ceiling over their heads and wherever they moved in their room, furtive and sly with their living, they heard the loud, loose mouth of the blind woman asking, even in silence, that they be affluent women in a house of decades of arrears. At any hour they closed the front door after them and hastened down to the gate, they went withered and small for the eyes that watched at the upper window: the eyes of the landlady waiting to be told, and the eyes of the servant seeing beside her, her hand scarcely raised nearly not-drawing the curtain's edge up to watch them going. In the summer the trees could hide a little of their convulsive haste, the boughs full enough to mask the throes of their proud escapes up or down the drive; but in winter their skirts rode down the walk, the sight of them unbroken through the twigs from the moment they quit the porch until they reached the carriage-gate. Still walking fast, Miss Fira opened her handbag and took the gate key out.

"Don't run, Grusha," Miss Fira said, without a movement of her lips.

"Run if I like," said Miss Grusha. "I'm younger. I've got a right to be spry."

They had their good hats on, the small, flat, velvet crowns sewn with jet sequins, and their good velvet jackets, embroidered black, their boas around their necks, their hands held rigid in their muffs. It was snowing and the flakes were drifting slowly, elegantly down, ready to pause midway in the garden over the bushes, turning and lingering in the cold.

Miss Fira and Miss Grusha turned together, and with their small hands in their cotton gloves they closed the gate. But even then, facing the house, they did not lift their heads towards the window.

"Walk like a lady, Grusha," said Miss Fira under her breath.

Without seeing they saw well the imperceptible movement of the curtain, without lifting their eyes perceived the two faces of the women watching there, and shrank like struck snakes into the refuge of their buttoned jackets until their courage walked, bodiless, embroidered and boned erect, across the avenue and made the corner of the street.

They did not speak again until they had sat down in the Métro wagon side by side.

"Little enough time left for us to walk like them!" said Miss Grusha. The two women sat swaying upright, their muffs held close against their jackets, their faces set, forbidding, against the swift, uninterrupted flowing of the cars. "Ladies!" said Miss Grusha with a snort.

"Whatever you become, Grusha," said Miss Fira, looking through the blank window across the aisle straight into the dark stream of air that passed beyond, "I am sure you will not forget your lineage."

"Other servants don't like it," said Miss Grusha grimly. "It makes them feel their place."

"The poor creatures," said Miss Fira in forbearance as they rode, "are penniless women who have been forced out of poor homes to make a living. You can expect nothing of them, but you can pity them. We may even have to eat in the kitchen with them," she added in grieved, resolute pride.

"Eat?" said Miss Grusha sharply. "Perhaps we will." She turned her head quickly on her neck and eyed her sister. "What kind of food do they give domestics?" she said.

Erect, inflexible, almost unheeding in her austerity, Miss Fira swayed with the ceaseless movement of the train.

"Perhaps soup," she said after a moment.

Miss Grusha's tongue ran out along her lip.

"Perhaps onion soup," she said. "With cheese grated on it." She looked in question at her sister. "What do you think?" she said.

"Perhaps," said Miss Fira, making no sign. "Perhaps fried potatoes. Sometimes servants eat what comes back from the family's table. You will remember that was the arrangement mother had at home."

"That would do," said Miss Grusha with a sudden spark in her eye, "if the man of the house was delicate like father. But some of these self-styled gentlemen wouldn't leave enough for a bird to peck at! And the way the French wipe up the last drop with a piece of bread, Fira! We'll have to be very particular about where we consent to go."

"If there weren't any children," said Miss Fira, looking straight ahead, "the vegetables might come back to the kitchen as good as untouched. A place where company comes in often is the nicest place to be."

"Would they ever," said Miss Grusha, her voice gone thin in an agony of hope, "leave any asparagus or fried tomatoes over?"

"That would be very unlikely," Miss Fira said, riding invincible, supreme. "There ought always to be sufficient carrots or spinach left. Spinach always did wonders for you, Grusha."

"What about the fish course?" Miss Grusha said.

"You never had a good night after sea-food," said Miss Fira quietly.

"Oh, thank you very much!" cried Miss Grusha in a pique. "I assure you I'll have my share of it just the same! Tartar sauce on boiled potatoes never hurt any one, and the way you used to dream on clams is a caution."

"It's your own fault then," said Miss Fira with restraint, "if you have nightmares all night about your teeth falling out."

"I never thought," said Miss Grusha, speaking with quick, savage, bird-like convulsions of her head, "to see you begrudging me the food I put in my mouth!"

Miss Fira, her face set in quietness, turned to her sister.

"Grusha," she said, "can you truthfully say that I tried to deprive you? Did I interfere with the soup or the carrots or spinach? Have I said a word to you about the dessert?"

"The dessert?" cried Miss Grusha. "I haven't so much as got a look at it!"

"No," said Miss Fira with dignity, "but you'll have to decide for yourself. If it's *soufflé* and you want to lie awake all night, then you can go right ahead and be a libertine over it. And if it's apple-sauce," she began.

"It might be *banane flambée*," said Miss Grusha wildly.

"We are at the Etoile," said Miss Fira in rebuke. The train had halted in the lighted station and Miss Grusha followed Miss Fira out the door.

Because of their muffs and their boas and their haughtily-borne faces, they were shown through the ladies' door of the employment office and not into the hallway where the servants sat. The young woman behind the desk was dressed up like an idle lady, and it crossed Miss Fira's mind that she might take a position of this sort rather

than go into service if there were anyway for Miss
Grusha to survive alone. A place of dignity and
quiet, and the salary paid once a month, with
Grusha keeping house for her, Grusha cooking,
keeping the place clean, Grusha eating. "Of
course, she'd have to keep an account of everything she spent out," she was thinking. "I'd have
my hands busy with the work here all day."

The young woman pulled out chairs for them
and sat down behind the desk with her ledger open.

"What is it I can do for you, please?" she said.

"We scarcely like to make a change," Miss
Fira began, rapidly snapping and unsnapping the
catch of her handbag, and Miss Grusha leaned
forward up and out of her seat. "We're eight
months behind on the room now," she whispered
quickly. Miss Fira took hold of her sister's skirt
and pulled her down from behind.

"Sit down, Grusha," she said sharply, and Miss
Grusha sat down with her head writhing in silence.

"We are Russian gentlewomen," Miss Fira
began again, speaking lightly. "The name would
doubtless be familiar to you. We have resided in
Neuilly for a year now, but circumstances make
it necessary for us to make a change. Of course,
the servant problem these days," she said with a
little laugh.

"Did you wish a cook or a *bonne à tout faire?*"
asked the young woman at the desk, her pencil
lifted so that this situation might be clarified.
She looked cordially, smiling, at Miss Fira's sharp
little face under the sequins.

"We," said Miss Fira, the colour gone from her mouth. "That is, my sister and I, we," she said, her hands gripped tight in her muff. "We had been considering placing ourselves . . ."

The young woman looked quickly up at them, from one shy, bright face to the other.

"*You* want places? You yourselves are looking for work?" she said.

"There must certainly be some homes or some places of business," said Miss Fira, raising her chin clear of her boa, "where refinement is required and where gentlewomen could perform light duties for a recompense."

The young woman closed her book, seeing at once in quiet impatience the indigence of everything they wore.

"You should not have come in through this entrance," she said. "You will have to wait your turn with the others out there."

Miss Grusha gave a wild cry of laughter.

"We haven't been servants yet!" she cried. "There's no reason why we should sit with them."

"You haven't had any experience, then?" the young woman said.

"None," said Miss Fira proudly. She sat erect, her muff lifted from her lap, her feet arched in her shoes.

"Father had quite a correspondence with d'Annunzio," said Miss Grusha, but Miss Fira let her go no further. She leaned towards the young woman's desk.

"We would, if necessary, instruct the young," she said.

The young woman's eyes were fixed in hopelessness and stupefaction on their faces.

"We can't stand children, either of us," Miss Grusha said, and she gave a snort of laughter behind her muff. "They wouldn't have a chance to get the upper hand, you may be sure!"

But the young woman had risen to her feet.

"If you haven't any references, there's no use," she said. She looked towards the door.

Miss Fira slid forward on the chair, her shanks gripped tense beneath her skirts. The young woman looked blandly at the door, seeing the glass pane and the winter light outside and the respectability of office places and people who went past. She stood looking, her fingers tapping the table, not believing in desperation, not giving ear to it or to the frenzy of starvation that was rising in the room.

"References?" Miss Fira said. "My dear young lady, you must try to understand what our connexions are. If family history is not sufficient, I may add that we both graduated from one of the most select musical academies in St. Petersburg." Her face was lifted sharp, imperious to this instrument of service which they had chosen out of all the ways and means available to breeding. "Paderewski was frequently a dinner guest at home; my sister still has her childhood fan on which he wrote his name. We have not come to this decision in haste. We have considered it carefully."

"We could join Mr. Sorrel's colony in Neuilly if we wished," Miss Grusha said, "but we have to have our comforts."

"There is no need to question our qualifications," Miss Fira went on. "We did not come here for that. We simply wish to use this commercial agency as a means of meeting a few refined persons who would understand and appreciate our influence in their homes. Then we could make a choice." She looked at the young woman, and suddenly her lip shook. "We are not difficult to please," she said.

" But if you can't clean or wash or cook—" said the young woman, spreading her hands. "There's really——"

"Cook?" cried Miss Grusha before her sister could speak. "When we left home we didn't know how to boil water, if you can imagine that!"

But suddenly the spasm of laughter left her face and she reached out her two black-gloved hands and seized the desk's edge, clawing wild there, clinging as if the tide were rising fast and would submerge them if they did not float with this.

"*Ecoutez*," she whispered sharp across the desk. "I'll take any place." This was between her and the young woman standing there. Miss Fira had been cast aside to perish or survive in any way she might. "I'll do whatever they want," Miss Grusha whispered, clinging rigid to the wood. "I'll clean their garbage-pails, I'll empty out their chamber-pots," she whispered. "I'll do any thing." She turned her face at the touch of Miss Fira's hand on her arm, looked slowly, savagely at the thin black fingers and then struck them away. Here in the lifeboat there was no more place; blood and kin could strangle on quarts of agony with their lungs pumped full until they went down and left the living in peace.

"I don't care what they pay me," Miss Grusha said in her hushed, high imprecation of despair. "I'll take their children out, I'll take them! I'll wash their feet and their floors and their water clos, out for them. *Ecoutez, mademoiselle*," she said, and her face was turned sideways and up, her voice whining. "I don't care about the money they'd give me. I'd give it to you," she said slyly, "that's what I'd do, miss. Whenever they paid me, I'd bring the money to you. Two meals a day without thinking where it will come from, that's all I ask of them. Coffee and bread in the morning, miss," she whispered, "with a bit of butter if they could spare it. I'd work myself to the bone for them, damn them."

"Grusha!" cried Miss Fira, and she rose to her feet, trembling. Miss Grusha turned her head with that slow, savage twist of cunning and clung faster to the desk.

"Shut up!" she said, and she swung her head back from her sister and faced the young woman standing there uneasy now. "I haven't any false pride," Miss Grusha began again in that shrill, wild whisper which seemed to fix them motionless in the sibilant fury of its sound. "I'm young still," she said. "I'll fetch and carry. I'll clean their foul boots for them. I'll wash their under-wear out if that'll keep them quiet. All I want is the meals they'll give me. That isn't much, miss, is it?" she said, wheedling. "I'll do it for the food, the lowest things in the house for them. That isn't too much for a poor servant to ask now, is it? I'll start working now, me, by myself, any-where you want to put me. Put my name down in the book, put it down, miss. Put it down," she said. She was edging along the side of the desk to the other one, her face stricken, her fingers clawed to the wood in frenzy. "Write it down, now, won't you, miss?" she was saying. "Grusha," she whispered, "Grusha. It begins with a G. I'm the youngest. I can do things an older person couldn't do."

With something like fright in her face the young woman pushed a bit of paper and the pencil towards Miss Grusha.

"Here," she said, "write your names out. Write the street where you live. If anything ever turns up we'll let you know."

Miss Grusha seized the pencil and wrote her name fearlessly across the paper. After it she wrote: *cuisiniére, bonne d'enfants, bonne à tout faire.*

"I'm ready any time," she said, lifting her head up. She wore the grim, warning smile all the way to the door. The two of them stepped out into the street, their muffs with their hands in them held close against the bosom of their jackets, the mince and jerk of their identical figures passing the length of the glass.

CHAPTER TWELVE

When Sorrel put his good wool tunic on after supper and did his hair over fine and smooth to go out in the evening, the others left the downstairs room, certain but playing with the uncertainty of whom he would ask to go. Those he never took out on pleasure with him, Cina or Gabrielle, Arthur or Peri, carried the grievance of it into the kitchen or into the glass-house or up to their own rooms and closed the door. It might have been only that he had forgot to ask them night after night, month after month, year after year since they had been there, for in his remote, abstracted, seemingly unthinking dimness he never put a meaning to it, nor ever seemed to see the wounds they bore. He put on his good dress, and once or twice in the week Matilde went to the movies or to a lecture with him; but the true abandon to preparation, the real festivity came only on the evening that Estelle and Edmond were free from the music-hall.

It was the sight in itself of Matilde's wife-like, complacent being, and the leather purse at her belt holding the money of the colony: her unhemmed, unclean veil, her watchful this, that and the other,

enough to make a commonplace of the evening
and the price of the ice-cream he must have on his
way home counted out on the table and the price
of her own strong cup of tea. When he walked
out the door with her twice in the week the eye in
his face was resigned to obedience; he went out to
his lectures a sharp, angular, old lady with his
hair done neat and his arm bare, and the bristles
showing in surprise along his chin.

But with Estelle and Edmond it was another
occasion. When the car was still at the curb in
front, Sorrel skipped quickly around it, his limbs
bewitched, the hem of his robe held up from the
condition of the street. The others could see him
from the windows, bending swiftly in his gown to
scrutinize the thin bicycle-like tires which framed
the car's light, wiry wheels. Edmond was sitting
in the back with his chamois gloves on, his light
fedora, and his cane between his knees, sitting
high and grand in the narrow, ancient, precar-
iously-swung car. Estelle sat in front in her
sables, with a short blue veil pinned soft across her
lids.

"*Ça va, mon chèri?*" they could hear her say.
And "*ça va, ma chère,*" Sorrel answered in his
dry and slightly-baffled mid-Western voice.

They could see him put one bare leg over the
bar before and fit the crank-handle in. His arm
with the wrist shapely and small, turned over the
engine, and then the awful, the unceasing palsy of
the car began. Estelle and Edmond sat upright,
shaken in the teeth of its convulsions. There was

no door on the driver's side, and Sorrel lifted
himself on the palms of his hands over the edge
and slipped in under the wheel. The blood came
red in his neck under the weathered skin, his lips
folded grimly in with a smile at the ends of them,
his hair shone smooth as silver on his skull, and
he put his sandal firmly on the clutch in the cold.

Whatever the weather was, the three of them
set out on Friday night for the automobile show
or the flower show or for an exhibition of modern
art. Beside him rode the silk hose, the foot's arch,
and the high voluptuous calf; the white, farded,
perfumed flesh breathing love as Matilde's never
breathed it. Out of devotion to Estelle and
Edmond or for the good they shared with him,
his heart was perhaps pure for ever of any vile
intent, but in his eye was waltzing in delirium the
ecstasy of bosoms under lace and limbs stainless
as milk, bleached out as if by wisdom of the senses
to a parchment nudity. On the way home after
they took him to a good place for an ice-cream soda
or a banana-split at any time of year, and on the
other side of the table they drank their cognacs
under his conniving, sweet, and uncondemning
eyes.

But on evenings when he was invited to the
houses of the rich or titled, then there was no
question of any of them going. He went alone, in
well-groomed and immaculate silence, like the
solitary existing member of a tribe. The others
of the sandalled and skirted house were left at
home to think about it, each in his own bitter-

ness: whether it was they were not clean, not handsome, not cultured, not presentable enough. Only Matilde had the vocabulary to say it out to them, and on nights like these when the others went upstairs to talk against the customs of the house, she opened their doors without knocking and walked in upon their sullenness, standing soft-fleshed, housewifely in their doorways, calculative of their impotence. She did not berate them for their faces' mutiny, but for the other things that she could seize on by right: for the colour put badly on the scarves, the posters Peri had not set up in type, the floors unwashed, the gas left burning in the kitchen all afternoon. She had the knowledge to give the truth to them besides, but that she did not tell. She did not say: there is too much written on your countenances, the history of dirt, rebellion, and discontent cannot be taken out in company for leisurely people to see.

"Arthur," she said instead, "there are duties in this house every one is to perform in turn. You have been twelve years here and you give no sign of understanding it. You were to do the stairway and the hall today."

Arthur, with his auburn helmet on, was paring a callous from the sole of his emaciated foot. He did not lift his head or speak; as she advanced he did not shift his place upon the floor.

"What are you here for?" she cried. "What good are you to the place? What work do you do that we have to put up with you here?"

He gave no sign, but carefully he pared the

deadened skin away. When she was gone on
down the hall, he looked up at Victoria. She was
sitting on a sheep's hide by the window, with her
coat on in the cold, braiding out Bishinka's hair.

"I don't believe in colonies," he said in that
hollow, quiet voice which filled the room with
sorrow. He stopped paring his callous and his
face was turned to her, pallid and cavernous under
his helmet of hair, the pale eyes rimmed with red,
the colourless lips moving as he spoke. "I am an
individualist," he said, quietly, ominously, as he
had said it a thousand times before. "It is unnecessary to waste words on either of them. They
are *arrivistes*. We are aesthetically opposed."

He wore a tunic coarse and grey as a rat's hide,
and under it stood the frame of his bones, long,
loose and plaster-white under his ailing, trans-
parent skin. He looked without emotion at Victoria and Bishinka.

"Sorrel's wife was a woman of poetic vision,"
he said deeply. "I have not spoken to Matilde or
Sorrel since she died."

But in the morning Matilde went with Victoria
to the shop and gave her a green and deep blue
woven dress to wear at night. She brought it
down from the loft where it had lain among all
the other things that had been worn by some one
else and discarded or left behind, or had been
waiting with the nameless peace of objects for a
time to be made use of again.

Matilde said: "You can wear this at night with
the sandals Peri is making for you, Victoria.

Sorrel would like you to go out with him sometimes."

It might have been that she had been till now
under probation with them, and whatever the
demand they made, she had quieted it, unknow-
ing, insensible to the virtue or the diligence they
asked. She held the dress up before her at the
mirror, and when she turned, liking the length and
feel of it, she saw the look that was neither one of
pain, nor of misdoubt, nor of sorrow but rather a
mingling of these in Matilde's face.

"I wouldn't know what to do with it," Victoria
said, and the colour came into her face. "I'm not
used to being gay and going out at night."

"Oh, but for Sorrel," cried Matilde, the smile
in her cheeks again, "you must do as he asks! He
gets lonely, Victoria. It's nice for him to be seen
out with a nice, tall young woman!" The round
little ha-ha's of Matilde's laughter came shaking
from her throat. "We're very pleased with the
way you sell things," she said. "But, my poor
Victoria, we don't want to make a shopkeeper
out of you! That's not the idea of the colony at all.
There's more to our work than that," she said.
"Sorrel used to get out a paper, you know, but in
the last years he lost interest in it. If he had some
one to work with him on it, perhaps he would
have the heart to start it again. You can see for
yourself," she said, "how hard it is to get the right
people around him. If you went out in the evening
with him, you could talk with the poets and painters
and draw them to him. He needs that kind of

interest now to keep him young and filled with plans."

Matilde sat down on the poets' bench, facing herself in the glass but seeing something else there, a thing too far and perfect in its death for Victoria to see.

"We used to have forty people in after dinner at night," she said. "We used to play Sorrel's Greek tragedies three nights a week, and three nights a week we had the dances and lectures. And then he used to stand up until two or three in the morning setting the paper up for the next day. You can't say it was because of any one thing, or any one person," she said, her heart and her will and her speech denying that Sorrel's wife had been there then. As she told it, it seemed that all that had belonged to them had dwindled without explanation: times had changed, money came harder now, as if these were reason enough for the great secession that had taken place. Once they had been in the heart of the city with a theatre playing and the doors thrown wide and the place standing ready, and now they were abandoned, they had withdrawn to themselves like a defeated people. Victoria was draping the scarves in the window and listening to the words she said.

"A few years ago, Peri took Gabrielle and the three young children off and they tried to start a place of their own," Matilde was saying. "But they couldn't do it without him. They went off to Italy and they tried weaving and painting and sandal-making, and when they had added Cina to the family and she was expecting her first baby, Gabrielle wrote to Sorrel. Peri was too vain to do it, but Gabrielle wrote and said they had nothing to live on, they'd been eating truffles and mushrooms for weeks then, and stealing from other people in the countryside at night. Gabrielle wanted to know if they could come back, and when Sorrel got the letter he went out and cranked the car and he drove all that night to get to them. Sorrel's heart never closes," she said, "no matter what people do."

Suddenly, as if a signal had been given, the two women's eyes lifted and they looked full into each other's faces. Matilde's gaze was dark and quiet, given so without preparation to Victoria, dark and entire, apprehending, as if in declaration that she no longer feared.

"We used to have a great movement of life and great activity all around us," she said. "You could bring painters to the place and arrange exhibitions of their paintings. If you brought young poets together, Sorrel would print their poetry, and print his own again. It used to be that way," she said. "There's no reason why it shouldn't be like that again."

CHAPTER THIRTEEN

In four days Antony came back in the evening. He did not come into the shop, but he passed outside on the pavement, walking up and down outside in the dark. He was wearing a fine fur coat in the early winter night, and he had an angular, thin curve and stride among all the other people passing. He seemed to be going somewhere with intention, and in five minutes, without looking in through the plate-glass, he was walking the other way. Inside in the light, Victoria sat still and watchful on the poets' bench with Talanger, listening to the voice that strayed high, thin, wanton across the hanging curtains, and waiting for Antony to pass again outside.

"Maybe I'll go on the stage," Talanger was saying. Maybe I will and maybe I won't, and wouldn't it take the conviction from their bone and split the house like thunder? "Estelle said I might become very rich and famous. I'd have to begin soon, wouldn't I? The good ones started very young. Estelle was four when she went on the stage. Mistinguette was better because she began at three."

Talanger sat close to Victoria, her soft, young,

golden muzzle lifted, the thick hair hanging straight in her neck. Her hands were as thin and dark as an Indian's hands holding Victoria's.

"I've never been to a theatre," she said, drawing it on the thin string of her voice, the history of the times and the places of other people, the theatres where Victoria had sat watching, and the faces of other children who had stood up to see over the heads of the people sitting watching; taking word by word from Victoria the memory of one man who made magic: his name was Thurston and there were red devils with doe-like horns that followed after his name. "Yes," said Talanger, "how old were you then? Who took you?" Drawing out of the heed for Antony passing and re-passing the words spoken in description of the fire that moved across the table on the stage and yet destroyed nothing, the water in glass that rose or fell obedient to Thurston, the watches, cuff-links, rings, coins, watch-fobs that he swallowed like a meal and then turned to the people. "Which of you ladies and gentlemen would like your watch, cuff-links, ring, coin, fob restored first?" And Victoria's own father had answered from the audience: "I'd like the nickel dated 1900."

"Then what happened?" said Talanger, and Antony walked by the glass. How has he the time for it, if he is anything but an idle, shallow man, or even for unhappiness or loneliness, which he never saw coming or going. Why doesn't he go home and ask the butler to tell the footman to have his valet bring him his letters, Antony Lister, on a silver plate so he'll know what he is and who he is and how many shops he's flirted in today. She saw the blonde ends of Talanger's darkish hair pointing on her shoulders, the weave of the tunic she wore coarse against her throat.

"He brought it up, he brought the nickel right up," said Victoria.

"Vomited it?" said Talanger.

"He gulped it up, quietly," Victoria said. Antony was taller than any one else outside. "And the other things afterwards, in the order people asked for them."

It did not come to an end there, but it went home to the family's house and up the stairs with Victoria. The nurse took off her hat and started to undress Victoria.

"How old were you?" said Talanger. "What kind of a dress did you wear?"

And the tears were coming down the face of the nurse because she was a Catholic, she was an Irish girl, and she had been brought to see a thing she should never have had to see. Victoria's people had taken her to see the devil at work, and she could never purge her soul of it. She had thought it was going to be a musical show, until she saw the devils with their horns on the posters inside. If they took the shoe off Thurston's foot they would find his cloven hoof inside it, and his tail coiled up in his trousers behind. The nurse lay down on the bed and cried all night for the shame and the sin that she had witnessed. She got up at five in the morning to go to confession and rid herself of the burden of what she had seen.

"If they left me here with Estelle when they went south," said Talanger, "I could get confirmed, couldn't I? Anyway, I could go to the music-hall and see Estelle and Edmond do their number."

Antony was going past the glass.

"They left me with Estelle last Easter when they went to Cannes to get the sun for Sorrel's ankle when he sprained it. I went to Mass on Easter Sunday with Edmond and Estelle."

In a little while they would get up and go back into the hallway where the stairs were, and climb up to fetch their cloaks from the loft. It was almost seven, and they would turn out the light upstairs and come down, groping in the dark together, and in the shop they would turn the gas-heater out and switch off the light and go out the street-door together, Victoria holding the key of it in her hand. In the street Antony would be walking up and down, waiting, or else not waiting any more. And then what will happen, what will happen then?

"Estelle let me use her lipstick after church," said Talanger. "Estelle gave me a medal from Lourdes last summer. It belongs to me really, but Estelle keeps it for me in her room so they won't know. If they left me here when they went south in the summer, then I could wear it on my tunic."

They went upstairs in the dark, and Talanger followed Victoria soft as a cat on her bare, sandalled feet. They stood before the mirror in the loft, arranging the cloaks across their shoulders. When Victoria smoothed the powder on her nose, Talanger stopped still, her slant-eyed, impudent gold face held fixed, like a cat's face, watching.

"Let me have a little bit of powder, too," she said. They went down the stairs, their hands out touching the unseen wall as they went, Talanger coming behind, her legs thin, bare, smooth as saplings in the cold. "I saw a crucifix I wanted in a shop behind the Madeleine," she was saying.

Victoria held the curtain aside into the shop, and Talanger passed under it. Antony was standing outside, his back turned, waiting close against the glass.

"Will you turn the gas off, Talanger?" Victoria said. What would he say, and why should there be anything more to say between them, or if he is waiting for speech I will say this street is full of shops, and the next one like it, with girls in them selling gloves, handkerchiefs, flowers. There isn't any time to lose, Antony Lister. Look in the windows for the next one to listen to you. I'm hard of hearing. I'm getting older every day.

Talanger crouched down in her tunic and cloak, and at once the blue flames of the heater died as if a wind had snuffed them. At the door Victoria turned the electric switch and when the light went out in the shop, Talanger came running over the thick, wool rugs to her.

"Wait, Victoria, wait for me," she said, "wait . . ." shivering a little for fear of the cold outside, or fear of the dark within. They put their arms close through each other's and went out on the step and locked the glass door behind them. Antony waited until the key was turned and then he walked up in his fine coat to Victoria.

"Hullo," he said. "Could you wait a minute? I have something for you in a car across the street."

He did not seem to walk away, but quick as a hand passed over a countenance he was effaced from where he had been, and in the mind's eye or the sight the pictures of him kept recurring, flashed swifter and swifter as though on a silver-screen gone wild: the grin racing in delirium, the face flashed short-nosed and paper-white, the hair brown, short, disordered above the empty loop-holes of the eyes.

"Who was that man with dead animals on him?" said Talanger, and Victoria stood still in the cold street looking at the place where he had been.

"That was an American called Antony," she said.

"Here you are," said Antony at once. He was carrying it in his arms like a baby, the cradled basket of whatever was inside. "I've been making money on stocks all afternoon," he said in apology. "They've got names cold as Maine water: American Ice, Lackawanna, Canada Dry, and what about Congoleum Nairn? I like it like 'Helen, thy beauty is to me'."

"If it's alive," said Talanger, stretching up to

132

look, "what will you do with it? They don't believe in animals, except goats or cows."

"It isn't a cow," said Antony, speaking French
because Talanger spoke it. "I couldn't find one.
But they're alive," he said. He lifted the lid of the
basket and they saw the flowers lying there inside:
the seemingly countless, tall, yellow-throated jonquils lying one against the other, furled at the
summit of their stalks. "All sisters," said Antony.
"Lovely, unascended towers. Where are you going now?"

Victoria put her hand in on the cool, clear stems.

"It isn't the time of year," she said. "It isn't
anywhere near spring."

"Flowers!" said Talanger, a little in scorn. "I
thought it might be turtles."

"It's almost time for turtles," said Antony,
looking at them as if in sleep, as soft, as unaroused,
the vacant eyes preparing to fill but never filling
with fear or curiosity or any other of the subter-
fuges that people carry for explanation in the face.
"It's almost time for anything," he said.

Victoria saw his face in the cold, hanging in
pallor and unrest like the face of a poor man set
incongruously in the prosperous fur of the coat he
wore. And for a moment it seemed to her that it
must be true: that he had borrowed everything he
had, the coat, and the good shoes, and even the
courage to speak out to strangers on the street,
and the things that were his own he was keeping
in shyness and humility for some other time.

"We have to take the Métro at the Concorde

now and go home," she said to him. Talanger was shaking against her in the cold.

Antony jerked his head at what there was on the other side of the street.

"There's a car waiting over there for me, if you'll have it," he said.

"It's too long a way to go. It's Neuilly," Victoria said.

"Nothing's long," said Antony. "I've been two hundred kilometres this afternoon."

He had his grin back on his face again and he was holding the basket sideways under his arm. The wind moved out in long draughts of the last of January weather from between the houses and Talanger's bare hand shook in Victoria's. Under her tunic, the childish bones were quivering in the Indian-dark, hairless skin. What did you wear in Ohio when you were a little girl was the memory of Talanger's voice saying, saying the word O-ee-o like the sound of a song beginning: how old were you, what kind of shoes did you wear? I used to walk up to art school at night for the classes in charcoal and the wind came like this right through any kind of clothes. I sat near the window doing the bust of Adonis. I was young then, I was so young I could rock the thought of it to sleep in my arms. Victoria put the side of her cloak around Talanger and held her.

"Come on, we'll get in the car," she said. "It's too cold to stand here."

It was a black car, closed like a case, with the chauffeur sitting out before. All of the things

inside were strange and glamorous to them, as
valuable as gold and silver: the beaver rug laid
over their knees, the bottles for perfume in their
cases, the hammocks for the arms to swing in, the
seat soft as a bed under them, and the name written
on the leather, etched on the glass, struck on the
silver, Fontana, Fontana said in rebuke to them,
spoken in sorrow over and over when the chauffeur
closed the door.

"I began believing in it after lunch," Antony
said, "I mean in the alteration in the time of year
or life or in direction. I called my broker up and
told him what to do," he said, talking fast, with
his eyes running out the window. "I need a lot of
money suddenly. I want to print a book about the
virgin passions of the soul." Even the breath of
Antony was new to them, warm and fragrant
with drinking in the car. "I believe in the word
now and in the transformations it can make. I
know that three lines of them at lunch changed
my course like a compass. Emily Dickinson open
beside the oysters. I would have climbed all the
walls in New England to get to her if we had lived
at the same time. I am afraid to say what I mean to
you," said Antony, "carrying her so thin, fragile,
delicate, modest inside me that talking might end
her. I started driving towards the country, persuaded that what had happened to me had happened as well to the mud, but, God, how I resent
trees when they haven't a bud to say for themselves, standing there hard-mouthed, crusted,
mean with their blood."

He was sitting close to Victoria, his long, elegant leg beside her unstirring, cool and seemingly unliving against her under the rug. Whatever comes, comes late, said Victoria in silence. I've seen grim things too long in my own face to put out my hand in gentleness now and say yes Antony, yes Antony. I've seen Lacey dead in Montreal and my mother is never done crying alone without any comfort in me. It is too late to say peace now and too late to say love; I should have learned in my youth to say it. I'm going to wilder, deeper places, Antony. Next week or the week after I'll be twenty. You might be afraid to come along.

"I knew gypsies once," said Antony. "They have a good name for us, but it rankles day and night in me. They call us 'trees' because we stand still, we can't move, we're caught rooted. Rooted in what? In rugs, books, walls, floors, possessions that cannot follow after. God, how I hated trees this afternoon," he said. "I drove faster to get away from them than I ever went towards them. They gave nothing, they made no promises, they kept their peace mean and hard inside them like all the people that drive me to despair. What I wanted for you I had to get out of a hot-house where the sun had been courted week after week by glass and the soil had been wooed by cow-flops and blossomed. That's how jonquils grow this time of year, not for love," he said, "but for money. It is not bitterness but hope that has taught me spring can be had at any time of year.

I have been too many times betrayed by the virtues I have strained my eyes blind for in reality and not yet perceived."

The houses were slipping past the windows in the dark, flowing evenly in a pacific stream of glass and stone.

"Victoria," said Talanger's high voice. "This is Passy. There's a shop for religious images at the corner of the street."

Antony did not turn his head, and his voice did not alter. He was speaking quickly, turning the empty bottle where his fingers fell below the window, twisting it quickly in its leather case.

"When I think of you, I am thinking of a thousand people I've imagined," he was saying, and when the bottle turned the name Fontana was written underneath the light. "So that when I think of you, even in January, I think of Emily keeping the wall between her and destruction or of me putting speech between you and what I want to say to you, and when I think of you, or any one like you, jonquils come out of my ears and flower and lady-slippers come out of my scalp and run through my hair. I can't bear music," Antony said when they stopped in front of Sorrel's house. The chauffeur opened the door beside Talanger and Antony sat smiling straight ahead. "Good night, Victoria," he said. "Music or the voice of any other woman talking interferes with the sound of what I'm waiting to hear you say."

CHAPTER FOURTEEN

Peri walked in and out of the open shop-door, bearing the tables out and the poets' benches. The embassy flags were not out yet at this time of the morning; there were only a few carts passing, horse-drawn by beasts already worn at the beginning of the day. Into the shop and the loft upstairs moved the dark, cold, shivering waves of city morning, the seven-o'clock voices of women with their vegetable and fruit carts rising, the icy tide reefing in, lightless, to the trembling curtains on Sorrel's walls.

When he had set the furnishings out on the pavement, Peri crossed his arms over, thick and hairy to the wrist, and watched Victoria scrub out the floor. The tunic hung below his knees over the muscularly misshapen limbs, belted at the waist of the sallow, narrow torso that had seemingly telescoped in upon itself under the weight of strength it bore. Arthur was standing in the show-window in his homespun dress, his helmet on, his mouth hanging open and his chin gone under his lower lip, working with the vacuum cleaner in his hand.

"Nice work here, eh, Victoria?" said Peri, standing short and thick in the doorway, the smile wide in the monstrous head, the eyes clear as beads through the shrubbery of hair.

"Fine work," said Victoria. "Makes the arms strong."

She twisted the rag out over the bucket and threw it down damp on the boards again. Arthur worked gaunt in the window, lost in the high, electric singing of the cleaner, his skin white as a leper's on his bleached, gigantic bones.

"We had enough of it a few years back," Peri said, smiling. "I told Sorrel what I thought of his place, and I took Gabrielle and the two children. We went down to Italy where the climate is good and started a colony of our own."

Victoria scrubbed the floor with the long-handled brush, following the way the boards were laid and the grain of their black wood.

"You'd never see a morning like this one down there," Peri said. Here he was out of his own country, bitter and soured with cold, and nothing left to him but his envy for fruit hanging big on the trees, and the vines swelling, and the ease that other men had. "And we were selling sandals as good as his too, and weaving cloth just the same. You see by this time who does the work here," he said. "The only thing I didn't try down there was giving lectures. I could have done that too," he said, "only I get claustrophobia in a crowded hall."

"It's starting to rain," said Victoria. "You'd better bring the benches in."

From across the street came the smell of solemn ambassadorial stone.

"But Sorrel couldn't get on without us," Peri said, smiling still as he carried the dark-stained furniture in. "He came down after us. He came all the way to Italy after us with a lot of apologies. He wanted us back at any cost. I told him we'd come back for so much a piece for the work Gabrielle and Cina turned out for him. Cina joined my colony in Italy. She didn't know anything about Sorrel until he came down after us. Prosperine was just born when Sorrel and Matilde came down. So we came back on that arrangement. I wasn't going to have me and the women working all day and night and getting nothing out of it. That's not my idea of a colony," Peri said.

Arthur closed his mouth and his chin came back, and he switched off the sound of the vacuum cleaner in the window. Having been a long time in another place and deaf to them speaking, he started when Peri's voice began again.

"I'm not here for ever," Peri said. "I've got another idea up my sleeve."

Arthur stood winding the cord of the vacuum cleaner around its silver stem, the Adam's apple quiet in his long, white neck, his hands incredibly bleached and mammoth-boned.

"The time is not far" he said as he stepped from the show-window "when the endeavour of a single individual will square the circle." The prophecy of his voice laid a silence on the air. "If it could be solved in the terror of communal living, it would be twice the victory——"

"Don't step in the water, Arthur," Victoria said.

He stood looking at her, the vacuum cleaner hanging in his hand. "Why don't you come and work in the loft when you want to be alone?" she said. "You can have it to yourself whenever you come."

"No," said Arthur, slowly. "I cannot be alone. I live as the member of a tribe."

"In twelve years," said Peri, smiling, "you've never tried to go away."

Arthur turned and looked at him, as if startled to find him there.

"And when you go away," he said slowly in a moment, "you go as far as another colony. You do not escape, my poor friend. You should denounce the conception of a colony as evil and see the isolation of the individual as the one release."

The rain was running now in straight white rails across the plate-glass window, and the poster on the inside of the glass said backwards that Sorrel would hold a lecture on Saturday night entitled: "*Pourquoi l'Homme Doit Chercher la Simplicité.*" Below it a smaller notice said in red and yellow that a dance and tea would be held as usual on Sunday afternoon at the colony's house in Neuilly, and on Monday night a reunion of the discthrowers at the *Salle Pigalle.*

"You compromise with fate," said Arthur in sorrow from the darkness of the hall behind as he climbed up the spiral stair. "Silence," his voice returned deeply sonorous as a voice about to rise in singing, "silence is as absolute as flight."

In a moment they heard the vacuum cleaner wailing and moaning overhead.

"No man can be a leader," Peri said as he laid the rugs down "if he's what a woman makes him. Maybe it's Matilde who's after the money, but that doesn't change anything if it's Sorrel who lets things go that way. Sorrel's wife was another kind of woman," he said. He was on his hands and knees, smoothing the rugs out. "That's why a man needs different women for the different things," he said.

Victoria was kneeling on the poets' bench by the mirror, rubbing the glass clear. She could see him reflected, squatting in his tunic, his full mouth smiling, his eyes bright as an animal's under his hair.

"In the bourgeois régime," he was saying, "there's the idea of the wife and being faithful to her. But for men like me, if you stay faithful to your art and your own needs, that's all posterity asks of you. I'm faithful to one thing in Gabrielle and to another thing in Cina and I could be faithful to another thing in somebody else."

He stood up on his sandalled feet and he came near to the bench. He had folded his bare arms over his breast again and shaken the hair back from his face, and he stood planted there, rooted powerful on his thick, spread legs, smiling under the dark nostrils that widened to take in the shop's cold air.

"Peri, will you light the heater?" Victoria said.

He walked to the corner where the heater stood and struck the sulphur match on the sole of his sandal, and the smile did not fade from his mouth.

"You, Victoria," he said. "You don't look like Cina or Gabrielle, so you're given a place to work in town where people can see you. They're kept up in the house doing the other kind of work because they're not good enough. They're not asked down to tea here, and I am not wanted once the customers begin to come. Estelle and Edmond go out riding in the Bois with him, but the rest of us aren't asked. We're not good enough to go."

Victoria stood up on the poets' bench to reach the top of the mirror with the rag in her hand.

"I'll ask you to tea, Peri," she said. "I'll ask all of you. Come down this afternoon with Cina and Gabrielle when all the Americans are here. It's your place as much as mine, isn't it?" she said. "It belongs to the colony and every one of the colony can come."

"It's Matilde's," said Peri, stepping close to her. "It belongs to the rich here," he said, speaking in a voice hushed to a whisper with malignancy. "I don't belong to the rich. You don't belong to them." His face had come close beneath her; his eyes fixed open, dark, fanatical, in the cold, yellow flesh. He was no longer speaking, but he was moving as if in wordless persuasion the smooth, colourless mouth which fear, or hope, or prurience had drained of speech.

It was the sound of Arthur coming quiet down the stairs again that sent Peri across the room in impatience, settling his girdle at the waist. Arthur held the curtain aside in the doorway and looked at Victoria. His eyes were glassy as a goat's eyes in his long, white face.

"Some day I will come and sit for you, Victoria," he said. His helmet had slipped sideways on his head. "I've run the vacuum over everything upstairs. Your paintings say that you are singling out the individual." Arthur turned coldly, hollowly, his voice a cavern of condemnation deep around Peri like a grave. "As fast as you and Sorrel put people into groups," he said, "I will remove them and give them their own life. You and your beliefs," he said; and the words shuddered in his mouth. "Putrid. Grasping. Foul."

"Saint Arthur," said Victoria softly, calling after him as he went, and he turned and smiled, "put your helmet on straight before you go."

The rain was still falling in the afternoon when Sorrel drove the car before the shop, stepped lightly out, and slammed the tin door behind. He came across the pavement, holding his skirt above his delicate bare ankles, and behind him a few people stopped to stare.

"You should have an umbrella when it rains," Victoria said, and she wiped the drops of it off his face.

"An umbrella!" cried Sorrel, shaking his toga out in the shop. "What a mad idea! An umbrella is just an evasion. Look out the window and see how silly all these people look! There's no need in the world for an umbrella, dear child, unless you're wearing dead birds or something just as horrible on your head."

This was the way he came to the shop on the Wednesday afternoon of every week, came clean as a swan in preparation, his hair smooth, his eyes mild as a woman's, his dignity in readiness for the Americans who came in for tea. He and Victoria locked the shop-door and went out into the rain together, hastening down the street and around the corner to Rumplemeyer's. This was the rite, whatever the weather was, this was the programme of how things had been and must always be.

"You see, my dear, I like the elements," said Sorrel as he pushed the door of the teashop open. The rain was running in beads across his brow.

It was too early in the afternoon for the customers to have come in from the rue de la Paix, or from the rue Royale. The tables were empty, and the girls in aprons sat behind the counter; the long room, velvet under foot, waited in cloistral silence. Under the glass cases the sandwiches and cakes were spread.

"Um—mm," said Sorrel. "Nuts and mayonnaise."

"We have olive and cheese, too, today, Mr. Sorrel," the girl said.

It was the sight of them so, spread under glass, endless in shape and size and their names spoken, that filled him weekly with tireless, unquenchable delight. The cakes as readily green and mauve as pink stretched the whole length of the left wall gave him something of the vast, varied, lavish landscape of what food might be. They had faces as different as young girls' faces, red-mouthed, milky-skinned, and almond-eyed; and they were the shapes of hearts, diamonds, triangles, or the ruby lips of icing saying, Oh, Mr. Sorrel, oh, oh, oh, Mr. Sorrel, in the different cries of love, or the teeth of sugar smiling sweet as honey at him.

"Darling," he said to Victoria in his indecision. "Just you pick them out as usual. I never can make up my mind." And he sat down sighing, for no matter how many went back to the shop with them to serve the American women there seemed small and miserly after the sufficiency of what he had seen. He wanted them all, his mouth full with them, and he sat down and turned his head away, his lips pinched sharp from the years of deprivation there had been.

"Victoria," he said now when their packages were done. He stood hesitant beside her, the soft, baffled, green eyes level with Victoria's, and in their helplessness dependent on her own. "Victoria, we might have an ice-cream soda," he said. It was as if life had confronted him with one of those strangely bewildering moments which only a woman's clarity could simplify. "I don't know how your money matters stand with Matilde. I never keep track of these things, you know. But perhaps it could be arranged, only I'm not efficient like you about it; perhaps the ice-cream sodas could be put down as part of what was spent for tea. Then we wouldn't have to speak of them again. . . ."

He could not bear to be made to face these things and speak them out, but once it was said it

was done and he would not have to make her
understand again. She would know very well
when he came to the shop with the shy, bright
look of helpless pride on his brow that he had
driven the whole length of Paris thinking of it,
his hands gloveless in any kind of weather on the
wheel, his eyes clear, visionary, far, seeing the
traffic but inward dwelling on the thing that he
was crossing Paris for. She would see him stop
the ramshackle car at the kerb and come past the
plate-glass window and through the shop-door,
coming to kiss her cheeks as a shy man might
come to his tall young daughter and stand there
scarcely daring to look into her face. But after he
had said it the first time, there was no longer any
need for him to ask it. Victoria said at once to
him: "I sold a scarf this morning," or "I just sold
a tunic, darling," and the purse that hung on his
girdle opened like leather-dark lips parting for
spring water, and his fingers took the money from
her and put it away. He said then, as if the
thought had just come to him, "Victoria, we might
run over to Rumplemeyer's and have a marsh-
mallow sundae together," or "what about a soda,
Victoria dear, if you think you have time?" Nor
was the money ever spoken of again, once having
passed between them, as faceless as invisible currency might have gone from hand to hand.

At four or five the American women began
coming into Sorrel's shop, dressed in their furs
and their high-heeled shoes, coming in singly or
together for a taste of what was simplicity to them,

bringing their friends to look at it, with a half-adoring, half-marvelling language of "the empty lives we lead" and "you, Mr. Sorrel, who have the courage to be free." Or French or Russian women in turbans of odd cloth: women who sang, with great, draped breasts of full, throbbing, organ sound; women who had known his wife well, sculptresses with straight, grey hair cut short, old princesses who brought their poets face to face with the homeliness of his reality; young women dancers who came in reverence for his implication in a revolution of living and of the dance.

These were the followers, the disciples whose number and faces altered from week to week, who brought him the homage which the others in the colony denied. Here he laid down his arms and spoke in that amused, musing voice of Yankee prophecy, quiet and sure and hilarious with strength before these women because they offered him sanctuary in their hearts. They gave him courage, for they themselves half-feared his garb, his pure, white wreath of womanly hair, taking as sinners the guilt of luxury before the clear, active, uncondemning judgment in his eyes. Or they feared the places he had been, listening to so much and no more of what he told, in evasion of the thought they had no wish to think: of barren unpeopled plains and wilderness which silence flooded until the female ear went mad for sound. He had been there, in such places, unafraid, without them; wherever he had to go he went, fearlessly, without them, taking only stronger-bodied, less-cultured women along. They must have beds and baths, they knew, and know at which hour, for how long, and what the weather promised. They took their tea with him, flattered and flattering, twenty or thirty of them speaking at once in the shop, coming close to him for the sound of his wit or his chastisement to mock them, seeing him unattainable, ready for what he had next to do with his life, and the muscle young still and hard as stone.

But it was not these women who stayed with him. They were fine women in elegant clothes, or they were artists, and they had other places to go. At seven or half-past the last of them were gone, and they took the tradition of what he had been with them. They took it out to dinner with them, and in the end they took the remains of it back to America, and when they came to Paris another year they came back on Wednesday afternoon to see if it was still as beautiful as it had been before. But now it was January, it was as dark as midnight, and the tall windows in the embassy across the street were lighted. And oh dear, oh dear, grieved the voice worn thin with saying I am this thing, believe in it, for I lived my life this way to prove that it is true. All the things said on Wednesday afternoons were the things he said the first night to Victoria: the olives plucked from under the leaves and pressed into oil by his people, the stricken that he had taken into his arms and nursed through the plague in Balkan countries, the following of a river to its source. Having said them once, he need never say them again to Victoria, but to the changing congregation of women he must say them every week anew.

Victoria could see the empty cheek, and the skin drawn thin over the nose's arch, and what does he ask, she thought, but the time to sit quiet at night talking, talking of people he had known before, of his wife and of other people, talking of her until a bead of grief hangs on the end of his nose; talking of the olive orchards that grow quivering, silver-branched down to the Mediterranean water, of other places and of other people, and in saying these things putting a condemnation on his old age. Because of the life he had known before, he was making shift with them: with Matilde and Peri, with the children, with the love of Edmond and Estelle.

"Listen," said Victoria, and when she kissed the side of his face the tears moved out on his lashes but did not fall. "We'll go home now," she said. "I'll wash the cups to-morrow."

Sorrel looked up at her in weariness and wiped his nose on the back of his hand. He had been a young man a long time, and now he was tired.

"I haven't a soul," he said. "It's like living on a desert island. Nobody cares at all what happens to me. I keep thinking there are going to be footsteps somewhere. I don't want to go home, Victoria," he said, and he laid his head against her. "It's Cina's day," he said, "and the carrots are always burned."

CHAPTER FIFTEEN

The lights on the avenue were blowing wild in Neuilly, were swinging in the wind like signals of alarm given, and the shadows of the trees raced gigantically across the light-swept street. It was nine in the night and Victoria stopped at the boarding-house gate and took the key from her pocket. In the garden the leafless shrub-trees bowed to the ground in frenzy, the shutters slapped at the sides of the house; the great boughs rose and fell on the maelstrom of the wind.

Victoria shut the carriage-grill behind her and ran up the gravel drive to the door. Her hair and her skirts were laid back flat against her in the pouring dark, blown cool and smooth as a rabbit's hide in flight. An oblong of dim green light was shining lustreless in the transom overhead, and in the hallway, as if the wild centre of the storm had been imprisoned in all its fury there, the voices of women or fiends or the elements gone mad were crying. Victoria stopped short inside the door at the sight of them: Miss Fira and Miss Grusha quivering in the open archway of their room, their voices darting quick across the scarcely-lighted hall, and

151

on the marble stairs the woman of the house
propped upright in the shadows on her cane, her
face dough-white, convulsed with passion, shaking
slack-mouthed and monstrously obscene. As if
blown on the winds of their delirium, the servant
spun on her short leg and her long across the hall,
screamed out her venom in the Russian women's
faces, jerked back to the blaring brasses of the
voice that swelled, anchored in blindness, from the
last tread of the stair.

"Everything you own," was the woman's voice
clanging in the convulsive power that death from
sightlessness and death from age had given it in
anger, "everything you have won't pay me for one
month of all the time you've been here!" And the
servant fled across the hall to them, crying: "Cooking behind the piano! Hiding the egg-shells and
the rest of the filth under the mattress so we
wouldn't know!" Flinging it in their faces until
they were bare and flayed leaping from it. Miss
Grusha sprang forward, wasp-hipped and warped
in her skirt and her shirt-waist, and savagely struck
the air where the servant had been.

"Pay *you*? Pay *you*?" Miss Fira cried, her lip
drawn back from her teeth, her neck stretched thin
as a string from its boning, and Miss Grusha's
piercing laughter cut wild across the hall. "We'll
pay when we are ready to!" Miss Fira cried; and
the eyes were ready to burst from her head in the
ecstasy of her passion. "I'll report you! I can get
the authorities here in five minutes!" she said.

The woman seized the bannister in one soft lax

hand and in fury her cane struck towards the direction in which they stood.

"You're sly filthy cats fouling the place!" she cried hoarse across the hall. Having lost the sound of them, her face was turned to one side, her eyes seeking blind for them in the echo of where their voices had been caught. "You'll get out of here," she said to the empty corner. "You'll get the money to settle or I'll have the police here after you!"

"Get them, you blood-sucker!" Miss Grusha screamed out, smiling as she danced in the doorway. "Get them! We'll have a fine reception for them!" And the servant spun across the hall at them, crying: "Prison's too good for you, for the two of you! Liars and thieves, stealing the bread off the door!"

It might never come to an end, unless by violence, for the fury of the women was transport as marvellous as love to them; was virgin anguish in them as exquisite as the pangs of birth might be. They could not turn now and close their doors and dwell upon their wrongs in bitterness, and speak calmly to each other of injustice, forswearing this rapture of devouring delight. It could only end in an orgy of attack upon the foully-seen and foully-hated bodies of the others, two women against two. The look was there in their faces, to rend the secrecy of clothing from each other's flesh and assault the vulnerable privacy of what their unwashed, ancient apparel concealed.

But Victoria came down the hall, suddenly stand-

ing between them, tall and austere, with her hand
lifted. She looked at Miss Fira and Miss Grusha
and she said:

"Go into my room, Miss Fira and Miss Grusha,"
speaking sternly to them as if to children. With
her raised arm she pointed towards the darkness
of her door.

Miss Fira fumbled her handkerchief at her lips
for a moment, and Miss Grusha's hand closed fast
upon her beating heart. Then the two of them
turned and fled down the hall before her, the
whaling upright in their collars, their posteriors
moving lean and small, the hair on their heads
wrenched without mercy from their napes and
pinned into the smooth, high buns behind.

"*She* began it . . ." Miss Grusha whispered
sharply at the door.

"We didn't say a word. . . ." Miss Fira said
with dignity.

Victoria led them into the room, turned on the
gas and lit it, and locked the door.

"Listen," said Victoria, turning to them as the
light gathered strength in the room. "There's
something else in life. You must believe it." She
heard her own voice, almost a whisper, in supplication. "There's something else," she said; and
suddenly she went to them, taking their hands in
hers, her eyes averted in confusion. "You must be
ready for it when it comes."

She could not say put your heads down here on
my knees, little women, let me take the pins out of
your hair, let me draw the bones from your lace

like taking splinters from your flesh. Whatever I do, I have enough left over, enough food, drink, love, time enough, enough to touch your hands and make you go to sleep quiet. You must believe in me for I am not afraid of anything the world can do.

She could not say these things, but the sound and the shape of them were moving in her.

"Listen," she said. "When I came down this street there was some reason for it. I didn't know you were going to be here, but something else knew where I wanted to go. You gave me what you had, dinner and everything, didn't you? You took me to Sorrel. I'm going to get money some-where," she said. "I promise it to you. You can get out of here. I'll see that you can. You can go away and be whatever you want, wherever you want to be it."

Miss Fira's quick little fingers were moving shyly in her hand, and Miss Grusha looked swiftly up at her and spoke.

"We've been thinking of Monte Carlo," she said. There was a small furrow of concern set between her brows. "There's such a lot going on for single women there."

"It does seem the logical place, doesn't it?" said Miss Fira modestly. "There's always the chance there of doubling one's income."

"We had a friend who lived twenty years in Monaco," Miss Grusha began in her high, wild whisper of hope.

"An acquaintance," said Miss Fira.

"She made both ends meet and something over

every afternoon by playing *trente et quarante* from ten till tea-time every day and Sunday," said Miss Grusha. "She said the price of life was cheaper in the Condamine."

"I'm sure one could live quite comfortably elsewhere," Miss Fira said, rebuking Miss Grusha in a voice as soft as silk. "There's no use being in a place if one settles in the wrong end of town, you know. I remember father speaking of the far end of the boulevard du Moulin as a neighbourhood where unattended ladies could find accommodations in all security."

"We'll need quite a little to start out on," Miss Grusha said. Her hand was trembling in Victoria's hand. "I'll have to have a coat. They're selling some out cheap now at the Galeries Lafayette."

"I'm sure, Grusha," said Miss Fira, "that what we have will do."

"Oh, it's all very well for the older sister to talk like that!" Miss Grusha said, and she went from them to the glass. She stood before the mantelpiece smoothing her hair up in her fingers, her eyes gone arch with pride at the small, neat face she saw.

"Listen . . ." Victoria began, and when she stopped the three of them saw it together: the basket with the green ribbons on it lying on the bed, the woven ribs, the golden straw of a strange thing that had somehow come into Victoria's room.

"Oh!" Miss Grusha whispered, seeing it reflected straight before her in the glass. "It came this afternoon. We saw a chauffeur bring it. . . ."

"We forgot to tell you," Miss Fira said, breathless, as if her voice might fall and break in pieces on the floor.

Victoria took her coat off and laid it down. Then she went to the bed and touched the elegant satin bows of what was lying there. The two little women came across the room and stood beside her, waiting.

"Were you thinking of opening it?" said Miss Grusha after a moment.

"There's probably something inside it," Miss Fira said. If she did not speak fast, her breath might be gone from her before she was done.

The ribbons came long and loose in Victoria's fingers and lay heaped as beautiful as jewels upon the bed. The two little women were almost beside her, not quite behind, silent as she lifted the long cover off, scarcely daring to see with her the thing that she would see.

"Good God," said Miss Grusha when no one else had spoken. "Good God, it's food," she said.

There was a great nest of soft green curls of paper, and in it lay the fruit, the cocoanuts, the pineapples, the grapes with the bloom still on their skins; the bottles of red-stuffed olives from America, the Boston baked beans in tins, the boxes of caviare, the pretzels, the shrimps in glasses, the anchovies, the peanut-butter jars. What's this? what's that? and what's the other thing? said the voices of Miss Fira and Miss Grusha. Peanut-butter, said Victoria in silence, peanut-butter, coming out with a knife like putty, with the oil left sitting in the middle, and it hugging the tongue and the teeth with taste like nothing else on earth. Heinz beans being born, one after another, hot in the mouth, a bellyful of food remembered good as food might never be again. America, she said in silence, touching the boxes of what had grown there, I want to go back to you. I want a father with a voice like baked beans and corn to put his arm around me. I want a mother warm as corn-bread to wash my ears at night.

"Listen," Victoria said to the Russian women, "we can eat a lot now. We can heat things behind the piano. We have everything."

"Even dates and figs and cheese," said Miss Fira, following the menu course by course in her mind.

"We haven't any bread," said Miss Grusha in a whisper.

"It's too late to buy any," said Victoria. She saw the small envelope lying among the things and she took it up in her hand.

"There'll be some left in the old woman's kitchen," said Miss Grusha evilly. "Sometimes the old skinflint saves a bit for morning."

Victoria turned the envelope over, and inside it was Antony's card, and written straight across it:

" 'Ah how the throat of a girl and a girl's arms are Bright in the riding sun and the young sky And the green year of our lives where the willows are——' Have you ever read a man named Mac-Leish? I've never read any one like him. I've a book of his for you if you'll have it tomorrow afternoon."

CHAPTER SIXTEEN

Antony said, "There are a few things we
have to say to each other. It's eight o'clock
now, we can spend all night talking." He
said, "Victoria, I don't know anything about you,
but I know so many things about so many women
that some of them must suit you and be an explanation. If you begin where I begin it will be something. Let's have some more clams," he said, sitting tall, thin, curved like a harp to music at the bar.
"Let's have some more cocktails, empty 'em hot as
vocabulary into the pit. Let's say it," he said,
" louder, wilder, fiercer than it's ever been said."

Or he said, "What I want more than anything
is this." He did not say "What is it you want,"
as if it came to the same thing in the end. He
said, "Let's have some more thin bread that folds
double. Tell me what things you are afraid of and
it will be some kind of a beginning. If you're
afraid of heights or mountains shouldering you
out of the picture it's one thing, or water it's
another and I'll make some kind of a fleet of history and get out to you. I'm scared to death," he
said, and he was laughing as if his teeth were shaking, "I'm scared of being pushed out of it, I can't

see myself anywhere in it. It's like looking at a
photograph of a ball-team sitting up to have their
picture taken and trying to find yourself in it. Every
one's there I like," he said, "but I'm never there."

The barman put down the little glasses full
again before them, and Antony said: "Every day
I'm in Europe or wherever it is, I can see the map
of America in my head and the mountain-ranges.
I think of State lines and I can hear the people
talking as well as I hear you and me. Nobody
over there hears it or sees it the way I do, the
men's spit hitting the stove in the hardware store
or the corn popping makes too much noise. They
can't hear what is going on the way you and I
hear it sitting here in a bar kissing the rock of
Plymouth, the stone breasts, the iron mouth of
Plymouth, because I'm for Plymouth, I'm for the
Puritan women and for the ancestors who were
not afraid of beginning there."

"There's nothing to take me back," said Victoria, and she felt the drink moving in her blood.
"I'll go back when I'm old, maybe, and it will be
like going to a new country because there's nothing
waiting for me."

"Keep on drinking, keep on drinking," Antony
said. His eyes were running fast over the tables
as if whatever was waiting there behind them
would strike if the drink stopped going down.
"Keep on drinking," he said, "and maybe something will happen. Maybe we'll recognize our own
faces in the newspaper or in a mirror."

"I'd like there to be a way of living without it

having a name to it. Not waitress or stenographer or salesgirl or painter," Victoria said. "I've been these things because they were there to do, and maybe I'll do them for ever. But there's something else that doesn't belong to that. It has to be carried along and set down in the end on the top of things somewhere."

"Keep on drinking," Antony said, and his face was as white as paper. There was no sense of place now, and the sense of time was drifting as if in sleep. The voices of people in the bar were as loud as the blowing of steamers calling deeply out over the water.

"It's given to you in the blood," Victoria said. "I don't know how it's given. But it has to be taken somewhere where it's never been before. If you know this, your face has two sides to it and one doesn't match the other."

"Keep on drinking," Antony said, and he looked straight ahead into the mirror. "The left side of yours matches the right of mine. They mixed us up somewhere in the beginning."

"I can't cry the way girls cry," Victoria said. "That's very hard on one's people."

"Fontana cries," Antony said suddenly, and then he didn't say any more. "Have another drink," he said in a moment, "and I'll start talking about Fontana." Everything he said came out in haste and was passed quickly over as if it were too humorous or too inconsequent to give it any time. "Fontana's my wife," he said. "Will you have a gin fizz?"

"Yes," said Victoria, and in silence the tumult of drink and confusion began speaking in her saying Antony why did you or what is a wife Antony or why should there be the word wife like something in warning said between us. Listen, Antony, said the three Martinis reeling, whirling, spinning on their light glass toes in silence, does everything come too late no matter how young you stay?

"Fontana cries like a bride," Antony said. "Have some potato-chips. Fontana wears white satin slippers and a lace veil, but otherwise she always forgets to dress. I never remind her because it is not necessary to wear clothes if you carry a bouquet. Fontana carries five or six bouquets because she always stops and gives one away to any one who asks." Antony's eyes went away and came back again. "You and Fontana," he said, "you and Fontana are different. You could exchange things back and forth with each other. You could give her austerity or whatever it is across your forehead and she could give you things like tears."

Suddenly one of his sleeping hands came to life on the bar and he reached out and took Victoria's hand.

"Fontana, you know," said Antony without looking, without moving, "is part of the bridal cortege that goes endlessly towards the altar. She's so beautiful that I'm lost somewhere in the crowd. I can feel my eyes cut out of my face like holes, standing staring in the crowd because I'm afraid of the function. If I could stand the faces of all

the people I'd walk with Fontana to the altar, I'd
be the eternal bridegroom, I'd walk straight to the
anointed place where the Holy Ghost is burning
in his little cup. That's what I'm afraid of," he
said. "Of people. And late at night when there's
no one left to talk to any more I'm afraid the Holy
Ghost does not burn night and day for ever but
expires. Victoria," he said, "this is the first time
I've touched your hand."

The barman put down their tall white glasses
of gin before them, and Antony put his hands in
his pockets and looked blind into the lemon foam.

"I'm not afraid of anything in America," he
said. "I've gone through the Catskills, walking
alone all night from one place to another. I'm
not afraid of what can happen to you in open
places. I carried a slinger. I was ready for wild-
cats or Dillinger or anything that came along."

He sat grinning at the drink before them, his
head small as a child's head, his nose short and
seemingly still unboned.

"I've been in blizzards, lost on skis, night on
the Arlberg. I wasn't afraid of that. I've had a
man freeze dead, standing up beside me. I'm not
afraid of the dead," he said. "It's the other people.
I'm afraid all the time of what people can do."

"What can they do?" said Victoria. The room
was moving soft as water on her face.

"They can come in between," said Antony.
"They can stand in between you and whatever it
is and you can go all your life down the length
of them beating your fists on them and it never

alters the look of them but it twists your own face up with fear. Ancestors, friends, strangers, all of them," he said. "I'm afraid of them. I go running up and down the ranks all night and day trying to get through. There's only Fontana," he said. "Something like our finger-tips manage to reach over the ancestors, friends, strangers, and touch. Let's go somewhere else," he said.

"It must be almost morning," Victoria said softly as if out of sleep. "I'll have to go back to the colony."

"No," said Antony. "It isn't midnight yet. You hooked me out of the water for a little while. You can't go off and leave me gasping here. Do you believe in fidelity?" he said. "Fontana believes in fidelity to the great. She believes I am a great man because I am not a great man, but I have stood outside looking at them so long that something they have has fallen in reflection on my face. If I were great I would not love the great, I would stay home contented the way the great stay home."

"Who are the great?" said Victoria, in her sleep.

"Captains of ships with compasses and charts," said Antony. "It's a good thing to know which way you're going and a little the shape of things ahead. Put a uniform on me," he said, "and, damn me, I'm still not there in the picture. There's nothing for me. I probably wasn't born to be," he said. "Fontana hears every word all night because it is said to her no matter how many things come in between us. She can even see you, Victoria," he said in a moment. He had turned his head from the bar and was looking shyly at her. "She can see your hair cut short on your ear like that and your eyebrow, and she knows very well," he said.

"What does she know?" said Victoria, her voice stirring like a still fish aroused in the deep, slow waters of sleep.

"She remembers," said Antony. "She remembers this time and the time after and the time before."

She looked at him smiling, the soft, drunken room moving in persuasion, the drinks in her blood murmuring softly, Antony, I will think a long time about you, I will remember your face a long time and your modesty bare as a white stone in the desert. There are not many stones, for conceit makes dust and sand of the others. But this is the end of it, Antony, this is the way things should end in sleep.

"It's late," she said. "I have to be up at six in the morning."

The street outside was dark and mild as if on a spring night and Antony's car was waiting. Antony said: "We'll go to the river for a minute. We'll go for just a minute to a boat on the river." They sat down inside and the man closed the door after them, and wherever we go, thought Victoria, this is not the beginning of anything, this is the end. They sat each in his own corner, looking through the glass at the streets passing. This is like floating at night on the water, thought Victoria, riding in the dark.

The car stopped near the trees by the river, and Antony stepped down into the ring of street-light that lay, clear-edged as shallow water, on the walk. There were no stars out, but a cloudy, spring-like darkness was drawn across the sky and river and the houses. He took Victoria over the little stretches of mud and through the wall above the river, and they went down the stone steps on the other side. There were canal boats swarming in stillness under the bridge's arch, lying asleep on the unmoving water, in the silent, unbreathing dark. Antony stopped under the bridge in the blacker shadow of the cool, wet flanks of stone and he laid Victoria's hands, open, against his face.

There he stood leaning against the stone, tall and thin in his black suit with his flesh shining white and featureless out of the merged, the perfectly passing stream of motionless land and water. "Victoria," he said, "I'm afraid of you. I can only say it to your hands in the dark. I'm in love with you," he said.

There was no cry, heat, spark, clamour of flesh, the words might have been written down on paper or stone and read by somebody else a long time after. He did not move and Victoria stood strong and cool before him in the dark, her hands held open on his face, listening to the pulse of the water lapping at the side or to the words written cold and motionless.

" I've never been in love," she said out of her

throat's pain. "I don't know——I don't know what it is."

Antony leaned over and kissed her mouth, and suddenly she saw Fontana clearly, saw her wondrously singled in his sight. He put his arms around her and he said:

"It's going to be history. It's going to be like nothing else has ever been."

But even in hearing this she could see the endless procession of the others : the quick, new, perishable innocence of their faces, the poverty of their faces once they had been given in embrace. There is no one, even now, there is no one but Fontana, she thought, and they moved out of the dark, hand in hand together. They went to the edge of the first boat where it rode bound to the thumb of timber going grey with rot on land.

"You'll have to jump here," Antony said. They went over the piece of dark water together and when they struck the deck, the boat stirred on its belly, but scarcely, as a crocodile might shift without awaking. They crossed the width of it and took the next boat, jumping the lane of water between, and Antony began laughing, high, sweet laughter like a boy laughing as they ran, his hand holding hers tight, thin, quick, like a boy's hand without ingression.

"We have six boats to do," he said. "Count 'em." They went over the water together and he said: "We're alike, Victoria. Our legs are just as long."

CHAPTER SEVENTEEN

When they came to the boat Antony knew, he called out a man's name in the dark, and they waited, their breath coming fast, harking, their hands held.

"Michel!" Antony called out, and in a moment they heard him coming up inside, coming up from the depths of what was below in the broad flat *peniche* on the water, the light he carried laying a line of white around the cabin door. The door opened out on the narrow run of deck to them, and the man stood on the last of the wooden steps holding his lamp up, standing waist-high at the open door, heavy and short with his hair oiled thick on his head.

"Hallo, Antony!" he said. For the sake of art or the work on the boat to be done, he was dressed in corduroy breeches and a flannel shirt, and he spoke an elegant, idle French. "Come in," he said. "There's a wonderful crowd here." He held the lamp up to show them the first step clearly. "*Bon soir, Mademoiselle*," he said. "Look out for the beam. Listen to them downstairs! *C'est fou!*"

Antony was laughing at the sound of it.

"Did the champagne come?" he said.

"A thousand thanks, Antony," said the Frenchman. "Two cases of it."

He went down before them, walking carefully in his canvas shoes, turned back a little with one hand held to guide Victoria down the stairs, the lamp he carried high opening out the hallway of the first descent as they went, the timber ribs, round as a barrel's, the striped curtains over the port-holes, the middle beam from which hung squashes as various as sculpture and Chianti bottles in their baskets, the crockery set on it thick to serve a purpose, chipped and split with use. It had the orderly demeanour of a place where people who were pleased with shape and colour remained and kept clean and scrupulous and in repair.

In the flat bottom of the river-boat, the bedroom opened suddenly out. They had come down three ladders of steps to it, and suddenly it opened, miraculously flower-like, petalled mauve and richly scented, lamps lit around it as if forcing it to bloom at night. The place was filled with smoke and the talk of people, and the bed, wide as three beds, stood to the side against the ship's curved ribs, covered in velvet, holding the woman in it propped higher than the heads and bodies of the others who lay stretched, smoking and talking, in evening dress across it.

For an instant the people in the room were not aware that any one had come to the door and did not turn to see. Their life went on unbroken; the woman in the bed lay on her pillows in a white lace gown and through it her angular, her almost

manly-boned body moved with the animation of
her talk and her hilarity; and the others lay there
lost in the murmur of their own talk together,
drinking, or lying harking to the voice of brass
that clanged between the two long braids of hair,
made artificially blonde, which hung across her
white and high-boned shoulders and her breasts.
There was the woman in her nightdress, and cast
across the velvet of the bed the slim, swallow-
like bodies of the dark-dressed men and the
women's bodies near them lying softly, volup-
tuously revealed.

The music that played filled the boat's belly
with languor, humming black skins are richer,
black speech sweeter, stronger, riper under the
tongue. It was coming from somewhere else, from
a night-club or from London maybe, and nobody
on the boat was dancing to it now but harking and
drinking the glasses of cold champagne. Black
girls are made for it, shaped for it, sweet for it, said
the music, and the woman in her white nightdress
jerked with laughter, sitting high and hard as a
corpse in the bed and the black music howling like
loose-lipped hounds at the smell of death on the air.

It was only when Antony turned to the Frenchman and spoke that the life in the bedroom halted
for a moment.

"Did Fontana come yet?" Antony said, and the
faces of all the people turned to the door, their
speech quiet for a moment, as if the curtain had
risen on the step where Victoria and Antony stood.

"No," said the Frenchman, "she hasn't come.

I've been waiting for her," and the woman in her nightdress lifted her glass of champagne and called out: "*Bon soir*, Antony!"

"Come in, Victoria," said Antony softly, and he felt for her fingers in his hand and they went together towards the bed.

The tide of smoke, names, voices, drinks taken quickly down rose then, the heat rose swiftly, insidiously, lapping first at the ankle, mounting the leg until the knees were weak with the palsy of drink and the air thickened, slow as sugar, moved from place to place in the room, laughing, snickering, leaning on a shoulder or the timber ribs, gasping with laughter. Even the air in the room went from mouth to mouth asking for breath, moving towards the port-holes of night as if the smoke would part and let them open, asking in a voice gone high and weak with laughing for a way into the darkness, for a way out of the sound of music playing on the radio and the light.

People had begun dancing in the bedroom, people had put their arms around each other and drawn their bodies close. The nap of the velvet stood like a caterpillar's coat against the white arms of the woman in her bed and the blue veins that lashed turquoise under her flesh.

"Who's Victoria?" she asked. The bones were big in her neck and the veins ran down across them to her breasts.

"Victoria," said Antony. He was lying with Victoria's hand in his, floating, his face turned up smiling on the dark belly of the water, his hair drifting and reaching, washed serpentine in the room's current from his brow. The champagne was breakable as crystal in their mouths, and through the music, through the heat and smell of love, Victoria could hear Fontana's heels coming across the deck outside in the darkness that was almost morning. She could see her cheeks clean as heather, and the flowers she carried in her ringless hands in bouquets of early-morning stars. She could hear Fontana laughing as she met Michel, a small, tall, stout, slim woman with her Saxon eyes black as ripe olives. In a minute Fontana would come in through the door, laughing like a farmer's wife at a clam-bake, dancing like Pavlowa, saying: "Land's sakes, you haven't been listening to Antony, have you?" crying like a bride crying, whispering: "Antony, I'm in love with you. Come home."

"Victoria's Victoria," said Antony to the woman in her nightdress. "Victoria's my next bride," he said.

In a minute Fontana would come in. She could hear her heels on the stairway coming down. She would come in without any hat on, with an apron on her stomach, her hair pinned back in patience but coming down in the heat around her ears. "I was up to Swiftwater making gingerbread for Antony to take to school tomorrow," Fontana said. "He never feels like he had a meal unless he's got gingerbread to finish off with." Antony was lying on the bed, his mouth speaking near Victoria's hand.

"I found Victoria," he said, laying the words in

softly under her fingers. "I found her selling things in a shop. We're going to run away together."

"Don't run too far," said the woman in her nightgown, touching the short locks of Antony's hair. "You'll have to be back next week if you're going to America."

In another minute Fontana would be in the room. She would run in with a boudoir-cap tied up in ribbons on her curlers, her chest caved in for coughing, and a dressing-gown with lace on it that she had dipped in tea for the antique look it gave it. "Christ, Antony, you can't do that to me!" she was saying, and the teeth were knocking in her head. "You can't do it, Antony, you can't do it, I tell you!" She was rolling the lace of her *négligé* into points in the wet palms of her hands. "You can't give me the bum's rush now, kid. You don't know what's the matter with me. I ain't told you what I got wrong. Listen, Antony," she said, and the marks were dark as bruises under her pale pink eyes, "you know you're going to stick by me, don't you? You know you don't want people going around saying the kind of things they'd say."

In a minute the door came open, swift and wide, and Victoria jumped up from the bed and put the piece of hair back from her face. The step on the other side was waiting, in preparation, and the dancers moved slow, as if slumbering in each other's arms to the music, the air beat heavy as blood in the temples and in the heart. She could hear Fontana's voice speaking, but only the Frenchman came to the step that was ready there, in waiting.

He carried the lamp no longer, for the port-holes were turning white already with the dawn. He said:

"Antony, Fontana sent the chauffeur over to say she forgot. She thought it was ice-skating in the Bois. She's been there all night with people."

"Perhaps it was ice-skating in the Bois," Antony said. His mouth was gone suddenly under the kisses of the woman's mouth, and Victoria put her hand out and held to the side of the timber wall.

The boat had begun to rock in the storm, you couldn't find the door out for the ups and downs of the briny, and Mrs. Coffee's voice was poured like Crisco on the troubled waters. She was saying "It's murderous the way the sea's going, Miss Victoria." "It's only going up and down instead of back and forth as usual," Victoria said. Only Rose Coffee's face had anything like faith left in it, with the pinks in her cheeks and mouth as flowerful as ever. She had a voice for singing, and she began The End of a Perfect Day with the vile green of sea-sickness blooming all around. Just then the wave went over the deck and took the soft-shell crabs and the bottle-fish and Mrs. Coffee's rosary overboard.

"They used to tie me by the middle, tether me to the mast," said Victoria when Michel put his arm around her. "Sometimes you caught bottle-fish instead of king-fish by mistake and the captain used to put his lips to the fish's lips and blow. The fish blew open once, split down the middle," said Victoria with the laughter coming out of her mouth. Every one else had stopped dancing and lay on the bed again, the soft knees of the girls and the men in coats with hairs across their hands, and a tide of sleep rising and falling on them. Michel was holding her strong against him, a short, thick man with perfume in his hair, holding her together as they danced.

"I'm going back over the boats now," Victoria said. "I remember the way to go."

"Every one goes to sleep now," Michel said. "It's the time to go to sleep." He was dancing, but his limbs were heavy with slumber. "You can go to sleep for a little while," he said.

"I have to open a shop at eight," said Victoria, with the grin stretched in her face. Michel had laid his face against her cheek.

"It's only six now," he said.

She could hear Mrs. Coffee raking the ashes out of the stove at Beach Haven. There was a mirror they were dancing past, languid as sloths to the music, and if I turn to it whatever is drunk in me will make a face at itself wild enough to rouse them, will give them insomnia as a gift to walk the floor with them all night.

"If you'll take me up the stairs," Victoria said. "I can go the rest of it by myself."

"What about Antony?" the Frenchman said. "What about him? You aren't going to leave him here?"

"Who's Antony?" said Victoria, holding on to her mouth to keep it straight. "Who is he?" she said. The air was cold as mountain water when she stood on deck. "Who in the world," she said.

CHAPTER EIGHTEEN

On Sunday morning some kind of stir was made to clean the downstairs room in Sorrel's house in preparation for the dancers. It was the women's work to do, but there had been trouble about payment for the tunics on Saturday night, and Cina and Gabrielle would not come down the stairs. So the woman's war cried on, unceasing, through the house; the fires were not lit, and the dishes from the breakfast porridge stood thick and cold in the dark, unstraightened room.

Sorrel was in the garden in his steel-grey tunic, and the frost scarcely off the winter bushes, his white hair hanging straight as an Indian's in his neck, his bare arms elbow-deep in the bath-tub underneath the eaves where the cloths for new tunics were soaking in a bath of powerful and icy blue. Whatever was going on in the house, he had closed his ears and his sight to it. He was working alone in the air, his flesh cold, mute, isolate, protected from any lasting outrage by the might of his indifference.

He was like a ghost in his own house, and it was perhaps because of this mystery in his flesh that the other people stayed. It was the mystery that did not seek to explain, that passed quickly, running down the stairs. The thing they could not touch, that did not eat at table with them, slept apart, that gave no orders, but whose identity had drawn them from their different ways of living to this house and held them captive, in awe, or pity, or resentment there. For Peri he had been the mystery and the vision, and through Peri so the women and the children saw him, but only for a little while. If they heard him speaking out at night to strangers in the lecture-hall, they were humbled by the presence which sat at ease, quiet, shepherd-like, leader-like, the ecclesiastical voice unshaken in its saw-mill, Yankee French opining: I have lived a simpler, a more honest life than you. Or they were awed by the presence that entertained at tea, or drove to other people's homes and gave no explanations, driving erect in the spindle-wheeled, old car, immaculately secret, immaculately clean.

It was only when they had learned his secrets from him that his dignity was shed. Once they could make sandals as well as he and colour cloth with his colours, they believed they had seen through what he was. They were sullen and bitter with the work they had to do, for they were disciples only so long as they believed they never could be like this man.

Now and again when the voices of the women cried too long and high, Estelle opened the door of her room and shouted into the hall. The quick,

M

female tongue of Matilde lashed in anger upstairs and down, and "You band of cretins!"
Estelle cried on the landing. "Can't you let us get
some sleep in the morning?" She had got so far
as putting her corsets and her stockings on, and
the black had run beneath her eyes from her lashes
painted the night before. "If you had to work for
your livings the way Edmond and I do, you
wouldn't have so much wind to spare!" she said
and she slammed the door on them.

The children were playing in the downstairs
room when Victoria went in with the broom and
the bucket in her hand. Bishinka lay on his back
in the dust, his arms spread out, his eyes closed,
and his short braids standing out from his head.
Athenia kneeled on the floor beside him, the
wooden hammer lifted, as if to drive the nails of
crucifixion in through his open palms. Prosperine
knelt as an angel of God beside him as he died, and
Talanger's head, with a scarf drawn over it, was
bowed to the floor in grief.

"Oh, my son, my son," moaned Talanger.
"You are dying to defeat the devil!" When she
looked up in agony to his face, she saw Victoria.
"Can't we finish the crucifixion, Victoria?" she
said.

"I'll start sweeping the other end," said Victoria, and Hippolytus came into the room with a
cup in his hand, carried it fearfully across the
boards and threw the water from it towards
Bishinka's small, dark face.

"You wanted a drink, eh?" said Hippolytus

in contempt. "Well, there's some vinegar for you!"

"They gave it with a sponge," Talanger looked up and said.

Peri and Arthur came in with the mops, and Peri was smiling at the sound of the women's voices screaming like gulls in the rooms overhead. Arthur's helmet was close about his ears and his tunic was girdled high for the cleaning.

"You didn't get very far with your Oedipus this morning, did you?" said Peri, smiling up under his hair in venom. Skeleton-like and majestic, Arthur walked silently to the crowded mantel and waved a cloth vaguely at the glass.

Hippolytus was playing two parts at once now: as Peri began to mop the floor, he was two of the Roman soldiers marching, and in a moment he was two of them lolling at night outside the tomb. He stretched out on the poets' bench, and for all the wild storming of the women in the rooms above, his voice sounded high and pure as an urchin's voice.

"We killed a dirty Jew last night," the Roman soldier said, and in Hippolytus's same clear voice the other soldier answered: "*C'est bien*. We ought to kill them all."

"This is the Holy Mother," said Talanger as she rose and with her hands clasped walked to the poets' bench in grief. "She's coming to mourn at the tomb. Move over."

Prosperine drifted after her, her arms waving like a bird's wings, and Bishinka sat up from the cross.

"What do I do now, Talanger?" said Bishinka.

"Hush, you're dead," the Virgin Mother said.

Estelle opened her door upstairs again, and Edmond in purple silk pyjamas followed her out on to the landing, neat and fresh and odorous after his morning bath.

"Matilde, we've had enough of this noise!" Estelle shouted. "Kick the two bitches out in the street and see how they like it!"

Edmond came quickly down the stairs in his suede slippers, fastening his little link bracelet on his arm. And now the voices of Cina and Gabrielle and Matilde seemed to break the walls, surmount whatever obstacles there were, and flood the hallways. In a moment the torrents of their virulence cascaded down the stairs. Edmond fled before it to the kitchen and lit the gas under the percolator again, and the children moved into the glass-house for peace, following Talanger's dreamy, devout retreat, seemingly deaf to the human words of the advance or to the woman's altered faces. There, under the tables burdened with block letters a hand wide, with half-made sandals, pails of drying printer's ink, the game did not begin again but, never having been disturbed, impassively went on, as if the anger of the women had struck them as a wind might and gone by.

And down the stairway came the wild clamour of the women warring, Matilde's voice, and Estelle's, and Cina and Gabrielle crying out, into the room where Peri and Victoria and Arthur were making the floor clean. Out in the yard behind, working in oblivion as if deafened by the cold, Sorrel with his hair undone was turning the limp, clinging forms of tunics in the icy blue.

"Why shouldn't the American clean up here on Sunday?" Gabrielle cried out. "She's down at the shop, dressed up all week. It's a good thing to see her doing a little work for a change!"

Her body was shaking as if from illness, and Peri looked up under the mane of his hair at Victoria, giving her a bright, animal-quick glance.

"Why don't you fight the women?" he whispered, smiling. He would like to see the lot of them at it, with no words left foul enough to be spoken, and their hands lifted and striking at one another's flesh. "*Allez-y, allez-y,*" he urged softly. "Don't be shy with them. Don't be timid. If they think you're afraid of them they'll always be at you."

Estelle came down the stairs behind them, came running on her heels, her pink underwear short on her thighs and her suave, tapering legs gone wild in the black gauze stockings. Her lip was lifted, smiling, and she held a siphon of soda-water before her high, full breasts.

"You're rich enough to have a servant here and pay wages to her!" Cina cried out, flinging into Matilde's face her black, Italian wrath. And "Psst, Gabrielle," said Estelle softly behind them, and when Gabrielle turned the jet of siphon water played straight into her eyes. "Psst, Cina," said Estelle, with the rich sol-fas of her laughter calling out across their outrage. She drove Cina into the corner with the gasping, croaking siphon's jet foaming across her face.

"Psst, Peri," said Estelle, and Peri got up from his hands and knees in haste, his eyes turned hard as beads again, having gone soft while he watched her legs' shape and the purity of her thighs where the stockings came to an end.

"I've been working with Victoria," he said when he saw her there, and he lifted his hand to shield himself. "I haven't done a thing."

"Just a little shampoo," said Estelle, wooing him softly as a dove. "Just to save you a trip to the coiffeur, Peri!"

He did not move when the siphon choked and spit on his hair, but whatever was venom and fury in him was burning in impotence in his face. There was nothing left to the curly mane but the writhing laces that fell on to his eyes and cheeks, with the tears of soda-water falling drop by drop upon his tunic's stuff. This too, this injury which seemed more than human dignity or vanity could bear, this too he must endure as thrashed beasts endure what they are given, knowing that except for this masterly subjection there is no protection, no certainty of shelter from the cold. Estelle had gone mad in her delight and she stood crying out with laughter beside Matilde, the laughter shaking ripe as fruit from their soft, female throats, as rich as money in the power they had.

Nor could he turn his face to Gabrielle and Cina and give them the sight of him with his crown of hair fallen in shame across his drenching mouth.

But his anger went over the room and into the corner after them where they stood wiping their faces dry.

"You women," he said, without turning. "You get up to the room, get up there!"

They hastened by and out the door in silence, and in silence Peri crossed the hall and mounted the littered stairs. As though he had waited for this silence to fall within the house, Sorrel opened the glass door from the garden and came in humming, bringing the cold red as dried apple-skins in his cheek-bones, and hanging beaded from his nose. He was moving quickly in the printing-room, seeking something, his senses deaf, blind, mute in his preoccupation, his being wilfully concealed from human sight or sound.

"*Mon Dieu*, Sorrel *chéri*!" Estelle cried out. "You missed the performance while you were at the North Pole! The women put on a singing act that brought down the house."

Sorrel lifted his head in the glass room and turned towards them, smiling gently as though just aroused from sleep, a screw-driver hanging from his hand.

"What is it, dear?" he said, and within him it seemed that his weariness and his despair were cocked for peace and quiet. He stood looking towards the three women and wiping his nose dry upon his tunic's sleeve. "Matilde," he said, "I wish the children wouldn't play in here. Pieces of my Meccano get lost and then nobody knows, nobody ever knows where they are. Edmond and

I couldn't make the suspension bridge last night."
He stood looking helplessly at the children underneath the table playing the nativity upon the floor.

" 'We three kings of Orient—are,' " Talanger
was singing as she crossed the desert. And Sorrel
turned, deaf, blind, mute to the big room and the
sight of Estelle's underwear. She stood smoothing
it down over her breasts.

"*Pas moyen*," she said, "to get a cup of coffee in
this place without fighting a regiment of cockroaches and women. Edmond's locked in the kitchen making cinnamon toast. Why don't you get
rid of the lot, kids and all, *mon chéri?*"

And "Hush, Estelle," said Matilde as she set
the benches straight, but speaking in indulgence
to her. "You mustn't talk like that." Her eyes
were quick on Victoria laying the sheep's hides
out. "You don't understand the colony."

"As for that," said Estelle, "I never have."
She leaned to stroke her silk calves smoother, and
her bosoms were ready to cascade from her lace
brassiere. "I can't see why Sorrel should feel it
necessary to live with a pack of dirty foreigners
he'd just as soon kick in the tail——" Suddenly
she waltzed across the floor to Sorrel. She put
back the thin white locks from where they hung
in his neck and laid her bare arms about him.
"Sorrel, wouldn't it be cute to have a colony without anybody in it?" she said. "You could call it a
colony just the same."

Sorrel leaned his brow against her cheek, and
slowly shook his head.

"That consarned tap's come loose in the bath-tub out there," he said. He looked in bewilder-ment from one to the other of the women, and the screw-driver hung down in his hand. The grey skirt of his dress came down just above his ankles, and there were the little bones of them held tight and narrow in his skin. He was like a ghost in his own house, moving around the edges of it in doubt, his voice not so loud as any of the others, the things he did done quiet and alone.

In the morning he ran out of it early when the sound of goats' bells came down the avenue be-yond the gate. He had his little pail in his hand and he ran quickly through the garden to the fluting of the goatherd's pipe as he drove the beasts along. The goats halted by the fence of themselves, and there they stood watching the smoke of the breath that ran between them, remem-bering the hay they left at dawn and returned to at midday, while the goatherd crouched by the side of one and drew down her milk into Sorrel's pail.

Sorrel did not touch them, and for their dis-parity with man he did not even seem to see them in the cold. He took his pail through the gate again when it was full and paid the goatherd out of the leather purse on his belt. So it would hap-pen day after day in the winter: he would latch the gate behind him and come quickly up the garden on his limber feet, his elbows out, like a spinster's, in the air. He would come into the kitchen, and when he saw Victoria at the stove, "My, my, up so early, dear?" he would say.

In the early morning he sat down on the stool in the kitchen, and the faces of the unwashed dishes looked at him out of the sink and from the stove and up from the table and floor. He drew his bare feet up from the touch of them, and there he sat drinking his goat's milk from the tin. His eyes were so beauteously lashed that a woman might have cried herself sick for them, for their colour and for the seas of languor and latency they held.

"We used to run down to the spring where the goats were and milk them ourselves," he said, speaking wistfully but with some kind of contempt as well for what the world had now become. He picked a goat's hair from his lip and wiped it in his dress. "On Cyprus," he said. "Well, well."

"There are just as many things ahead for you," Victoria said. She was stirring the oatmeal on the stove. "There's no end to them, Sorrel. There's the printing-press, whenever there's a little money ahead to go on with it. We could find young poets and print their work and sell their books in the shop for them, and it would all pay for itself when it was really going."

Sorrel sat on the stool, sipping his milk from the tin and listening.

"I've got poems of my own that would give these young ones a jolt," he said, and he chuckled. "Stacks of 'em," he said. "Waiting to be put into print. I'd show them a thing or two!"

"And paintings," said Victoria. " We could have people bring their canvasses to you, and if

they were exciting we could give them shows.
We could take down the scarves and tunics for a
week and give young painters a chance by having
exhibitions in the shop."

And what about my pictures, the mystery in his
eyes was asking. Talk about me, Victoria, said his
skin and his bones. Every one else is young with
time enough ahead of them, poets getting their
books printed, young men getting their pictures
hung. I've worked harder than any of them,
there's nothing they can teach me. Young men
callow and raw with no life in them, nothing to
take them the places I went to when I was young.

"I haven't an ache or pain in me," he said,
drinking the goat's milk. Everything's like it was
on Cyprus twenty years ago. "I've thought of
writing my life," he said, looking up. "What if
we did it together, Victoria?"

She stood turning the oatmeal over the fire.
When she put her hand down on Sorrel's shoulder,
she could feel the bone hard as wood under the
woven cloth.

"Yes," she said. The oatmeal was bubbling,
thick and slow, like lava at the source.

"I'll have Peri and Arthur get the hand-press
cleaned up," he said. "We could set it up, page
by page, in the evening."

"Yes," said Victoria. Like any woman, I belong to the thing I have undertaken. She felt the
bone in Sorrel's shoulder, good as a weapon under
her fingers. I don't belong to idle people. Antony
Lister, she thought, watching the lava gasp thick

and slow on the flame. Take the best boat back to America, six wardrobe trunks in the hold and pigskin bags breaking the porters' backs, and a different face every night on the upper deck in racoon fur or whatever's smarter. Take it back, Antony, give it to some one else. There's nothing in common between us except America.

"Peri can clean up the alphabet," Sorrel was saying. "We can start any day now. I've got enough poems to make Homer look like a piker once we get them set up," he said.

CHAPTER NINETEEN

Mrs. Brookbank came into the shop in innocence: she did not know the colony had been waiting since its beginning for her to come. It was for her that the scarves had been painted and the show-window dressed with care every morning; it had been for her, or elusive manifestations of her, that Sorrel had shorn the wool from his flocks in Cyprus and woven rugs of it. All the words he had spoken to American women at tea on Wednesday afternoons had been a rehearsal for the great performance, an immaculate design shaped syllable by syllable for her. She had a face of over fifty years, and a lady-like white skin filled soft with loose, quivering flesh upon her shy, her almost retiring body. Her cheeks were papery to the eye, and pure of artifice, and her voice was soft as a grandmother's speaking of Cambric tea and cretonne slip-covers for the wicker chairs at home. She was dressed in grey with chains about her throat and an embroidered handbag in her pearl-grey glove. Only in her feet could anything be seen of the intention and authority she had: she wore low, black, walk-over shoes which did not falter. She sat down on the poets' bench facing Victoria, her features scarcely seen, scarcely remembered, trailing a shy scent of lavender behind her on the air.

"How do you do?" she said as beautifully and timorously as if it were the rector who upheld her faith standing on the rug and not Victoria.

"How do you do," Victoria said. Now I shall have to say things I do not believe. "It really looks as though the sun were trying to shine, doesn't it?"

"Oh, I'm so glad there's an American here!" Mrs. Brookbank said, and her smile fluttered on her face. Hollyhocks were growing all around her and white butterflies pausing as they passed. She put her hand out tentatively and touched the sun-dial with the ivy on it. "I'm not very good at French," she said in apology. "I've travelled quite a bit, but always with our own people, and you don't have the same opportunity, you know. . . ."

Her voice died word by word between them. There was nothing they could do to sustain its failing life.

"I'm so glad you came in," Victoria said. "Mr. Sorrel wants Americans to feel that way about this place."

"What a great man he is!" she said. "What a great artist, isn't he? What a privilege it is for a young girl to be working with him! Why, I don't know of anything else I'd rather do if I had my life ahead of me," she said.

She came from the south and her voice had the sound of it, and her skin, for all the care it was given, was shrivelling a little as if in recession from the cold. She must have set the silver spoon deep into the sweet potatoes with a fragile, lady-like hand when they put the steaming dish with a napkin tied around its neck down on the well-appointed table before her; she must have broken the brittle edge of cinnamon and candied sugar that ran around the top, and turned her head with the milk-white hair on it to see if the corn were coming through the door.

"I'm going to St. Moritz tomorrow," she said. "Not that I expect to find it warm there, but at least there'll be some sun, and that makes a world of difference to me. I don't expect to find any-thing there that will mean what this—what this——" she said, and she lifted her hands helplessly to the glory of the tunics and scarves that hung around them. "That's why I want to take what I can along," said Mrs. Brookbank. "I'll have to have one or two tunics for the fancy balls they have there, and a scarf or two to cheer my old things up. I haven't bought a single new dress this year because, as I told my daughter, I feel I've come over this time on a—on a mission." She said it almost in apology, and then her voice expired.

"Mr. Sorrel has made a lovely mauve and silver one," Victoria said. "He might have been think-ing of you when he made it."

"Why, isn't that lovely!" said Mrs. Brookbank. "It sounds like just what I want. I hope it isn't *too* expensive. *Nothing* could be too much to give for Mr. Sorrel's things; but this year, like everybody else, I'm just not allowed to be as openhanded as I'd like."

Mrs. Brookbank stripped off her gloves and laid them on the table, and set her grey velvet hat down upon them. Her hands were shaking a little in suspense and wonder as Victoria slipped the long silk tunic over her white hair.

"Oh, isn't it beautiful, beautiful?" Mrs. Brookbank said. She stood before the glass, scarcely breathing in her reverence for what she saw. "It's really too beautiful for me," she said, and her smile fluttered to Victoria's face. "Some one tall and young should wear it," she said. "I can't express it the way I should because my limbs are so short."

"It's made of all the colours that go best with you," Victoria said.

"Is Mr. Sorrel's name woven in it?" asked Mrs. Brookbank, looking shyly into the glass.

Victoria leaned over and turned up the fringe at the hem.

"Here at the bottom," she said. There was the name Sorrel, stamped in block letters across it, not woven in.

"Oh, lovely isn't it?" said Mrs. Brookbank, touching the silk. "How beautifully he has blended the black silk of the letters with the rest! Now, tell me, where was this tunic woven, what is the history of it?"

"This one," said Victoria, turning away to choose a scarf from among the others, "was woven in Mr. Sorrel's colony."

"Oh, in the colony!" said Mrs. Brookbank, her voice hushed. "Oh, how interesting! I must remember that. And now tell me, please, did Mr. Sorrel himself weave it?"

Victoria put the scarf softly about Mrs. Brookbank's shoulders, and she stood looking at the sight of herself mild and quiet in the glass.

"He wove every bit of it," Victoria said, and Mrs. Brookbank touched the tunic with her fingers.

"I feel so proud, so proud," she said in her frail, reverent voice, "that Mr. Sorrel is one of our very own artists. It makes me feel different inside just to have these things on me. What a pride to America he is!"

Mrs. Brookbank chose two of the tunics and six of the scarves to take away with her. And then she sat down on the poets' bench in exhaustion, smoothing the milky wisps of her hair back into place under the white horn combs and under the hat with the pearl-headed pins run through it.

"I can't feel I've been extravagant," she was saying gently to Victoria. "I can't think of anything so beautiful that I could buy for the amount these cost. I'm not only buying them for me and for my life-time," she said, and a faint blush of shyness came into her delicate cheeks. "They'll be my daughter's one day—and then, you see, after that they'll go to our museum in Richmond. I've come over on a sort of mission," she said in apology. "I've come over this time to collect the work of our leading American artists abroad. I

want to take the very best things I can find back
home with me. You see, I've given a new wing to
our museum and I want to start the collection off
so I can see some of it with my own eyes before—
before anything happens to me."

Victoria had put the three hundred dollars in
the cash-drawer of the table, and her heart stood
still in hope a moment. No one had ever bought
so much at once; perhaps no one would ever buy
so much again.

"We have some fine long panels, painted by
Sorrel. Could I show them to you?" Victoria said.
Mrs. Brookbank's voice faltered and shook a little
in her throat.

"Why—you're very kind," she said. "How
much—how much are they?" she said, with the
lengths of them stretched out before her on the
floor. She was watching in timidity the stag done
to death in linen by the lion as yellow as mustard
on a purple ground.

"This one is two thousand francs," Victoria mur-
mured. "There are hand-printed books, printed
on Mr. Sorrel's hand-press, which tell the history
of each panel. The books cost one hundred francs
a piece."

Mrs. Brookbank sat very still, looking. She was
lost in the jungle of great bladed stalks which
pierced the storm clouds of a tropic-heavy sky.

"I don't know, you see—I don't know," she
said, almost unbreathing. "I'm not quite sure how
the exchange works out. I'd have to—I'd have to
figure a bit on paper." She looked up in helpless-

ness to Victoria's face over the writhing figures
on the panel. "I wanted some of Mr. Sorrel's
rugs, too, you see. I'd heard about them from my
daughter who had tea with him last year. But I
don't want to decide in too much of a hurry. I'd
have to pick and choose pretty carefully. I only
have a certain amount to spend, you see," she
faltered. "I couldn't afford to spend more than
five thousand dollars here. I'll have to go very
slowly and see how much the things I want would
come to altogether."

"Five—five thousand francs? Five thousand?"
said Victoria, keeping her voice cool and clear and
the smile steady on her face.

"No," said Mrs. Brookbank, shifting uneasily
on the poets' bench and smiling in apology. "I
don't understand francs, you see. I've always had
Cooks take care of that part of my trip. I'd have
to ask at Cooks how many francs five thousand
dollars would give me to spend."

Victoria sat suddenly down on the floor with
the linen panel clasped tightly in her lap.

"Five thousand dollars," she said aloud, and
she looked up into Mrs. Brookbank's modest,
retiring face. She thought of this coming to Sorrel,
entering note by note the dark lips of the purse at
his girdle, paid out for handmade paper on which
poems would be printed, paid out for parchment
covers for the books they would set up together,
paid into the thwarted intention of what his old
age should be for him, the thing restored to him
by the miracle of money, whatever it was that had

been there in his youth and in other places. And suddenly she began speaking to Mrs. Brookbank, not of money or of what could come of it, but of the things they had planned to do together, speaking as if Sorrel stood at night, or stood till dawn in the glass-house setting the poems of other people on paper, as if the pictures other men had painted hung on the walls of the colony's house and people came in and out, seeing and giving understanding, as if next week there would be another exhibition of a young painter's canvasses as there had been the week before, and Sorrel sitting alone by the fire with the manuscript of younger poets open on his knee.

"Oh, the colony!" breathed Mrs. Brookbank; and Victoria went on speaking of the house in Neuilly as if it stood fair and clean in pride, with vegetables cooking in the broad white kitchen, and the women painting the scarves and weaving in the common room, and the men at work in peace and quiet carving the sandals out of the fresh, sweet slabs of leather. Or she spoke of the children, giving them the clean tunics, the flesh, the new-washed locks of hair that she would have for them, sending them out to dance in the garden for Mrs. Brookbank, having swathed them warm as Eskimos in Grecian white, taken the gooseflesh from their skin, the dirt from their ears, and stayed their hunger for the afternoon. Don't tell her about Talanger's crucifix, she thought with cunning. Don't mention the *Catholic World*.

"Oh, I should love to see it all!" breathed Mrs.

Brookbank, and as if these things had not been taken stillborn from Matilde's mouth, or from Sorrel when he talked to strangers, Victoria gave them to Mrs. Brookbank's reverence, saying: I believe in Sorrel because he has kept humble and pure in a time when there is little purity, because his heart is open the way his house is open, because I went to him in need and he withheld nothing, because he believes in the expression of what cannot be bought, broken, deceived, destroyed. She did not say: He is some one to sing lullabys to, to touch gently. I can rock him to sleep with his memories, I can take him in my arms and comfort him when he cannot remember where he is going or why he came this far alone. She said: See him this way, Mrs. Brookbank. See him the way he wants it. Maybe it would be true if anything like money ever came to him.

She had come to the end of it, and Mrs. Brookbank's face was hanging there, tender and soft above her. Mrs. Brookbank had leaned forward, far out over the strong, swift stream of living that passed like a torrent, impassable between.

"It's so beautiful, the way you feel about him," she said. "You've made it all so clear and wonderful. I think of my own life," she said in her shy, faltering voice, "and I think it is one of the loveliest things to meet some one who has found her *right* place and is in it so young. I can't tell you . . ." she began, but her voice expired. It did not revive again until she said that she was stopping at the Crillon. "This is a day I shall never forget," she said gently at the door. "You have made the beauty of life come very close to me. I feel I have felt her skirts brush against me in passing."

"Please," said Victoria, cold with the fear now that this would slip away for ever from them. "Couldn't you come in and meet Mr. Sorrel before you go to St. Moritz? I know what pleasure it would give him to talk with you."

"That would be wonderful, to really talk to him," said Mrs. Brookbank dimly. "My daughter said his presence was an experience for her. But that will have to be when I come back—perhaps in March, perhaps before. It all depends on if I find the sunshine."

She went out the door of the shop and down the street, not lingering at the other windows as women did but moving forward hesitant, her soft face lifted, her body a little stooped beneath her elegant clothes. And Victoria looked again at the money in the cash-drawer, thinking in panic maybe this is the last of Mrs. Brookbank, maybe I've let five thousand dollars go out the door and down the street, stooping a little, the pearl-grey gloves buttoned, maybe I should have said something else but what I did, maybe I should follow her home in supplication, coaxing her, wheedling her, Mrs. Brookbank, write it down in a cheque for him, let him have the flock of goats and the six Meccanos for Christmas. Victoria turned in small, quick circles in the shop, stopped at the mirror saying "This was my big day, this was my one chance and I missed it." Matilde would have locked her in until Sorrel got here and bewitched her. Matilde would have bound her hand and foot, gagged her, knocked her out and dragged her into the privy. God, let Mrs. Brookbank return, said Victoria. Let her come back to me with her five thousand berries, let her waltz into the shop again and I'll never ask anything more.

It was dark and the lights were lit in the embassy windows when the tongue of the bell rang out in the loft. Victoria ran down the stairs, wiping the paint from her fingers into the rag in her hand. Antony stood in the middle of the shop without any look on his face at all and he said quickly:

"Look, Victoria. Will you have dinner with me? It's a special night. It's February."

When she saw him her heart moved strangely with elation in her.

"I thought you were on a boat going to America," she said, and she rubbed blind at the cobalt on her fingers.

"Everything I own is on a boat going to America," said Antony. "It sailed at five o'clock this afternoon."

CHAPTER TWENTY

They went into the restaurant together, and the women wore evening-dresses at the tables, and their furs were lying on the backs of their chairs. But Antony's eyes ran over them sightless.

"On Saturday night," he said, and he sat down facing Victoria, "the rue Mouffetard might as well be Marseilles or the back end of Genoa. We'll go there after and find something to put on me. I haven't a suit left to hold me together except this one on me and we can get rid of it tonight. Everything in the hold or the cabin of whatever the boat was called. We'll go to the rue Mouffetard together after and find a face and figure for me. We'll pick out something for me that will cut me loose from what I've been for thirty years."

Victoria opened her hands on her lap below the cloth and looked at them, the nails worn close from work in the cold and work in paint, as thin and dark as a boy's uneasy hand.

"François, bring us things in shells," he said without turning his head. "We're afraid of something. You joining a colony in fright, me a social

order. It's time we were through with it. I keep
going home to Massachusetts to find some other
aspect of me, thinking maybe if I lift a turkey's
wing I'll find it like lice under the feathers. I
was going back for it this time again, but now
that all the accoutrements of me have sailed I can
alter. You stopped me," he said, and his eyes
escaped, running from woman to woman in the
radiantly-lit place. "You must help me now that
you've kept me over here."

"We aren't the same kind of people," Victoria
said.

"Pieces of us are just the same. Have some
chicken and asparagus," he said.

"I can't eat," said Victoria. "It's physical, as
if Miss Grusha had me by the neck. I'm hungry,
but I can't get rid of Miss Fira and Miss Grusha."

The chicken and asparagus were there, and
François was sliding the mushrooms into the
browned butter in the chafing-dish.

"I can see them," Antony said, "absolutely
twins, plump as Jewesses, both seventeen, with
that rich, heavy skin like cream laid on them with
a knife."

"Miss Fira and Miss Grusha never have
enough," said Victoria. "They've been hungry
ever since the Russian Revolution."

"They ought to eat," said Antony. "We can
send them things in dishes. We can send them
wine. François," he said, "you must make a dinner like this one for Miss Fira and Miss Grusha
and have it taken to them in a thing to keep it

hot. Take it quickly to where they live. Where do they live?" he said to Victoria.

François wrote it down on a piece of paper: he wrote Miss Fira and Miss Grusha and the address in Neuilly.

"Don't bother saying who sent it. They wouldn't know my name," Antony said. "Miss Fira and Miss Grusha," he said, and he took a piece of chicken. "I can see them very well without you telling me a word. They should have beautiful dresses, too, so that all the things you never dreamed they had would suddenly blossom out and burst the seams. I can see them, potatoes in their ugly jackets."

"The things they wear were new last century," said Victoria, eating.

"Don't tell me, don't tell me," Antony said. "You make my Miss Fira and Miss Grusha go away."

"They want to go to Monte Carlo," said Victoria.

"We can drive them there," said Antony, "whenever you would like to go." Suddenly his eyes stood still, and he said: "Fontana's gone to Rambouillet. I'll call her up tomorrow and tell her where I am. I'll tell her I'm on board and how the waves are and that the weather's grey with gulls going along the edges. She says something over the wire and it's like somebody turning a light on inside me. I'll tell her about a face I've fallen in love with playing shuffle-board, and then I'll drive down and have lunch with her, and she'll be so surprised when I walk into the place her two bosoms will take hands and jump up and down in her dress together."

The rue Mouffetard ran down as if going to the sea, cobbled like a village street, and even at ten at night it was alive with lights in the shop-windows and thronged with people moving up and down it, buying the food for Sunday and carrying their full market *filets* home. If you walked in the middle, the places on either side were close enough to touch, with their crocks and their china set out on the sidewalk, their ropes and their serpents of sausage hanging in festoons, their winter apples and pears nesting in brittle, glassy straw, their eggs by the dozens tasteless and cold as billiard balls; here was the stench of honest people's flesh and food, and refuse in the gutters so profuse and richly intermingled that it was like a south wind blowing. The meat in the butcher shops stood unbleeding on the mar-ble slabs (having been packed in Argentine), the smooth columns of butter were cut by wires thinner than a hair, and overhead the working-men's coats and trousers and aprons flapped for sale, lifeless as hung men jerking by their gullets.

"Whenever you see me, let me know," said Antony. He was holding her arm fast in the bend of his arm. Across the narrow avenue of night which ran between the houses beat the banners and pennants of clothing in a grotesque mimicry of taken life on the air.

"I like it here," Victoria said, and they went down the rue Mouffetard together. All about, as if they were swimming in it, was the uneven diverse melody of these voices of the others, these people without leisure who walked on the dry, summery cobbles on Saturday night without complaint. "Maybe New Orleans is like this," Victoria said, watching the people pause and dawdle and meander. They were not gay, but the women's heads were bare to February and they were slow enough in their choosing for this to be a summer evening in a southern town. Around the corner, bleak with winter, Paris was hiding in the dark.

"We wouldn't be foreigners in New Orleans," Antony said. "Not the way we are here. We'd have to act like every one else, and maybe we wouldn't know how."

In one shop they bought him the black corduroy trousers, and in another the flannel shirt and the carpenter's jacket with the pockets running sideways like a fisherman's blouse.

"This one's for my awl," said Antony, from behind the rack of raincoats. "And this one's for my jemmy."

"What's a jemmy?" Victoria said.

"I don't know," said Antony. He was only a voice left, speaking in the overhanging caverns, the grottos of working-men's dark clothing that were pendent back to front, front to back, identical, seams, shoulders, pockets, belts, alike as miners standing one behind the other, patient, featureless, defeated, at the entrance to the pit. "We'll have to buy a jemmy," said what was left of Antony, "and find out."

He came out from behind the raincoats, looking quickly for Victoria, and his face was small and perishable, like a child's face, above the labouring jacket and the corduroys. He was carrying his good suit over his arm, and he said:

"I'll have to give my suit to somebody." He looked a little shyly at the salesman behind the counter. The hanging garments cast shadows on them, gigantically shaped like men. "Could I give you my suit?" said Antony.

The salesman put his hand out for it.

"I'll just wrap it up for you, Monsieur," he said.

"No," said Antony, and the colour ran over his face. "I don't want it wrapped up. I want to give it away. I don't want it any more."

"It's not an old suit," said the salesman. He pinched his glasses on his nose and looked closely at the cloth. "The stuff is very good," he said.

"No, it's not old," said Antony. "Why can't you take it? Take it just as it is. It's very simple, you see. I simply don't want it any more."

The man looked sharply up at him. "*C'est simplement que je ne le veux plus!*" So that's the way the wind was blowing.

"Look here," said the man, very sharply. "You'd better not go around talking like that."

The colour went out of Antony's face and he stood quite still, with his suit laid down on the counter between them, waiting for the sense to come in what the man had said.

"People don't like it," the man said, and he

reached sideways for a piece of paper to put around it. *C'est simplement que je ne le veux plus!* "My God," he said, "there're too many people without a suit to cover them in this part of town. Nobody'd see the funny side of it."

"I'm not funny," Antony said; and because he was sick with shyness he was white enough to faint. "If you wouldn't mind taking the suit— and giving it—giving it——"

"Come," said the man. "Write down your address here. I'll have my son take it around to you tomorrow."

"But I won't be there, you see," said Antony, in confusion. "I won't be any more where I used to live." Suddenly he picked up the suit and put it over his arm. "I'll just take it as it is then," he said, and he took Victoria's arm and they walked out the door and into the street together.

There were a great many people passing in the little space between the hung men and the winter fruit and the pigs' feet rolled in batter and waiting for hunger and fire to melt them soft in the mouth. The men and the women, the women and men together, their arms held fast in one another's, the woman bound to the man and the man bound to the woman by their histories of days and nights and poverty and pain together. And we are only intruders here, Victoria thought as they stood on the narrow piece of the sidewalk watching the people passing. The bodies of the women leaned in some way to the men, and the men leaned to the women, as if whatever had passed over had shaped them to each other's shelter in its course. Touching each other's hands is like making a parody of them, Victoria thought and she drew apart from Antony. Here we come, mingling with them, making the same signs as love; like lean horses against a fence-post, we come rubbing against these others for the sound and smell of what love is. We're nothing to each other. Everything in me is too hard to break, and Antony has a wife like these men have to go back to in the end.

There was a young man playing a violin in the street, standing to one side and turning on his feet as he played to keep the blood moving in him and to catch sight of any one who might drop money in the violin-case that stood open by the kerb. His chin with the stubble on it lay close on the deep curved shoulder of varnished wood, and the cries of the strings were thin as lost cats asking, their spines drawn out in grief in their tails with asking, their claws and their fish-bone teeth gone wild with asking that death from starvation and death from weather be given mice or birds, be tacked open on the barn-door in warning, but that they be spared it. This was the thin, the ailing, the ignoble complaint the violin was making in this public place.

In a moment Antony walked to the man and touched him on the elbow, but he could not speak to him at once when he turned around and put his violin down. Antony's lips were dry and his eyes ran up and down the street.

"*Ecoutez, Monsieur*," he said in a low voice. "I have a suit of clothes here I want to give away."

The musician looked at him in the light from the *charcuterie* window, his violin hanging from one hand and his bow hanging from the other.

"Why do you want to give it away?" he said, with something like suspicion.

"I'm finished with it," said Antony quickly, and he held it forward a little on his arm. "I haven't any places to wear it any more."

"Perhaps Monsieur was ill and now he wants to get rid of it?" said the musician. The cold was there like a physical thing, like a scar marked on his face.

Perhaps Monsieur has lost his money, said the man's small, arrogant eyes, or has the plague, or has loaded the pockets with venom and spite. Perhaps there's a trick in it, said the stubble springing out black upon his chin, and he passed his hand warily over his jaw while the violin bow hung down in his fingers. Perhaps if I lift a hand to take it you'll tell that cop to ask that officer to call a policeman, said the ebony in his finger-nails, the mother-earth leering at them in contempt from under the cortical heavens in which the moons had set for ever.

"Does the shirt go with it?" he said, and his mouth went sideways in his face to point this out as a joke to them. He gestured with his forefinger at the tails of the white shirt hanging out of the suit's pocket, and then he put his violin on his shoulder again, and the cats of its strings came fawning and wailing and writhing on their backs for comfort, came shuddering against the ears, crying in whispers in the February cold.

"That's the way it is," said Antony, and he set off down the street with Victoria walking fast beside him, cold and hard and separate because of the torment in his face. Only women grow up, Victoria was thinking; men go on remembering the time when their families stood on guard about them, or the books on the table, or the silver, and there was no need for explanation. Haven't you learned that once cut out of the family's life you are a single thing given to yourself and other people, carved out separate to stand alone or not to stand at all?

"Listen, Antony," she said, but she could not say the words out. "Does any man or woman you stop in the street know what your people were or the weakness or might that were given you at birth, or take your dissipate, stubborn innocence for innocence? Now you are away from home, you are alone with nothing but your shadow. There is no one to say it for you in explanation unless you speak." But his mouth was frozen tight in pride and sorrow and he was running quickly away from the cold.

"You'll have to be ruthless, you'll have to be," said Victoria in impatience. "You can't give the same thing to every one. You'll have to learn it."

Suddenly Antony stopped walking and sat down on the kerbstone, his legs long as a grasshopper's drawn up to spring. He pulled Victoria down

beside him, their feet sitting side by side in the
frozen gutter. He was laughing, mixing the high,
aimless sound of it with what he had begun to say.

"My God, Victoria, I'll have to be something.
Ruthless, you say? You yourself see that I shall
have to be something. That is what they are afraid
of with this suit of mine."

Victoria looked at him, at the little pieces of
his face very near and the hair that stood up in
rags at the centre of his head.

"You are Antony," she said; and when she said
this for a moment she believed that it was true:
that this was the beginning and they would be a
long time together. He put his arm around her
and held her close for warmth.

"They are afraid of this suit," he said. It was
lying across their knees, lifeless, like a friend who
had suddenly died. "If they put it on they are
afraid they will become nothing. Can you imagine
anything more ridiculous? One cannot be nothing.
One has an obligation to one's flesh. That is why
I have made the attempt," he said. "I did everything I should have done, everything people like
me had done before. And it has always ended up
in the same way. It has always collapsed against
the granite and the resolution of life. I am not
resolved," he said. "You see, I am not absolute.
I am relative. I am the only thing that does not
remain." They sat close to each other on the side
of the street, closer than they had ever been before,
and the feet of people passing were of no importance. "What do you think happens to a man," he

said, "if his country has no place for him? Do you think it means there is nothing else, no place left? Do you think I am intended to stop being?" he said. "Do you think that is what is expected of me? But I wish to remain, you see. I do not want to be the only thing that goes past. I wish to be here as long as any one else, perhaps longer, so as to see all the institutions go back to their elements. I wish to remain," he said, holding tight to her, "but I do not see how to remain.

"Last year," said Antony, "when I went back, I went out on my uncle's ranch. I really believed it might happen there. I was in the saddle all day, I was there for the round-up, but I was like something spurious. The men were leading their own lives there and I was somebody else dressed up in imitation. It made me sick, like an illness, and I couldn't speak a word to them. I was sick with fear because for the first time I saw it very clearly. I saw there was no place anywhere that wrapped me close and held me fast for ever. I'm shy because I'm not needed, not wanted," Antony said, without complaint. "I would like to be needed. I would like the place where I go and work, and I would like America, and I would like civilization to need me. As it is," he said, " I've never been needed anywhere."

They sat quiet for a little while, and There is Fontana, there is Fontana, there is Fontana was played out like a tune by the beat of the people's feet in passing. There is Fontana hung unsaid between them, and presently the street had emptied itself into darkness; it was getting late now and there were no more people passing by.

"I am not needed," said Antony, "by peace or war or labour or education or any of the things there are. They are bearable to some people. To me they are not even possible. You see how unnecessary I am? I do not believe comfort or danger or ambition or love even are possible now. And although I believe this entirely alone, I must be right because I live curtailed, bound hand and foot, destroyed by my relation to every one of these things that is said to be. I do not admit that they exist, but I am as dishonoured as if they did because they are unshaken in the memory and habits of everybody else. I have never caught on to the unintelligible explanations that are made for living as we do, or else I am the only one whose racial memory has failed. I was absurd enough to imagine that being born had some significance for oneself. I believed some individual effort could be made. The truth is that being born offers no opportunity at all."

"Then what can strangers give you?" said Victoria.

"I go after them like mad," said Antony. "Like a dog after a bitch in heat. I go after them, but I do not know. I listen every time a man opens his mouth and tells me about an issue so vital in his life that it quiets me for a long while after, and then I suddenly jump up and shout the truth: that it is of no importance, it has no meaning, it is the final assault on dignity that men allow themselves to speak gravely of matters as weak as water when the entire shape of living is being lost to sight."

"Antony, your hands are cold," Victoria said.

"We'll have coffee somewhere," said Antony. He sat looking down between his knees at the gutter, and then he reached over and laid his suit down gently before them. He stretched it long and empty across the pieces of thin white ice that roofed the cobbles in the gutter, the loose limbs of it curved in weariness and the arms fallen open, the white shirt laid in at the neck, the jacket buttons buttoned, as if the man who wore it had lain down there and wasted to nothingness within.

"I like you, Victoria," said Antony. "I like the way you don't say things," he said.

CHAPTER TWENTY-ONE

Matilde came quickly into the shop with Hippolytus running beside her. She glanced swiftly, shrewdly at the show-window as she passed it, and in the room looked quickly over the benches and the mirrors for any sign of dust left on them.

"Ah, Victoria, you didn't come back for supper last night," she said. She stooped over in her white nun's dress and cloth and turned the gas-heater lower in rebuke. "You didn't come in for breakfast," she said. She did not look at once at Victoria but went here and there in the shop, shaking out the curtains, setting the lecture-cards and notices straight. "Sorrel was worried about you," she said. "Estelle went over to your room and Miss Fira and Miss Grusha said you hadn't been there."

She looked suddenly full into Victoria's face, as if to startle the truth from her.

"I went out to dinner with a friend," Victoria said. "I didn't know it mattered."

"It doesn't matter, it doesn't matter," said Matilde, her full, smooth cheeks smiling. "But you should feel like bringing your friends back to the colony. You know that we like to share everything together. It isn't the idea that one goes off in one direction and another in another. If you want to go out in the evening, bring your friends to Sorrel's lectures. It would not cost them much and it would please Sorrel to see new faces there."

"I'm sorry," Victoria said. "It was dawn when we came walking past here. There didn't seem any use going back to Neuilly then. He came in here with me and helped me clean the shop out." Her hand fell on the sheeps' hide cover on the bench. He shook this out when it was just getting light, she said in silence. He sat on this bench, he unrolled that rug, he hung those scarves across the easel. "We had special things to say," Victoria said.

Matilde stood shaking her finger, a little in mockery at her, but under this playfulness there was another look like censure lurking.

"You mustn't be afraid of talking about things before other people," she said. "That's childish. You must get over that. There's nothing you want to say, is there, that you wouldn't want Sorrel and me to hear?" She stood looking with a warm, bright, playful smile at Victoria. "You're not getting interested in a young man, are you?" she said, and she laughed to take the gravity and the suspicion from it. "You're not falling in love with some one we don't know anything about?"

"Perhaps I should," Victoria said, and she pulled Hippolytus against her and looked abashed into his small, withered face. "Perhaps I ought to begin. I'll be a spinster in a little while."

"What do you talk about with your friend?" said Matilde in bright, friendly mistrust. Now Victoria was suspect to her for ever; suspect of what she did with her nights and of betrayal to them all.

"Oh, life, and things like that," Victoria said, braiding and unbraiding the dry ends of Hippolytus's hair.

"You should talk about such things to Sorrel," said Matilde. "Sorrel has lived better than any one. He is the best one to advise you about life."

But the remembrance of Mrs. Brookbank's money suddenly came to end it. Victoria took it out of the drawer quickly and put it in Matilde's hands. The words stopped in Matilde's throat, and she sat on the poets' bench in the sunlight as it came scarcely warm through the glass behind her.

"Three hundred dollars!" she said. She sat smoothing the bills out on her knees in wonder. She could not get it close enough, she could not touch it, hold it, bring it near enough to her flesh. "One day, four years ago," she said, gaining the time necessary to believe that this was true, "we sold for two hundred and twenty-five dollars. This is very good. This is the first time. This is very good," she said. She looked up, smiling eagerly from under the unhemmed, soiled veil pinned upon her head. "So much money should not be left here overnight," she said; but this was not reprimand, for she was smiling with true love at Victoria. "What if your friend had gone off with it!"

"Ah, but he wouldn't, he couldn't possibly," said Victoria.

"You never can know about people!" said Matilde, holding the lovely, the sweet-scented bills. "Wait until you're a bit older!" she said, laughing outright in her joy. "Wait till you've seen as many as we have in the colony! I've even caught them stealing scarves here from the shop!"

"I think there will be more money from this lady," Victoria said. Hippolytus was leaning sharp and warm against her knee. His eyes at the apple were hollowed perilously deep, as if the destruction had begun already. So she sat watching Hippolytus's eyes and telling Matilde of Mrs. Brookbank, telling her of the panels and rugs that Mrs. Brookbank wanted, of the mission that had brought her to them, of the museum, and of the money Mrs. Brookbank had to spend.

"Five thousand dollars!" Matilde cried out. The smile had gone from her mouth now and she jumped to her feet. "Five thousand dollars! Where is this woman? Where is she now?"

"She's going to St. Moritz today," said Victoria. "But she's coming back. She'll be back in two weeks if the weather's not good."

"But where is she now?" cried Matilde in wild despair. "Some one must see her before she goes!"

"She's at the Crillon," Victoria said.

"Ah," cried Matilde, pacing the room in her full white woven dress, "this is the worst thing that has ever happened." She wrung her hands slowly, bitterly as she walked the length of the shop. "It was a mistake for me not to come down here more often. One puts too much faith in others. You should have let us know, Victoria! You should have kept the woman here," she cried. "You should have sent us a message to let us know!"

"But there's no telephone," Victoria said. "I told Mrs. Brookbank how Sorrel felt about telephones——"

"You could have sent us a *pneumatique*," Matilde said sharply.

"I couldn't close the shop up while I went to the post office," Victoria said.

"You could have come home to supper last night," said Matilde, at last. "Then we would have had time to think over what is the best thing to do."

The three hundred dollars had fallen on the floor unheeded, and Victoria stooped and picked them up for her and Matilde closed them away in the purse at her belt. She caught up her white wool mantle from the bench and swung it over her shoulders, and she stood blind before the mirror buckling it at the throat.

"Don't leave the shop for a moment," she said to Victoria. "Send Hippolytus out to buy the lunch. And if the American woman comes back, keep her here. Don't let her leave until Sorrel or I return."

"I haven't any money for lunch," Victoria said, and Matilde took three francs from her purse and put it on the table.

"Two-fifty's enough," she said; "but, never mind, I haven't any change." She went out the door, and then on the step she turned back again. "Dress the window over," she said. "Put some of the panels in it. Take the wrappings off some of the rugs upstairs and have them ready."

She opened the shop door again and the little bell rang out in the loft above them.

"Move two of the benches into the hall back there," she said, "so that we'll have room here to show the things."

Victoria and Hippolytus stood watching her as she waited, impatient on the edge of the sidewalk, and when a taxi came slowly down the street she lifted her hand towards it, and the fold of her mantle lifted gravely like a great white wing.

"Why was she angry this time?" Hippolytus said.

"Because I'm stupid," said Victoria. "I'm stupid as my feet."

"Why don't you wear sandals?" said Hippolytus, and he looked down at his. He was leaning hard against her hip, with his thin arm laid around her. "We're going away," he said. "Peri says so. He doesn't like Matilde and Sorrel any more."

"Where are you going?" said Victoria. There was a tooth gone from the front of his mouth and it made the words whisper on his tongue.

"We're going to Italy," he said. "It's farther than Neuilly. I don't think Bishinka could walk all the way."

"It'll be warm there," said Victoria; and suddenly she put her arms tight around him. His bones were ready to come through his skin at any time, and his head might snap the threads of his neck in another minute or two. "You must eat a lot and get fat there," she said.

"Cina says there's fruit on the trees there. You can eat all you want and nobody stops you," Hippolytus said.

He sat down on the step of the show-window and watched her as she took the panels out. The end of his braid was in his mouth and he sucked it softly, looking into the street beyond the glass.

"Talanger wants to go in a convent. What's a convent?" he said; but once it was said he did not remember any more. He sat watching Victoria spread the scarves out and the automobiles passing in the street. In a little while he said: "Where do you want to go?"

But the two little Russian women had come into sight on the other side, skipping furtive past the embassy's archway, their hands in their muffs, their heads darting in trepidation at the slow, sparse traffic that went by them. Across from the shop they drew together for courage, and faltered hesitant on the brink. Victoria stood motionless in the window, waiting until they flung themselves wildly from the kerb and gained the street's centre in alarm. There Miss Grusha spun about and fled back to the pavement before a taxi's slow advance, and Miss Fira hastened forward with solitary resolution, her head lowered to forestall catastrophe. Once on the kerb, she turned and lifted her muff on high to direct Miss Grusha's desperate and giddy course.

"Matilde and Sorrel have a lot of money," Hippolytus said. With dark, blank, seemingly sightless eyes he watched the Russian women as they came side by side along the pavement to the tall glass door. "Peri says they have a lot of money and they don't give us any," he said. Miss Fira and Miss Grusha slipped through the little piece of it they dared open and closed it swiftly behind them as if they had outstripped the enemy at last.

"Victoria," said Miss Fira, scarcely aloud, and Victoria stepped down from the show-window as Miss Fira sank upon the poets' bench.

"By God, you missed it!" said Miss Grusha, sitting down and pushing her hat back off her forehead. "We saved the plates to show you."

Miss Fira looked at her sister on the other bench and shook her head in grief.

"Grusha, it's gone far enough," she said.

"It's my business," said Miss Grusha savagely. "You thought they'd made a mistake in the address. I knew who it was meant for all right."

"Victoria," Miss Fira said with dignity, "I would not have come here this morning except for the dreadful thing that has occurred. Grusha will not tell me the truth. I know you can help me prevail on her. For months now, perhaps for years, Grusha has been living a life that I had no suspicion of. But last night a thing occurred for which there can be no other explanation. Grusha has been—she has been—Grusha has been debauched." Miss Fira wiped her quivering lip with her handkerchief and her hand in its cotton glove was shaking. Miss Grusha sat very still on the other bench, her hands braced open on her knees, her eyes fixed bright with interest on her sister's face. "I don't know what to think," faltered Miss Fira. "I am afraid to think, Victoria. I am afraid that Grusha has a—has a lover," Miss Fira said. The implication of it hung on the air in terror, and then Miss Grusha gave a cry of laughter.

"I've got my life to live," she said, and her mouth shut grimly over.

"And what about my responsibility to mother and father?" Miss Fira cried. She looked in her affliction at Victoria. "They put their trust in me," Miss Fira said. "There's no one else to protect Grusha from what an irresponsible man might do to her. She doesn't understand what men can be, Victoria. She's like a child, a plaything in the hands of any scamp. She doesn't know that a man's promises are just as lightly broken as given——"

"You ate the chicken fast enough," said Miss Grusha sharply; but Miss Fira went on with her sweet, stern complaint as if she had not heard.

"If it were any other sort of attachment, I would rejoice with Grusha," she said. "But this —this is a thing outside the experience of any one we've ever met. Men don't make gifts to ladies," said Miss Fira, the words spoken slow and terrible, sensational with the meaning that they bore, "unless they've been bought and paid for at the price which every gentlewoman holds dear."

"Let them pay that will," said Miss Grusha grimly. "The asparagus wasn't any the worse for it, was it, Fira?"

"As long as what happened *did* happen," Miss Fira said in explanation, "I saw no point in refusing to share the meal which Grusha's—Grusha's acquaintance sent her last evening. He had been thoughtful enough to include me as well. But I suffered all night for it. After Grusha had partly confessed to me, I sat up turning the thing over and over, trying to convince myself it could not be true."

"That was the lobster," said Miss Grusha, taking a toothpick out of her bag. "You didn't divide it equal."

"I believe there was no difference in the portions," said Miss Fira with dignity. "I cut it down the middle. You got one claw, I got the other."

"You got the whiskers," Miss Grusha said. She was sitting there with the toothpick worked between her teeth and suddenly she looked up sideways, evil and sly, into Victoria's face. "He's quite a man of the world," she said with a smirk. "I suppose he wouldn't seem much of a catch to a flibber-jibbet, because he's going a little grey at the temples and he thinks the morals of today are worse than Louis XV. Anything American gives him a turn," she said, "so I couldn't introduce you."

"Grusha," said Miss Fira sternly, "tell us now,

and speak the truth to us: has he ever broached marriage to you?"

"Yes," said Miss Grusha, "if you have to know everything. I refused him." She looked at them both with a gleam of triumph. "Not on your tin-type, I told him."

"Grusha!" said Miss Fira.

"The Spanish Count used to say it," said Miss Grusha smartly.

"He learned it from the Americans in the Quarter when du Maurier was writing that unfortunate book," Miss Fira said. "He always said it with a twinkle in his eye."

"Twinkle or not," said Miss Grusha, and suddenly her voice was bitter as gall. "I told my beau I couldn't marry him. I told him I had my sister on my hands," she said.

Sorrel's car had halted, quivering and gasping at the kerb outside, and when the tin door of it slammed Miss Grusha's voice stopped short in the room and they turned their faces to it. Matilde and Sorrel were coming across the pavement in the cold.

CHAPTER TWENTY-TWO

"Well, my dear," said Sorrel coming in upon them. "Well, my dear Victoria," he said, and Matilde averted her face and set to draping the scarfs on the easel behind him. He settled his toga uneasily on his shoulder and his mouth was thin as a wire drawn up under his nose. "What is this I hear about you allowing a customer to leave the shop without buying the things she had come in for?"

Victoria looked at him from where she stood by the show-window. He had lifted his hand to his girdle as if to steady it from the palsy that was shaking him because he must say these things.

"Why do you imagine you are here, my dear Victoria?" he said, in this prepared, this high, cold, sneering voice of reprimand. "I suppose you think you are just to sit on the bench there and look at the young men who go past the window? But that is scarcely our idea," he said. "Perhaps you didn't know you are to sell things, Victoria. These things that I have worked my fingers to the bone on are here for sale, my dear." His voice had gone so high in its strange, unaccustomed flight that now it split in the rare atmosphere. "Even

Hippolytus here," he said, pointing his unsteady finger at the boy, "would have known better than to let an American lady who had come in with the intention of spending money fly off as fast as her legs would carry her!"

"She spent three hundred dollars," Victoria said. But even when she spoke to him with humbleness his eyes were masked, inscrutable as a stranger's, bold and uneasy with the necessity of mimicking what circumstances now demanded that he be. He must turn up and down the room like a man in anger, his lips curved exquisitely with scorn; he must borrow the speech and the high, indignant laughter from some one else, from God or from Matilde's impatience with him, wear the markings of temper mottled on his cheekbones; he must hold back his pity for himself and his tears for a little and be what followers recognized an outraged leader to be.

. "Three hundred dollars!" he cried out in derision. And behind him Matilde moved, soft and potent in her silence, as though absorbed in the arrangement of the tunics on display.

"She's coming back to buy other things," Victoria said, and "ha, ha, ha," said Sorrel, and the laughter rode up and down in his neck, endlessly, as if he must laugh on in ridicule for ever. "Just listen to her, Miss Fira!" he said. Suddenly the laughter stopped and he turned to Victoria. "Are you speaking seriously? Are you really pretending to believe it?" he said. "No, no, I cannot believe you are as stupid as you want us to think, Victoria." He opened his hands before the little Russian women. "What do you think of it?" he asked them, and again he began laughing as if the joke of it were more than he could bear. "A customer comes into the shop to spend a certain number of dollars and this young woman here lets her walk right out again! I think she's lost her senses. No, no," he said, "there's no use expecting others to look after things for you. Every man for himself, isn't that it, Victoria? The colony means nothing to you. Every one of them just alike, get what you can for yourself and let the rest go hang."

"If you had come home last night at least—" cried Matilde, swinging about in her wide skirt to face her. Miss Grusha lifted her hand up and jerked her hat down to her brows.

"She was home last night," Miss Grusha snapped, "if that makes any difference. She had supper with Fira and me."

"Let's have no lying now!" Matilde cried out. "Sorrel is always too good to his disciples! He's been robbed by girls he's put down here to run the shop! He puts too much faith in every one. And now Victoria has failed him!"

Sorrel walked quickly across the shop and set the lecture programmes straight with his shaking, unhappy hand.

"This isn't a place to entertain your friends at night, Victoria," he said, and his voice was trembling, having been lashed to venom as gentle as Sorrel in his grey dress sitting in the chimney;

as Sorrel buying an ice-cream cone and wiping what ran over off his chin; as Sorrel ready to cry when the dry pea-soup burned thick on the stove.

"I didn't come here with friends at night," said Victoria to the high, amused, unheeding scorn that was empty of anything he was. He went to the door, settling his fine wool toga over, and his dress beneath it was woven of white silk, pure and heavy as cream. He paused at the door in his party dress, clean and immaculately prepared, and when he looked back his eyes were unveiled for a moment. Have I or have I not, his eyes uttered, do you now fear, revere, honour, have I made the loud sound long enough a man makes in a room? Will you believe now, have I persuaded, will you applaud me in your heart at night for what was wrath, for what was towering passion? When I am gentle and untowered, will you remember the violence of this?

"You've made such a blooming mess of things," said Sorrel, and he drew the fiasco of his anger like a cloak about him. "I'll have to go over to the Crillon and try and fix it up."

So it went on, one night after another in the colony; when she sat down at the table, his face was set against her as if it could never turn her way again. He sat with Estelle and Edmond at the table apart, and however the talk began it ended in the same way, of other women who had failed him in other ways somewhere.

"I remember Ruth," he would say in that high, cold, that perfect voice of amused and bitter contempt. "She heard me say I wanted a canal boat one day. So poor Ruth decided she would get me a canal boat. She used to spend hours walking along the Seine," and he smiled helplessly at Estelle as she filled his plate again. "Poor Ruth, poor Ruth," he said; and he sighed with laughter and shook his head in despair. At the length of the common table sat the others, Cina and Gabrielle and Victoria, Arthur and Peri and the children, and Matilde sitting at the end wilfully partaking of the daily, humble fare. "Poor Ruth," said Sorrel, and when he lifted the fried potatoes on his fork, the children stopped for a moment and watched him put them in his mouth. On their own plates lay the winter carrots and stewed turnips, cooked fast so that their hearts were hard and done to death in flour in the cold. "She was another of those American girls with too much of the family to live down. I could talk to her by the hour about philosophy, but she wasn't ready for it," Sorrel said. He finished off the steaming *ratatouille* which Estelle and Edmond shared with him at the little table by the fire. "She was bourgeois, Edmond, you remember how she was," said Sorrel. "She *thought* about philosophy, but it was all up *here*," he said and touched his forehead. "She wanted to do something for me no disciple had ever done, poor Ruth," said Sorrel dreamily.

"She had a good figure for a girl of her age," said Edmond, wiping the butter off his ruby lip. He was wearing his dress-shirt under his dressing-gown, with the little diamonds sparkling down the front. For the sake of economy or to comfort Sorrel for Mrs. Brookbank's loss, they were eating in the colony before the show.

"Well, Ruth was set on finding me a canal boat," Sorrel said. "She used to come back wringing wet at night if it'd been raining, and I'd say 'Well, Cap'n, been trimming sails again?' " Sorrel wagged his head on his hand and Edmond laughed with him. "Ruth'd say 'I think I'll have something to show you tomorrow'. To-morrow, it was always tomorrow. That's a word I never used when I was young and full of sass. To-morrow was always just about twenty-four hours too late to suit me. But things change around till you don't know where you are, Edmond. Why, when I ask Victoria what she's sold down in the shop, she tells me the customer is coming back in two weeks to do her buying!" Sorrel looked in sweet, bright bewilderment at Estelle and Ed-mond. "I declare the Americans have a sort of sense of humour nobody else can get on to. I guess I've been away too long to know what it's all about."

Because he spoke in French to Edmond and Estelle, the whole colony listened with interest to the story. Only Arthur sat with his head lowered, giving no sign, eating what was there to eat, the carrots and the turnips. His spirit was gone from them, it gave no ear, it was swathed in a grotesque silence, a quiet as immune as death's, which the speech of the living could not destroy. But Cina and Gabrielle and Talanger listened, and Peri glanced up at Victoria under his ambush of hair.

"Well, Ruth had her heart set on that canal boat," Sorrel said. "But it couldn't have been set hard enough or that tomorrow might have become today some time. Week in, week out, it was always going to be tomorrow!" Sorrel shook his head and sighed with laughter at the thought of Ruth walking up and down the Seine.

"It gave her *des belles cuisses*, that exercise," said Edmond, and with the little bangle swinging on his wrist he dished out the apple-sauce.

"One night she came home," said Sorrel, "and she'd sprained her ankle."

"She certainly had nice ankles," Edmond said.

"She was as pleased as punch about life," said Sorrel. "She came hopping in here on one leg and she said 'Sorrel, I've got the canal boat for you'. 'Where is it?' I said. 'Tied to the gate-post outside?' " Sorrel stopped to laugh again and lick the sugar off the back of his spoon while the children watched him. "But, no indeed," he went on. "She had nothing like a boat to show me. She had a tiny little clipping from a newspaper advertising a boat for sale! She'd been down to see the boat and interviewed the owner!" said Sorrel, his voice rising high with scorn. " 'He only wants a thousand francs for it,' she told me. 'He wanted more at first but I talked him down!' 'Talked him down, my dear Ruth!' I said. 'Sounds to me as if you'd talked him up! That's just about nine

hundred and ninety-nine francs too much to pay.'
And then I told her: 'It's not a matter of francs
and centimes. You've gone the wrong way about
it. That was never the basis I did things on in
my life. It's a matter of who I am and what value
that can have for other people. Anybody can pick
up a newspaper and find advertisements for any
old thing in it. But it's one person in ten thousand
who can see right off what's the right thing to do,
and that's the person I'm interested in.' Now,
Ruth," said Sorrel, his fingers playing with the
breadcrumbs left on the table. "In a case like
that, Ruth should have gone directly to the French
Government. She should have put it up to them
as a proposition: 'Here's a canal boat for sale. You
can get it for next to nothing. Mr. Sorrel is eager
to start a canal-boat colony on your Seine. You
make it possible for Mr. Sorrel to have this boat,
say, for a period of twenty years, if you're going
to be stingy and won't give it to him outright.
And you'll not only double but you'll triple your
tourist trade this summer! Do you know what
you'll be doing? You'll be adding more to the
artistic value of Paris than fifty of these modern
painting fellows like Picasso. You'll have people
coming from every corner of the globe, flocking
on to that one little boat to see the weaving done,
the dyeing, the painting, to join in the dances,'
and, by Golly," said Sorrel, "after awhile one
boat wouldn't be enough to hold that floating
colony! There'd have to be a string of them right
up the river! Isn't that so, Edmond?"

"Edmond and I will have one of our own," said Estelle, settling her bosoms in her brassiere.

"Well," said Sorrel, bringing his hand down open on the table. "I can't get it through their heads once and for all that there's no two ways of doing a thing! You do it the right way or else you don't do it at all. If you're hunting up a canal boat, or if you're selling things in a shop, there's only one way of doing it. You don't say to a customer, 'Oh, please don't spend all your money today! Oh, just come back in a couple of weeks from now if you want to buy any more!' "

Victoria got up and started collecting the empty dishes from the common table. Matilde looked up and unpinned her white veil from her head. Under it, her hair lay down her back, long and oily and uncombed.

"Victoria, you'll be getting ill" she said "if you stay out all night and never eat your supper."

"I'm not hungry," said Victoria, and she carried the plates out and set them down. She stood there in the kitchen watching the dishpan fill with water in the sink, and in a moment Peri came out and closed the door.

"Victoria," he said under his breath, and he was smiling, "why don't you clear out?"

"Is that what people do?" said Victoria, and she slammed the full dishpan down on the gas-stove. "Do they stay just so long?" she said. "So long as every one's polite to them they stay? And then when they get their feelings hurt they turn traitor?"

"Traitor?" said Peri. He jerked his head back towards the door. "You don't owe anything to *them*," he said. "They're capitalists," said Peri, and his teeth were yellow as corn in his head. "They use you like any capitalist with a walking-stick and a tail-coat would! They've got the money. They're not letting any of it get away."

He was a short, thick, swarthy, covetous man, and if there were no evil in his heart his flesh was there evil to smell and see. His nostrils were spread, taking the air out and in, and his neck seemed thick as a woman's waist but muscular as a stevedore's.

"What would you do with money if you had it?" Victoria said. She cut a sliver of soap from the cake and dropped it in the water heating on the flame. Money, it is the one word left, it is the blood running in our veins, it is the springtime that has promised to bloom some time some other month somewhere. It is the need for spring, the trails frozen over by winter, that has trapped us here huddling close for shelter from the cold. They have taken their heavy clothes off and slipped tunics on so as to pursue it the more swiftly, they have put sandals on so as to be more fleet. "Money," said Victoria fiercely to him. "I'd like to have bags of it! I'd give it to you in handfuls and I wonder what you'd do? I'd give it to you all, to Cina and Gabrielle and Matilde and Talanger, to every one of you! But it would be enough to make the heart die for ever to know what you'd do with it. There would be Sorrel, and he would be the only one who would turn it into something purer! He lives in his own house like a stranger among you, trying to use words poor enough for you to understand."

Estelle opened the kitchen door and her eyes went sharp on Peri. She came in, her breasts standing high in her *negligée*, patting the hard, brass waves of her hair with her open hand.

"Time you cleaned your teeth, you," she said to Peri. "Did you ever hear of toothpaste?"

The Pomeranian came after her into the kitchen, stepping eagerly, the nails of its feet clicking like a bird's feet on the tiles.

"Some day I'm going to get extravagant and buy you a comb for Christmas," said Estelle, staring hard as china at Peri. "With directions for how to use it," she said.

He swung his bare leg under his skirt to kick the Pomeranian as he went out the door, but the dog skipped aside with her lip curled back and a growl like a bee's hum in her throat. Estelle lifted her foot and closed the door sharply behind Peri. Then she walked to the stove and lit the gas with her cigarette-lighter and pulled the covered pot back over the flame. She stood stirring the food that was in it while Victoria scraped the dishes, and when she turned around to speak there seemed no alteration in the French metallic music of her voice or in the bold blue heavens of her stare.

"Don't you give up eating," she said. She took a plate off the shelf, blew the dust from it and wiped it against the apron tied around her hips.

"Give up mamma and papa if you like, or give up living like a natural human being if Sorrel wants you to, but don't let him make you give up eating." She served the food out in spoonfuls on the plate. "Here's some *ratatouille* I cooked for our supper. You finish it, Victoria."

She set it down, the rice, the eggs, the hearts of things cooked delicate as a Chinese dish, on the table beside Victoria.

"You needn't let the others know," she said. She did not look around again but walked on her high, rhinestone-studded heels out of the kitchen door with the Pomeranian behind her. Victoria stood eating quickly by the stove, eating the sweet beans and the separate kernels of the grain, and she could hear Estelle's heels overhead, tapping fast across the bedroom floor as she put her clothes on for the evening show.

Part Three

FONTANA

"Bathe me in the vision of my youth, communicate me for ever. Do not let me go back with the rest to fornicate and forget."—
EMANUEL CARNEVALI

CHAPTER TWENTY-THREE

There was a wall beyond the trees in the garden, and beyond the wall were showing the tops of other trees on the other side with white sky forked in their branches. It was early, but now that it was April it was light at this hour; but for all that it was spring nothing had seemed to stir, nothing had begun yet, nothing had turned to action. There was still the bleak, unfruitful solitude upheld in the branches and the withered, tarnished look of the wall against the sky.

Victoria lay under the boarding-house sheet and the quilt that was stained with other people's living. I'd give the feel of my skin to any one as a gift, she said. She could feel the dirt in her knuckles without lifting her hand. The air was chill in the room, and the green silk tunic Matilde had given her to wear was lying on the floor by the bed, collapsed with her blue cloak in orgy on the scars, the vermin, the disembodied disease left by strangers on the carpet that was saturate with age. I'd give the taste of my mouth to whoever asked for it, she said. She put her bare feet down on the planks and the three photographs on the mantel

239

swung around at once, as if the women were running fast to face her on the other side.

"It hurt me," she said aloud when she stood up. "It still hurts," as if asking pity of their relentless eyes. She could hear her own voice whimpering in the room.

The air was coming freshly born through the windows, and the pure look of the sky came, but there was nothing good enough to clean the whole place out. She went over the foul piece of the rug to the washstand and held on to the scaling tin of the table's top, deep in the valley of the swinging room. You're still drunk, she said through her teeth, and the table slipped away from under her hand.

She set the broken basin on the floor and took off her shirt, and she stood upright, cold and still, with her feet unclean, in the basin edged with dirt. Around her the room was turning, sick and slow, like a halting Ferris Wheel. She lifted the pitcher and spilled it over her breasts: she held it tight and the water fell out of the pitcher's unwiped snout and over her body in an unacknowledged, scarcely felt agony of cold. That'll do it, she said. But even after it she could feel the skin of her hands still parched as she took the soap from the dish. The three women on the mantel were behind her, waiting for her to turn, or for the room to turn her facing them again; waiting they watched the soap go white on her body, watched the water pass over her, resolved in the shadow with the indifference, the grief and the blasphemy of their features ready to give her when she turned. The drought of despair within her had blasted her dry before she took up the towel to wipe the water from her skin.

She stood naked in the chill on the rotting floor by the washstand and cleaned her teeth four times over. If I had clean linen, clean things to put on me, not to wear anything I've worn before. But it was the end of the month now and time for the salary that could not last a fortnight to be paid her. A clean shirt, even a man's clean shirt, anything not worn before, then I could start off new this morning. Then I would be saved, she said, and her teeth were shaking.

"What would you be saved from?" said Lacey's voice, high, clean, scathing. "What in the name of God are you shaking for?"

Victoria swung suddenly around on the three women.

"Look," she said, "I've washed everything off me. I'm as good as the day I was born." But her mother's face was lifted in grief under the brim of rolling mole-skin. "Nothing's happened to me any different than what happened to any of you, over and over. It happens to every girl who sits out in a hammock in the summer, sometimes it happens every evening to her and her people upstairs in bed don't know it, or if they do know it, it never changes anything for her. . . . It only happened once to me . . ."

"What happened?" said Lacey. "What are you getting the wind up about?"

Everything in the room is dirty, Victoria thought. Everything here is refuse, except the photographs. Even my own face in the glass, a mistake, ready to simper, ready to smile, ready to make its poor apology to God. It is too weak a face to cry, for tears are shed only by the strong; the weak ones snicker in amends and twist their skirts like servant-girls. I might as well bring everything to an end, once and for all be through with Antony, with Sorrel, with my own mug in the glass, through for ever. Only fine ladies have the dignity to bow their heads and weep. She saw her handbag streaked with mud and lying open on the table. Perhaps I fell down in the street, my face and neck red and thick with drink, my hair standing up with it. Somebody tripped over me where I was, she said, and suddenly she saw there was money in her handbag and she reached out her hand in wonder and touched the smooth, new, silky bills.

These were as pure as angels' wings, the pale golden leaves, the Indian-summer foliage, the fortune of one hundred franc bills which flowered among her lipstick and powder and her handkerchief. She took them out slowly, and laid them one on the other neatly on the table; and deeper within the bag there were others, the long, mauve petals of still another vegetation. Here were the thousand franc notes with no end or reason to them; they had come there without explanation, merely as if it were at last the time for them to come. She looked at them, and the words came too as if born of themselves, of necessity with no thought behind them. She said: "I'm going to have some clean underwear."

She picked up her blue cloak from the floor and put it around her, and she rang the servant's bell by the door. Then she ran quickly across the room and put the money underneath her pillow and smoothed it out. She sat waiting, quiet in the sagging hammock of the mattress, holding the one bill folded in her hand. She could not think of the money in her mind, but only of the explanation of the other thing to give to Lacey.

"Whoever it was," she said, "it wasn't Antony. I didn't see him again after we got on the boat. I was opening the bottles of champagne in the kitchen with Michel. I don't know where Antony was," she said. The day was entering the room in smooth, unbroken waves that made no mark or sound. She sat holding the hundred francs in her hand, and she said: "I wanted it to be any one but Antony. I can't tell you why."

"You're smug as your grandmother," Lacey said in contempt. "What is it you think you have better than any one else has to give? What good has it done you, keeping it to yourself for twenty years? Passing off pride on the lad for purity! You'd be singing a different tune if it wasn't for Fontana!"

"Maybe I would," Victoria said. She heard the servant coming down the stairs. When she came in through the door, Victoria looked up at her and said: "Here's a hundred francs. Will you please buy me some underwear?"

The servant stood wiping her hands in her black apron, her teeth out, dull as bone and yellow, hanging over the eaves. The money was very beautiful to her; she was rocking on her short leg and her long leg, and you could see the love for the money gnawing like cancer at her breast.

"I want a shirt too," said Victoria. "A small-sized man's shirt." Once I were a man, she said, it wouldn't matter any more. "One about right for me. And some good, white underwear. Nothing with lace on it. I'll give you ten francs for yourself. I want it right away."

"The stores aren't open yet," the servant said.

"They'll be open in a minute," said Victoria. "By the time you get your coat on and get out to the avenue, they'll be open."

The woman crossed the room, the gait of her short leg and her long swinging her head like a bell, and her rank hair slipping. She took the bill in her fingers, looked closely at it, and suddenly her lips went back in a smile.

"They brought you home in a bad way last night," she said, her voice gone thin to a whisper. The long, work-worn, bony face came close in strained and clandestine insinuation. "I opened the door," she said. "I didn't let on to Madame. She'd put you out quick enough if she knew you drank."

She put the money in her pocket under her apron, and she watched Victoria.

"I'll close the window for you," she said. She went over the room to it, her shoulders twisted as if in the grip of the deformity she bore. "Maybe you'd like a fire in the chimney this morning while you dress?" she said in that hard, cringing whisper which seemed to fear the sound of its own passage on the air. "*He* gave me something for my trouble last night. It's not every day you see one with a car like that and a chauffeur to drive it for him."

Victoria watched the door close after her, and then she took the bills from under the pillow and she said aloud: "This is Antony's money."

"Antony looks as if he had a hell of a lot of money," Lacey said.

"I'll give it back to him when he comes into the shop," said Victoria, and Lacey said: "You're talking through your hat."

"Antony brought me home," Victoria said. "I remember. Maybe he didn't know what happened. Maybe it happened to me in the foc's'le, to starboard or to port."

"Maybe it didn't happen," said Lacey, smart and slick.

"Yes, it happened," said Victoria, and she looked away from her mother's face. "But Antony brought me home. He sat on one side of the car and I sat on the other, and I was feeling sea-sick. He was talking about Fontana, and there was room enough for her to be sitting there between us on the seat. I heard a woman's voice saying his name aloud all night, she kept me awake with it. Maybe it was myself saying Antony Lister is the name of a man I want to be there and who isn't.

He will never be anything to me except a few words strung together. Antony Lister is a name with holes at the other end and everything poured into it runs out the other side."

She got up holding her cloak around her and opened the door and went barefoot down the cold tiles of the hall. At the door of Miss Fira's and Miss Grusha's room she stopped and knocked softly on it.

"It's the police," Miss Grusha said quickly on the other side of the wall.

"It's me," said Victoria, her mouth speaking close to the wood.

But even speaking through the barrier of the door to one another, there was no deliverance from the presence of decrepit harking that dwelled blind on the floor above them, the white enormous ears laid open to ringing silence or to the passage of footsteps or escapes below. The cane might even now be moving on its solitary toe down the upper hallway, the slowly-manipulated burden of flesh be laid against the bannisters in monstrous, auricular possession of the breath and being of the Russian women who tossed off the bedclothes and ran across the ballroom floor.

The key turned in the lock and Miss Fira opened the half of the door to Victoria. Here was the arched, pilastered, high room where tea had been served to other generations and where, the balls once danced, the dinner ended, the empty and then the loaded coffins had been set among funereal bouquets. Where cakes and spun-sugar had once been passed with remarks about the weather, Miss Fira's and Miss Grusha's dental plates were soaking now in separate tumblers of water.

"Look," said Victoria, whispering still to the little women who had climbed back in bed. Miss Grusha had drawn the covers to her chin and Miss Fira was buttoning her flannel nightdress over at the neck. "I've got some money," said Victoria. She laid the bills out, one by one, flat on the marble top of the table where the teeth studding the red gums smiled in lascivious delight. Miss Fira, sitting close against Miss Grusha, with her hand lifted to her throat, began speechlessly to shake in the uneasy bed. "Some one gave it to me," said Victoria. "I don't need it. I took a hundred of it without thinking to buy some underwear."

"We can leave," Miss Grusha said, but something else shook out of Miss Fira's mouth.

"Who gave you the money?" she said. The lips of her emptied jaws were drawn in tight as silk over the bone, marking her with a rectitude and inflexibility different from any she had worn before.

"Findings is keepings," Miss Grusha whispered sharply. The three of them watched the money lying on the table.

"It may not be good money," said Miss Fira, her lips sucked in, her eyes buttoning and unbuttoning in their lids.

"Money's always good," said Miss Grusha, and her eyes did not move from the sight of it.

"I don't know how I got it," said Victoria. She held her cloak closed around her. "There were a lot of people at a party on the river. I drank too much. I felt very sick."

"The young man with the chauffeur brought you home," Miss Fira said. The words could be seen as she spoke them, taken like objects in her empty mouth.

"He came up the garden with you," said Miss Grusha, "and the chauffeur holding you up on the other side. It was three o'clock in the morning. We heard it and looked out the window."

"We opened the door of our room, but the domestic wouldn't let us near you," said Miss Fira, folding her lips in.

"He spoke to us. Your young man spoke to us," Miss Grusha said, and she looked coyly at Victoria with her lips drawn back from her gums. There was no sound, but in the strong, white silence of what was left of memory and things told, the harking presence stood blindly in possession of the house. The woman might have been close on the other side of the door with her ear gaping wide for it, the strokes of her heart in her flesh subdued to hear it. But Miss Grusha whispered it with a snicker between them.

"He said he was going to a wedding," said Miss Grusha. "He said he was the bridegroom."

CHAPTER TWENTY-FOUR

Sorrel rose like a meteor in the night, swung his fine skirts over the oratorical heavens, his face exalted by the fervour, the divinity of living with the gift of the dance, the gift of painting, the gift of the gab done up and ready there within him. He had been bowed a long time in sorrow, and his lectures had died of it; Mrs. Brookbank had come and gone and left him with the sad, subdued speech of an apostle of forbearance and gentle dignity. But this was a night, sweet, high, and clear with stars, and he swept fresh as a daisy into the hall with his love-me's and love-me-nots all amorous, his arms thrown wide in his toga to take the whole world of women into his embrace. Even Victoria was taken into it, standing by the door handing out the programmes; even Victoria borne on the great current that brooked no opposition, that eddied three times around the lecture-hall and returned on itself with loud, loving calls of laughter as it took the falls. Grand Rapids, Cedar Rapids, with the cedar trees still growing tall in that part of America, still cone-bearing, and the rapids passing swift and cold, and an Indian's voice or that of a salesman travelling for fertilizer better than horse-manure and richer speaking out with the same stallion trumpeting that now was Sorrel's in the lecture-hall.

"My friends," said Sorrel, settling his skirt under him as he sat on the poets' bench on the stage, "if joy is a worthless thing, then I am indeed a poor man as I sit here in my tunic and sandals on this bench before you. If love of my fellow-men is a thing that cannot be weighed or converted into terms that your Rothschilds and your Krugers would understand, then my heart is empty tonight and other people's pockets are filled with something very valuable. Or it may be that I have something wrong with my eyesight," he said with a whimsical smile, "or that I'm not clever enough to have got on to what it's all about; but although I've come into this place with my hands and my pockets empty, yet I say to you that I am not a poor man."

So the strong, angular voice of Sorrel's America speaking the French tongue to the students, the old women, the stern young women and men, struck like an anvil striking the weary, the trade-bitten hearts of these poor failures who had come to hear the words said that would sweeten their defeat. The poor, the hopelessly poor, it was who came and paid their money out at the doorway and sat there listening to the sound of what was given like another coinage to them.

"Today," he said, "has been one of the greatest days of my life. It has been great because some one from my own country came to me and said

'It is time that your work and the history of your work came home'. My country," he said, and even Mrs. Brookbank with her French-English dictionary open on her knees beside Victoria could not mistake it, nor the emotion which seemed about to break. "America came to me today in the person of one frail, gentle woman, came into my shop where I was working, waited until I had wiped the signs of my toil from my hands, and said those words to me. She said, 'I have come from America to ask you to give us your best things to take home.' It is things like this," said Sorrel looking down into the audience at Mrs. Brookbank, "which are worth living for, worth working for, month after month, year after year alone. I left my country many years ago to live where I could with people who understood my ways, and now my country has come after me, America has crossed the ocean to me, America has come calling on me with an invitation. 'There's a great museum standing open for you,' she told me. 'We need your work at home.' "

Sorrel wiped his nose on the back of his hand and looked for a moment around the lecture-hall.

"My dear friends," he went on, with the tears sucking hard at the ends of his mouth, "the thing I have to impart to you is a very simple thing and a practical thing. Although I cannot take it in my hands and give it to you, still it is a practical thing. Even if I cannot write it down in a thing men call a cheque-book and say 'Here, take it. There is just so much behind it in a forbidding building men have learned to call a bank', still it is as practical as currency. I can only say to you that I believe in man—not in what man has erected all around him to keep the truth out, but in the reality of man, and I believe that in living a life which casts out all but the simplest needs of man that the way will be cleared to the necessities of the heart and so the revolution of love will be performed."

It was such a gentle, quiet, little revolution, asking no more of them than their own frugal living asked, that they could believe in it too. It made no noise, it shed no blood, it was all very tidy, though quite vague, and the old ladies crawled out of their backrooms to hear it talked of week after week; the old gentlemen left the poor-house of an evening to hear it and went back contented for another day or two; and as for the young, they were working their way through college and their faith in Christianity had not survived. There had to be something except trigonometry to combat poverty and hunger and the awful, the lasting defeat they suffered at the hands of the well-dressed and the well-fed. The revolution of love offered some kind of solace for what had happened to them.

Even Mrs. Brookbank could accept it because of the humility of his voice and mien. It was dressed up differently from anything else, in a white silk tunic and sandals sitting on a poets' bench. It was really quite a nice little revolution to take back to Richmond and talk to the Civic Club about.

"I took stock of my life," Sorrel was saying "and I cast out what was superfluous: store clothes, store books, store furniture, store ornaments. And out of my digestive system I cast meat. If you wish clothes, shoes, books, then I say to you, you have two hands like any other man to make them, and whatever you make yourself, those are the questions you put yourself and answer, for everything in its raw element asks you a question and in the answer you reveal who you are. Wood asks it when you pick up a knife to carve it into something; leather asks it when you start to shape a shoe; wool in the raw asks it, paint asks it. Things in their elemental form ask you to tell them object by object what sort of a man or woman you are. There is something very good," he said, smiling at his people, "in having every object in your house answer you solidly when you walk into it, as solidly as *that*," he said, and he thumped the bench on which he sat.

So he told them of the trees the wood had been cut from, and how he had stood in the sunlight in Dalmatia planing the sweet wood down. And how the sheep had come in from the barren scrub to yield their wool to him and his followers, and how they had dammed the water to clean the sheep in, working in loin-cloths in a high, clear air, higher than these people in their poor city clothes had ever been. So he went on to speak of the children and how they were growing up in the colony's house. The gift he would give them, he said, was the gift of selection, given so young that later the flesh of itself would make the choice for them and their minds would follow docile behind.

"There are children in my house," he said gently, "but they do not belong to this or that woman. They are not property. They belong to life, and that's the secret of their joy. I have no children of my own, but I say these are my children because I have opened my house and my heart to them." And if this were denial, then it was denial of the slender, Yankee bones of Talanger, and the golden muzzle, the broad-set Mongolian eyes. It was denial of the way Talanger's hair fell in her neck, as his hair fell, and of whatever passion she carried, the Easter Mass and the crucifix hidden, it was the casting out unseen, unrecognized of the core where the seeds lay, of the thing which said I am me, I am Talanger, I will not lie quiet, I will not be still. "I have no heritage to give them," Sorrel said, "in what the world terms heritage. But I believe they will have something better than most men receive from the fathers of their blood—they will be equipped, they will be ready to take standing whatever life brings them."

His voice had hushed of itself as he spoke of the children, and his eyes were bright with tears as he looked out over the people in the hall. And is it that he has not seen the truth ever, thought Victoria, listening, that it has not been shown to him; that he has in purity been kept apart from seeing the betrayal in other people's hearts; that he has never heard the voice of Peri or the voices of Cina and Gabrielle speaking, or the silence of Arthur speaking against him, or the voice of Talanger not asking from him the things she wanted but the sound of it going elsewhere so fast that none of them could follow; does he not see the disorder, the threshing of his people in confusion, or does he say This was a bad day but tomorrow will be better, and carry his bewilderment over the night into the daylight again?

"There is not a child in my house who is aware of the conventional manifestations of life," he said. "Elaborate clothes, social standing, theatres, cinemas, churches mean nothing to them, for we have given them a relation to life, not a relation to the standards made by men. They have learned to read and write of themselves, for their toys are not these hideous and meaningless gollywogs and jumping-jacks, but day by day they play with the type from my printing-press, with paints and brushes and cloth they have woven themselves, with our shuttles and looms. . . ."

Victoria could hear it growing, increasing, gathering power, gathering truth almost as it grew. The spirit had denied the flesh, had surpassed it, and now he could sing the hymn louder and more melodious than he ever had before. If the memories of Cina and Gabrielle had come listening, or the face of Peri stood in the backrow of chairs near the doorway, still the hymn must rise oblivious to peril or rebuttal. It must be sung long and wide to the presence, to the shy, modest comprehension of Mrs. Brookbank with the dictionary open before her; and if the words of it were nothing in her ears, the torrent of his virility and love must say it. It was a paean of praise to the wealth of America, a wedding announcement of his soul with hers.

And now might the whole colony have arisen, the children in their shaggy tunics, the men in their dark work robes, sombre, deep-eyed, unshaven, the sulky women crouched on their stools over the scarfs they must paint hour after hour for a living, Estelle in her black lace step-ins, Edmond with eau de Cologne and brilliantine on his hair. They might have come in like prisoners in their uniforms and faced Mrs. Brookbank in accusation, the accusation the poor must make the rich for ever, and would she have summoned the courage to put out her lily hand and touch their unwashed garments or put back the children's hair? Sorrel had brought her to the lecture-hall in recompense for the money she had given, but the colony itself was kept from her like a running sore. She was not taken to the common room to sit quiet in the cold while the brussels sprouts cooked in the kitchen and Sorrel read his notices from the clipping-bureau aloud. She did not hear his voice saying with the newspaper in his hand "the well-known husband of the famous dancer, the late Ida Sorrel, was seen yesterday with a group of apostles among the visitors to the Foire de Neuilly" and the scissors lifted, the scrapbook open; but she heard instead these other things, said with his arms thrown open: "My people are

simple people, they are people of the soil, but
they have become artists by living day after day
within the sight of art."

Mrs. Brookbank leaned towards Victoria and
pressed her arm gently and her voice passed
hushed between them.

"This is such a great experience for me," she
said. "I'll never forget it, even though I can't
understand a word."

From the first the young French poet had been
looking at Victoria, and when Sorrel and she left
the hall, the last to go, he was lingering by the
doorway. And "Ah," said Sorrel in the street, taking the air in as if it blew the smell of the people
out, "ah, ah, ah," he said, his sound chest swelling with it. He put his arm through Victoria's
and held her close, for now he could never make
amends enough to her.

"Ah," said Sorrel, "I really feel the spring for
the first time tonight. It came later this year. It's
a very good idea," he said, with a little laugh,
"to have April come back over and over the way
it does, year after year."

Now he was alone with the young and he could
speak like the young. He spoke of the spring in
other countries; for the things that had happened
to him then and the seasons of his youth were
clearer to him than any there had been since his
wife had died. They had crossed the bridge together, the three of them arm in arm, and come
into the park where the moon was beginning to
shine. The French poet had dark, quick eyes and

a Spanish skin, and short, dark, Latin hands. He talked of poetry as if it had been begun a long while ago somewhere, like a pyramid, begun wide and beautiful at the base and had grown tapering, dwindling, until now there was no place left to build upon; it had come, before the eyes, in tenuity to its end.

"Why should it be so?" said Victoria, and she turned her face and smiled slowly at him. I'm no longer a girl, she was saying. I'm out for a good time. Did you ever hear of a man called Antony Lister, she said.

The Trocadéro towers were standing up before them as they walked, dark and monstrous, ludicrous in the white-lighted park. The grass was soft and new, and the three of them took the paths that wound between the lawns that sloped down to the river, climbing arm in arm together, the young man, and Victoria in her long silk tunic, and the old man in his flowing robes.

"And here," said Sorrel, pausing before the archway of the building that held them in its shadow, "my wife walked out one afternoon in the summer time with fifty of our dancers behind her, little girls and big young girls who had always danced with her. My wife walked out of here," he said, and the corners of his mouth went down, acrid with his loneliness, "and the whole city of Paris waiting in the streets. They had put flowers down for her, and she ran across them with her arms out. . . . She only had to move," he said, and his voice was small and fine as if a knife were being drawn along it, "and people knew they were seeing something finer than they'd ever seen before."

They stood quiet in the shadow of the Trocadero, and they were listening to Sorrel's voice, but their hands had met and were holding fast to each other. The French poet's fingers were interlaced and holding fast to Victoria's fingers and my wife, my wife, my wife, Victoria was thinking. It came from men's mouths like a rebuke to her aloneness. Antony said it, and Sorrel said it. However much they gave, this thing was laid like a barrier: beyond it nobody could go. She held tight to the young man's hand and she was saying in silence: I'll be old in a little while, I'll get old alone, without knowing. Whoever you are, stand between me and my fear of being alone.

But suddenly Sorrel turned quickly on them, and with his bare arm through Victoria's, he drew her close against his dress.

"Victoria is the honey that draws the bees to us," he said. In the moonlight he laughed his gentle, high, old woman's laughter, but his fingers were closed fiercely on her wrist. "She draws them by the dozens," he said, with his smile worn sideways under his nose. He put her a little behind him in the beginning of the shadow and settled the toga on his shoulders. His body was straight and lean as a boy's with the Indian, hawk-nosed head set strongly on it. *"Bon soir,"* he said with the flat American tune in his voice. "We walk home from here by the rue de la Tour."

He put out his open, guileless palm with the callouses set hard across the cushions of it, and he shook the young French poet's hand. "You live back there over the river, don't you?" he said. He was standing between them, strong and white in his garments, an impassable, moon-drenched wall, his muscles waiting as hard as stone.

He watched the young man go down past the sloping flower-beds and lawns, grow smaller as he neared the river, and vanish in the shadows under the trees, and then Sorrel turned to Victoria. He was strong and sure now, there were no tears left in him. He put his two hands on Victoria's shoulders and his eyes were level with hers, large and wide in his high-boned face, soft and miraculously lashed.

"Victoria, you are beautiful," he said. "Has any one ever told you? You are a pure woman," said the preacher-like voice in benediction, and he put his arms around her.

"No," said Victoria, "I am not pure."

She put her arms tight around his shoulders and held him, and in the back of his neck his hair was turned up, as white and neat and virtuous as any old lady's hair. And this is the way I would come to my father and say it, she thought. This is the way I would tell him that the nights have become a search for it, one night linked to the next like a train with unlighted windows going endless through the dark rooms gone into without the face of the house or the name of the street known, and the way to take to the shop alone in the morning and a taste left in the mouth for ever that the cold of no mountain water running fast can alter.

But "Victoria, kiss me," he was saying, "kiss me, kiss me." His breath was coming short in his body. "Kiss me," he said, and his mouth was an old man's mouth moving over her face.

She went running down over the grass alone, jumping the little iron barriers in her sandals, cleansing her face in what was moonlight and what was quiet nightly air. On every bench there now were lovers sitting, clasped to each other like a single body, and Antony you made it sound pretty, she said, passing over the wet grass and the earth in which the flowers sprung. You put the paper lace and the tinsel on it. If you'd been a poor young man sitting on a park bench reading the want ads. in Oklahoma, we might have grown up together. We might have said something simple to each other once in a while. Now I can squat foul as a toad, rot in my own juices. I can stay out all night, I can stalk the streets for it, unsanctified by love or anything that has that name. She could see the end of her life and how her life would pass, clearly as only the young can see these things. She could see the passage of days leading to the end, small, dusty, yellow mats thrown down all summer upon the threshold of each fearful night's beginning.

One evening when she went back there was a letter under the door of her room, lying clean on the planks that had been a long time grey with

age and splintering off with thirst. She came in
tired from the shop, her face white from the heat,
and there was a letter pure as a sail on the dark
unaltering tide. She sat down by the open window
in the late light with it, and when she had read it
through she tore it up and threw the pieces away.
It said "Dear Victoria John, Antony sailed for
America five days ago and asked me to let you
know he will be back some time in June. He has
talked a lot about you, and it would be nice if you
would come and have tea or a cocktail or something with me. I'm always home between this time
and that," said the letter, "and it would be marvellous to meet you." It was signed "Fontana
Lister," and Victoria stood up looking at the little
pieces of Fontana scattered in the empty fireplace.

"That's the end of both of you," she said, and
she was tired. "That's the end as far as I'm con-
cerned of Antony and you."

It was the end of them, and soon it would be
the end of Sorrel for her. She knew very well
that they were finished in her life and that the
finish with Sorrel was drawing near. I'll go away,
she thought, I'll go somewhere else and it will
never change what any of them have meant to me.
I will have to carry little pieces of them around
with me for ever. She could hear her own voice
saying again to strangers "Now we have enough
money to do the things we want and Sorrel and I
are starting a printing-house together. We are
beginning something very great together. We are
going to do books in French and English and

young writers who have been waiting a long time for recognition will come to us. . . ." She had said it so often that now it had an empty sound, as if it had been drained dry by speech and only the memory of some one saying it remained. I no longer believe in it, she thought. I no longer believe in Sorrel's intention. I must say it louder. Perhaps if I say it loud enough it will come true again.

CHAPTER TWENTY-FIVE

Hippolytus, Athenia, Prosperine and Bishinka with their tunics shrunk sideways, their hair plaited stiff from their dark necks, their hands turning nervous as minnows in Victoria's hands, crossed the wet bridle-path to the lake on Sunday afternoon and stopped there staring at the swans. It was spring now, they had been told by everybody that it was spring, and they were out to get a sight of it after a long time of playing in the refuse of the garden.

"We can play games together on the grass," said Victoria in the common room at lunch.

"I've seen grass," said Hippolytus. "Is it alive?" said Bishinka, his head almost lying in the shadow of his shoulders' hump, the hump which he carried like a burden of precocious despair.

So off they went to the Bois de Bologne with Victoria who might have been a long, thin stranger gone to the slums out of charity on Sunday to promenade a meagre handful of the underfed, unjoyful children of the eternally poor. The children were dressed for simplicity, it would seem; dressed in tunics for fleet games, for open spaces, for competition in naturalness with all the things that grew. But the grass, and the trees with their new-born leaves, and even the smell of spring, still moist after a night in sweet and painless labour, even the young uncertainty of spring, like a calf on its first legs with its coat aglisten from the dew of the other, the unborn world, were ordinary enough things to the ordinary people, and the four children who were dressed for it did not know what to do.

People out in their Sunday clothes turned to look at them, for the ordinary French wore shoes and all the other articles of dress which now seem essential to an appearance in the street, and these children were decked out for Rome or Greece, but for a poorer, more disreputable Greece or Rome than any the promenaders had read about at school. They stood on the strip of grass, holding fast to Victoria, anchoring her there with their uncertainty, as if they feared she might escape and leave them in a world of alien things.

"You can sit down on it," said Victoria. "It's grass."

The four of them sat down obediently, sat shyly, uncomfortably on it. It might easily have been the first time they had crawled out of their cocoons, and their eyes were still unused to what they saw.

"We had something this colour around the Christmas tree," said Hippolytus, but scarcely aloud. "Only it was made out of paper. I've seen grass before."

Victoria sat down and the children moved close

on her skirts to watch the proud, mechanical line of swans that opened toward them from across the lake. They were coming close to the edge, their necks arched smooth as wax, their heads jewelled with golden eyes and tapering to the black wooden bills, the feathers pure as heaven on their lovely throats. Were it not for their hard faces, vain as women's faces, they might have been taken for angels fallen there on the lake and graciously, miraculously proceeding toward the land. But the vanity in their faces was almost enough to rob them of their beauty. Like the rich, they took everything for granted, looking down even on the lake which they accepted as a mirror for their charms. The four children in their dirty tunics sat quite still on the grass and watched the monstrously clean, fair birds swelling proudly near the shore.

And up from the earth beneath them came the wonderful movement of what was stirring and groaning in its sleep, of trees toughening from saplings overnight, of water breaking and rivers rising, of some momentous arousing as if a man who slept curved under the mountains and the plains and the waters was awaking and brushing the pine-forests and the world's endless spider webs from his eyes and preparing to stretch yawning from one continent to another. The shivers of spring that ran through his blood were now an excitement in the earth, more wonderful each year because of how completely they were forgotten, and more voluptuous because of the centuries of fragrance and blossoming they had gathered into themselves. The incredible power of what was alive beneath was knocking now at the skin and the bones, at the pitiful rumps of the children dressed for Greece. But they did not leap up and run about for pleasure, or wing like birds, or skip like lambs; they sat quiet, shyly holding on to Victoria, and Hippolytus and Athenia, the older ones, were even a little shamed by the looks which ordinary people gave them. Other children, dressed in sailor-suits, stood by the rail grinning at them, but the children in their tunics and sandals did not smile.

But there are alleys in the Bois de Bologne where one can escape every one, even the lovers, and everything except the spring. They went back by these wide paths, and Victoria ran quickly through the trees, but the children were afraid to run after. They had been audience so long, they did not know how to be the players. They were dressed up for it, their slight, breakable bodies bedecked in all the imitations of white, but for them the show had never started, the holy communion of living had never yet begun. They were not young any more, which did not matter, but if things went on the evil was that they would never be young again.

Victoria ran back and took their hands, and Bishinka was crying. His feet hurt because the ties of his sandals had been badly sewn. His toenails had not been cut, had never been cut at all perhaps, and they were growing inward like great yellow sabres. Along the paths they went with

her, puny and dark, with hollows in their faces:
four little overtures made timorously to death,
their feet whispering over the mosses an invitation
to the grave. There were a thousand different
greens and dews in the foliage, and the light
through the unfurling boughs was now a clear,
icy green, the green of light lichen on a stump
moist with black rot, the green of stone crypts,
the green of cold decay.

Victoria made a story for them out of the sound
of them coming through the woods with her.
Their feet, having so little to carry, made no mark;
she might have been accompanied by four blowing leaves. This was the Congo, she said, the
serpents lying warm and slumbrous along the
branches, this the undiscovered continent aching
with plants too heavy, smells warm as honey in
the nostrils, droning louder than any, this was the
promise of rich fruits, too languorous for bursting.
Hippolytus, Athenia, Prosperine, Bishinka, this
is the promised land. There were no black boys
to beat the way for them, and yet they were not
lost, having been eternally lost, only now seemingly smaller and more defenceless in their white
garments under the tall, closely-planted trees.

The little caravan went on, weaponless and
separated from the main body of human expedi-
tion which kept to the wider roads, wandering to
the sound of Bishinka's crying because his feet
hurt and to Prosperine's complaint against the
wet. Only these things were softly done, not as
the children of the secure might have made pro-

test; even Bishinka's tears were shed humbly, in apology. They looked up through the far, high branches above, for at least the sky was not a stranger to them; they had seen it from the yard in Neuilly every day. But there was little of it left here in the forest, nor did they listen very well to Victoria's story of them, for the sound of that too was unfamiliar: they could not recognize their own faces unless they were Hippolytus, Athenia, Prosperine and Bishinka waiting in the common room for supper or lying down at night to sleep upon the floor.

"When I grow up I'll have a lot of houses," said Hippolytus. "I won't have any trees around getting in the way."

He slapped at one with the flat of his hand, but it threw up its arms and shuddered at him.

"I don't like trees," he said, and he jumped back to hold on to Victoria. If this was spring, they had had quite enough of it. They could do very well for awhile without having any more.

Sorrel was sitting in the common room when they came back in the evening, and Matilde was eating figs and harking to what he read aloud. His feet were up on the bench across from where he sat and beside him was a stack of catalogues with pretty pictures in colour on them. Matilde held out the paper of figs to Victoria, and the children went slowly off, seeking Cina and Gabrielle upstairs.

"You're not going out again tonight, are you?" said Matilde.

"No," said Victoria. No to the figs and no to the round, sly face of Matilde squatting there in her woven dress and veil. "No, I'm going to bed early tonight. I'm tired."

Sorrel looked up, gentle and weary, grateful to her as she smoothed the white, patient-seeming side of his hair drawn smooth across his head.

"Just listen to this, dear," he said. For a moment there was a pause, as if he were going to begin telling her, as if it were on the tip of his tongue to say it, and then it passed. The coloured thing was open in his hand, and instead he began reading: " 'At first it seems a little strange,' " the pastoral went, " 'because you're not used to so much vision. An invisible power seems to pull you along. But soon you get the feel of it. And then you find yourself wondering why you ever liked a conventional older-type car.' " He cleared his throat. "It just goes on to say 'go to any Chrysler or De Soto dealer. Let him explain the air-flow type of construction, the Floating Ride that has a rhythm like a walk. Then decide for yourself whether you want to buy a modern or an old-fashioned car.' "

Then it was that Victoria saw Arthur sitting in the corner in the darkness, sitting like a figure cut from wax, the eyes and the cheeks scooped out with shadow and emaciation, the pale arms folded plaster-white across his tunic, the hair helmet pulled down close upon his ears. He was sitting there silent, as he had sat twelve years in silence with Matilde and Sorrel, but now his legs shifted in his skirt and his voice came deep, stern, denunciatory, across the common room.

"Sorrel," he said, taking the man's name as if it were a curse upon his tongue, "where would you get the money to buy such a car?"

Matilde jumped up with a cry of fright and quickly closed her little paper of figs over, and Sorrel gave a short, dry laugh and took his feet off the poets' bench.

"Why, I was just reading a bit about these newfangled autos they're bringing out," he said, pleasantly. "That's all."

"And as for that," cried Matilde in anger, "Sorrel can buy all the cars he wants to! It's his own things that are going to the museum, not anybody else's! He's worked hard for the money the American woman paid."

Edmond was in the hall, standing near to the kitchen door, waiting. When Victoria left the common room she saw him; he had his good grey flannel suit on and his hair was brushed back clean, and when he saw Victoria he slowly closed one eye.

"*Pernod*," he said softly, and he jerked his head toward the stairway. He lifted his hand and thumbed his nose at the sound of Matilde's voice berating Arthur's silence; he had drawn it around him like a cloak again, the square and the circle, and the area of some other place where no one else could come. The laughter was shaking under Edmond's watch-chain. "*Pernod*," he said as they went up the stairs. "*On vous attend.*"

Estelle was on the divan-bed, in her nightgown

still, having been asleep all afternoon. She lay
languid behind a delicate curtain of smoke that
rippled from floor to ceiling as they entered. The
ends of the cigarettes of all the admirers who had
not come were crushed out in a saucer. The lilacs
Edmond had brought home one evening were
dying for water in a glass and the cock-eyed hat of
Chevalier was floating dim in the smoke above
them.

"You look as if you need it," Estelle said, yawning. "Open the bottle and give her a glass of it,
Edmond."

He put his cigarette-end down with all the others
in the dish, and he took the bottle out from under
the bed. He was pulling the cork out, his back
turned to them, the bottle held between his knees,
the grey flannel coat tight across the shoulders,
the roll of flesh red as apoplexy over his collar at
the back. Victoria sat down on the bed and suddenly she began talking to Estelle, quickly, under
her breath.

"Estelle, I think I'm pregnant. I don't know
what to do," she said.

Estelle had begun to yawn, and the yawn
stopped short in the middle. She lay still for a
moment, expressionless, looking at Victoria, the
eyes fixed in their blue, callous, stony stare.

"My God, you would be," she said, slowly.
Her square red mouth was a little open, like a
chipmunk's mouth, wanting the yawn again that
she had left midway. It was swelling at her jaws,
like a mouthful of nuts. "My God," Estelle said

to Edmond. "Victoria's pregnant. Victoria would have to get pregnant, wouldn't she?" She took a nail-file off the table by the bed. "Edmond will get you some pills the kind the girls at the theatre use."

Edmond was filling up the glasses, carefully pouring the green drink out into the three of them and adding the water from the carafe. He watched the milkiness gather and spread, watched the absinthe-pale tide mount in the tumblers and the flat gold halo lie high along the rim. When he turned to them with their drinks in his hands, his lips were bunched up ruby-red under his neat little greying moustaches.

"You'd better not let on to Matilde," he said, tasting his *pernod*. "She'd put it on to Sorrel."

Victoria took her drink in quick, nervous swallows, sitting on the edge of the divan by the firm, white, languid body of Estelle who lay at rest in her black chiffon gown. The nail-file was busy in her fingers, but the china-blue eyes were examining Victoria, were turned in opaque speculation on her face, her hands, her breasts, her hair. She observed it all, scrutinized, considered without question, without a flicker of emotion the details of what Victoria's life had been.

"How long?" said Estelle lazily at last.

"I don't know," Victoria said. "Perhaps two months—I can't say exactly."

Estelle lifted her glass and sipped it evenly, her eyes unaltered over the thick tumbler's brim.

"If it's Sorrel," Edmond went on, "Matilde will

s

put you out in two minutes. She's done it before. There was Ruth," he said, and then he cocked his eye under the tufted brow at her. "And if it's anybody else," he said with the laughter beginning again in his belly, "Sorrel himself won't like it. That would hurt his feelings more than anything."

"Of course it isn't Sorrel," Victoria said. She could scarcely believe that Edmond said this with any gravity. "It couldn't possibly be Sorrel."

"Sorrel or no Sorrel," said Estelle suddenly, "keep it under your hat, Victoria."

"*Un peu plus haut que d'habitude*," Edmond said, with his laughter shaking in his vest.

"It's your own business," said Estelle and she looked at the enamel on her fingers. "I'll get you the pills tonight. They make you sick as a cat, but they do the trick. Once they get going they don't leave anything behind. I'll bring them over to you when I get back from the show."

CHAPTER TWENTY-SIX

The privy behind the shop was a deep, fecund green, and the hole in the pavings that stood for ever open like a corpse's eye was as much the earth's gangrened navel as a thing for any human use. Out of it issued the myriad, dark smells of the earth's bowels, incongruously dressed in the rags and tatters of the daily press: *Le Journal* from the conçierge's loge, *l'Ami du Peuple* from the florist shop next door, *Les Nouvelles Littéraires* from the bookshop at the corner, and *Detective* from the sport-shop that opened on the other street. The donations from those who came out the back door of Sorrel's shop varied from ancient lecture programmes asking "Le Poéte, doit-il Recônnaitre l'Empire de l'Age Mécanique?" to torn pages explaining "Comment J'ai Suivi un Fleuve à sa Source". On visits to the place, the face of Serge Stavisky might be found with all its suave smiling elegance drenched and defiled on the flagstones of the flushless cabinay, or Albert, King of the Belgians, dead and on the eve of an ignoble departure down the drains. It might well have seemed that the printed record of that year was day by day, and several times a day, being intentionally rammed down this foul tributary to the earth's most private recognition.

It was Edmond's pills which brought Victoria to an intimate knowledge of it. They removed whatever there was twelve or thirteen times a day: round, coffee-coloured pills of promise, so like the buttons off the leggings of children on their way to school that they were hard to swallow. Two of them six times a day until the murder is committed. In them they had fine limber blades concealed which they whipped out and flourished once they had reached the nine miles or yards of entrails coiled secretly in the belly's soft white skin. They removed whatever there was to take, but waltzed in their wary abandonment around the small burden of flesh and blood, leaving it sacred, miraculously untouched. They would have food and spirit and the body's pain, but absolute flesh itself they would not have. Having a heart that beat and small, clutching, vein-like hands of life, it was too good for their vile, absolute ends.

Women came into the shop and touched the bright scarves, and while they hesitated between this colour and that, the war the body waged against the pills' destruction stood beside them, the scars of it written on Victoria's face. Or Sorrel came on Wednesday afternoons for tea, wearing his smile for ever now, surrounded by the alien women who seized upon this sign or any other of art, creative art, feeling their own lives slipping from them year by year no matter how feebly or how frantically they clung. Not many men came in, except American husbands brought there to breathe for once the atmosphere their wives inhaled. There's another air back there, Victoria thought, watching in anguish the quavering indecision of their minds; she was sick for it, stabbed for it, she could not wait until the door had closed behind them to run groaning to it. The gooseflesh was all over her, like a broken string of beads.

Between these times she lay on the poets' bench upstairs with a sheep rug over her to stop the shaking of her bones, or visited the privy place behind the shop until even the soul fell to retching when it set nostril to the green blasts of corruption which made a climate of their own in the roofed-over, moulding alley-way. And on the eighteenth day, Antony took the habit of walking into the shop whenever she was alone and lying down. He came in, a little nervous still, but smiling. She could see him without opening her eyes, without stirring under the sheep's skin, and when he came in she said: "It's no use, Antony, I know now how little use it is. There are two kinds of people in the world, there are the rich and the poor, and if you're the poor you're finished from the first, even though you don't see it right away. You can make a little struggle, very brief, and after awhile you begin to see. You see they've got you down and they certainly aren't going to let you up again. It wouldn't be clever at all. Once you got up and were still young enough you might tell what you had seen down there."

I might tell you about Hippolytus, and Athenia, and Prosperine and Bishinka and then you wouldn't be able to sleep at night. I might tell you how Miss Fira and Miss Grusha lived for years. The fever was making a drum of her skin, drawing it tighter over the bones and beating louder on it. This was the music that began with the parade, with the procession of small agonies from the loft down the stairs to the customer waiting whenever the bell rang out. She pushed the sheep's cover off and then the bugles of pain were played out, sweet and shrill, and the little pearls of gooseflesh were cast out not before swine but before the swinish bartering of one bad thing for another just as bad. It was the one way there was of making a living as long as it was important that a living be made.

But Antony was saying that the rich and the poor were not the issue; it had to be something better than that or else he might as well be dead. If you had no money at all, you were finished, but also if you had money it was possible you were finished too. Rich or poor, every one was stabbing every one else with hate, stabbing in envy and in terror. "It isn't a great deal to ask, only that every one put down their weapons," Antony said, grinning and saying it quickly as if it were really of no importance. Or else he said: "I ask everything, I ask that people give up their brides. The whole universe on a honeymoon of horror, wedded to their daggers, stabbing their way from one betrayal to the next. Even your own family and friends eager to do it to you," said Antony, as if his wound were running wide.

"That's weak, that's weak as water," said Victoria. "You should keep your fears for the dark, alone, like your lovers. Lacey said that to me. It's only the people who speak the truth you remember in the end."

She had brought water up from the tap in the alley-way in the morning, and she crossed the loft to the pitcher and lifted it to wash the three pills down. Three pills eight times a day because the murder will not out, and each of them offering such a wide area of experience, as if they were small, terrible, faded eyes that had seen into the depths and widths of degradation and despair. "How would you like a tunic or a scarf," said Victoria, smiling at the customer. How would you like a pill or two to keep you busy?

"Is this one signed by Mr. Sorrel?" said the student from the School of Fine and Applied Arts who wanted a tunic to take back to California to her mother.

"Yes," said Victoria, "at the hem."

She leaned over to lift the tunic's edge and the fever struck like hammers in her temples. It went up into the loft with her and crawled in under the sheep's hide, not to be left alone without her, hugging her close in fear that she might get away. In great Atlantic breakers of mid-winter sea it rose, shuddering, shuddering, shivering out at the ends like the spread fingers of a hand. How would you like a scarf to hang you, said Victoria to

Stavisky lying polluted but smiling still, side by side with Madame Curie, in the dark forest of the cabinay.

"I am weak," said Antony, "too weak to take up a weapon and go into the orgy, unless I turned it upon myself and shed my own blood."

"You don't have to," said Victoria. "You can always get on a boat and leave the country. You can always keep on going."

"I can't go far enough," said Antony, "nobody can. Wherever I am, just looking out of the holes in my skull is enough to scare me. I'm scared of what's happening to every one and I can't do anything to change it."

"Keep on with it; keep on with it; it'll have to start coming," Edmond said.

"For two francs a day," said Estelle, pulling her stockings up, her eyes on Victoria seeing it, the hopelessness and the agony and the fifteen times a day in the alley behind the shop. Her voice was as hard as money in her throat, but she was saying: "If you had it, you could keep it in the *pouponnière* for forty sous a day."

"Two francs a day is a lot of money," Edmond said. "You'd better keep on trying. Where could you have it if you had it, and who would feed and house you?"

"I could take her food, wherever she was," said Estelle, putting the black on. "I could manage."

If I stopped taking the pills now, the pain would stop, said Victoria. A peace would come soft and tender as somebody's arms around me. I could lie down and sleep and be quiet for a little while. But she got up and crossed the loft and lifted the jug of water. Four of them ten times in the day now for the strange, inhuman kernel of life which sucked blind, featureless, unskulled at what they would not let it have.

"Gabrielle tried with an umbrella rib before Athenia," said Edmond, taking another glass of pernod.

Hippolytus, Athenia, Prosperine and Bishinka had been the same, had been mistakes made in the dark. While still unstirring they had been attacked in bitterness, and stubborn as wilful beings they had clasped faster to what was promise, to what was mamma, to what was the event of birth. They had desperately seized shape and bone within, while about them all the impotence of motherly hate laid waste.

"For two cents I'd have the baby," Victoria said to Antony when he came into the loft. "I'm not afraid of anything they can do."

But Antony was talking about what they had done to him when he was too young to see it coming. He walked uneasily over the boards; he walked up and down in his black suit with his hair standing up in the middle, watching Victoria with her hands up holding the pain tight in her face.

"Where I went to school," he said, "the conversation was the most elegant you could find for the price. The boys used to talk about how many cocktails their mothers served at home in the evening to how many people, and how many bridge tables they had. There weren't any black people being hung in the south, the Supreme Court was the highest, the supremest. Buddha had never sat quiet, year after year, reflecting. Nothing was sacred enough to kneel to, not even a mountain, nor an element like the wind, or the rain, nor an astral body."

The nights were little deaths, quite complete in themselves, animated by conversations with the dead, and slow, dim journeys down the hallway from the tomb to the doorway that promised a relief that never came. Opposite it stood the door of Miss Fira's and Miss Grusha's ballroom, bolted upon the confusion of their flight. And in the night Victoria leaned in pain against it, making no sound, shaping no wish, but remembering, as if the objects had been taken one by one and set before her in illumination, the bits and pieces that were left when they had gone: an end of black moire ribbon, a length of thread, and a pin-cushion shaped like a strawberry on the mantel. The mornings came very light and mild, almost summer mornings, with birds beginning early in the trees. And Victoria got up again and put off the shroud and the cold, sepulchral clingings of the grave. Fever was weaving together the dark and the light now, the nights and the days, so that time moved past like water flowing, a narrow stream of slow, sick water carrying a little reflection on it, passing underground.

One day she fell down in the Métro train going

to the shop in the morning. She fell down from weakness, and the train was turning fast. She fell down among all the people hanging to the straps, and her head went under the seat, and the coffee she drank at the corner for breakfast came out at the other end. They lifted her out under the arms and they put her lying down on a bench at the Place de l'Opéra station, and people came around and looked at her. She lay there with her eyes closed, and she could not open them now, she thought, for Antony might be standing there among the others looking. She lay with the murmur of strange voices like a tide murmuring and rising, and she began explaining it to him, taking the words as they passed on the water, saying: "This is something else, Antony. I didn't go out last night or the night before that. I haven't been drunk, Antony. This is just Victoria from Ohio wanting to go home."

When she sat up everything was foul in her dress, and a woman came over to her and opened a pocketbook before her, a poor woman with shaking hands and warts around her nose, and she put a clean handkerchief and five francs in Victoria's hand. It was a beautiful morning in June, and when she got up the steps to the air the waiters were making things ready for all the Americans who would come for breakfast on the terrace of the Café de la Paix. Victoria stood in the island, looking, and the traffic passed wild as steers, and toward the west she said America's that way, over there, and her teeth were knocking together. Listen, America, she said, and her nose was running. America, listen, listen, she said, but there was nothing more to say.

She stopped a taxi with the five francs in her hand, and inside it she took the woman's handkerchief and started rubbing at her legs.

"It shows, it shows everywhere," she said. "It shows."

CHAPTER TWENTY-SEVEN

I t was Saturday evening and she sat up under the sheep's hide in the loft, and the bell was ringing, it had been ringing a long time in sleep. She got up and pushed her hair back with her hand, and she went slowly down the spiral stairs, slowly, with her fingers feeling along the wall. The curtain was hanging motionless in the doorway, and there was some one waiting in the shop beyond, but now there was no promise in it. It might be Sorrel, or a stranger, or Antony come back again, and it would make no difference. Whoever it was, they would be drifting away too fast to help or hinder, travelling lifewards with the current, their voices heard calling back, strange, and faint, and far.

Victoria passed under the curtain and there was a woman in the shop, a small, pretty woman with a big hat on and a jacket like a little boy's. She was dressed entirely in black and white, very smart, with little ruffles at her wrists; so like a bright, saucy little boy, with the lipstick scarcely showing. A Russian wolfhound was lying in sorrow by her feet, ready to mourn if any one touched him, while the young woman herself was on the edge of laughing; it was in her mouth already and shining in her eyes. The two of them had nothing to do with each other: the sorrowing lonely dog ready to speak his lean-faced grief and the woman he must follow after with the little tendrils of her perfume lingering in his nose.

She said "Hello, there, I'm Fontana Lister", and in spite of the little rushes of laughter to her eyes and the hops and skips of her speech, she did not seem a very happy, foolish woman. It was more that she was there, right out in the front with every one looking on and she was going to give the best performance she had. "I forgot you couldn't get away from your work," she said, "and I was waiting for you to come and see me. But I waited so long and you didn't come," she said, and her teeth when she smiled were a little crooked, a little askew, which gave her another look of honesty. She was laughing outright about nothing at all, and the dog got up and turned around and sighed.

"Yes," said Victoria, and she sat down. She could think of nothing else to say. But Fontana was talking, as well-bred women talk, of everything else but of what was there before them; not of the white, shy face of Victoria reflected in the glass in silence, or the poor clothes, or the heels of the shoes turned over, but of places they might have met all spring, or names of people they might both have known as equals, said in the crowded presence of all their differences. She sat down neat and sweet in comfort, with her lovely hat and her fresh things giving a new taste to the highly-coloured room.

"I've had a cable from Antony," she said in a little while, and she did not seem to be looking about in curiosity or query, not taking things apart or putting two and two together. She put her hand in the pocket of her coat and she took out the cable. It was three pages long, typewritten in blue, and she began reading it out in bits: " 'Wall Street narrow as the bier . . . Horace believes in the future of gold, silver, copper, steel and other metals . . . They've put bars on all the windows because so many people committed it this year now it seems more like a prison than last . . . Nijinsky should have stayed sane long enough to create the dance I see myself doing in wreaths, garlands, festoons of stock quotations on white ticker ribbons . . . I walk all night after parties or when there're not any'," and Fontana looked up again at Victoria. She was smiling, but something had happened to her eyes. They were swimming as if to shore and safety, and in her face her mouth did nothing but stay there and look on and smile. "It's so stupid," she said, "he has to go back every year and pretend. Every one wants him to be something he isn't. He has a father called Horace," she said, "and he has to be some kind of a son to him. 'I am not' " said the cable in Fontana's voice " 'gold, silver or copper, I am something waiting to be set to music . . . Mozart forgot me in his eighth year . . . hummed me over between Don Juan and the Magic Flute and forgot me going upstairs to bed in Salzburg . . . Anaconda Copper, Carro de Pasco, Seaboard

Oil are passwords for departure . . . New York explodes inside me every time I step out the door . . . I can't do it. . . . I can't do it . . . I can't do it,' " Fontana read, and then she stopped reading. Her eyes were shining, clear and bright as glass. She took her handkerchief out and then she put it away again, and her fingers turned the cablegram over. "A little bit farther on," said Fontana, "he says 'have you seen a girl called Victoria John she's trapped in ancient Greece'."

Fontana laughed, and Victoria laughed, and the dog looked up at them in grief.

"Cities break him up in pieces," said Fontana, "and the country puts him together again. He paints when he's in the country. I'd love to show you his paintings." She was smiling quickly at Victoria and patting the dog's lean, lordly head. "We have a place in Rambouillet," she said. "Perhaps Antony told you that." I don't know how much or how little, said the rehearsal of her face, or what sort of things he told you. "We got the place out there so Antony could come to the country every night from work. He lives the kind of life he wants in the country, but every morning he has to get up and come in to work in Paris. He has to be a good husband, and a good son to Horace, and——" Her voice stopped speaking. "He wants to be a good everything to everybody," she said.

"I didn't know," said Victoria, and her own voice sounded strange to her. "I didn't know he painted. He said he used to paint. I didn't know he came in to work every day."

288

"I thought," said Fontana, smiling, "you would come out to Rambouillet with me. I've got a car outside. It isn't as nice when Antony isn't there because things stand around waiting for him and looking. Horses' heads out of stalls," she said, with her eyes squeezed up with laughter, "and jockeys getting bowlegged with waiting. The thing is going faster and faster every minute—the jockeys want horses, the horses want hay; the hay wants acres, and Horace wants Antony sitting behind bars making more and more of what there's too much of already. Antony provides everything in life; but according to some law that Horace understands, Antony must provide money too. Some day Horace will die and then nobody will be very sorry. It won't be too late then, do you think, for Antony to begin living the way he wants? Does it ever get too late for people to begin living the way they want to live?"

Everything sounded quite possible when she spoke of it, for she was prettier and cleaner than any one else alive and, being so, she could perform such miracles as the miracle of the song she was singing now for Antony. It was playing like a harem-dance in the little, white lifted tents of her lids, it was throbbing, transfixed to the points of her bosoms like living butterflies.

"Antony gives everything he has away as a present," Victoria said. Why don't you keep him home, Fontana? "To strangers. He ought to keep something for the next time."

"But there's always enough when the next time

289   T

comes," Fontana said. She was sitting there with the picture of him very close, blinding everything else before her eyes. "He said you used to walk all night with him and let him talk himself quiet."

"Antony was very good to me," Victoria said, and Fontana said suddenly, "You look tired, Victoria John," and she was smiling.

"I'm a bit ill," Victoria said.

"Oh, I'm sorry," said Fontana. "I hate being ill." She said things very simply as if that were the quickest way of saying them. "Why don't we take you to a doctor? I have a very nice doctor. Antony said you worked hard. Perhaps you would like to come for a week and rest in Rambouillet?"

"I don't work hard," Victoria said. What I won't have is pity. Fine ladies coming in with their gloves on to prod and poke at my wounds whatever they are. And now the wild bugles of pain were unwinding in her; they were crying high and shrill throughout her blood. They were stayless as arrogant riders, booted and spurred, riding ruthless over the country, the crops broken under as they passed and the slow quiet toil of the seasons ravaged. The elegant horsemen had taken their swords from their scabbards and were turning them slowly in her flesh.

"I don't work very hard," Victoria said, holding tight to the poets' bench under her. I'll sit where I am, she said: "I've just been a bit stupid." She would give her the truth, like a dirty rag in her face; for once she would have it to fondle instead

of the wolfhound in her ladylike hands. "I'm
taking some pills," she said. "I'm trying not to
have a baby."

Everything stopped moving in Fontana's face.
She sat there very quiet with the performance of
gaiety gone from her mouth and out of her eyes
even. There's the door, said Victoria in silence.
You'd better pick up your skirts and go. There's
the door, she said, and she held on tight to the
poets' bench to stop her shaking.

"But I don't think you should try not to have
it," said Fontana. She had begun to smile again,
but her voice was very small. And Victoria sat
laughing, holding on to the hard, the unadorned
seat for the posteriors of poets. In the alley the
privy was waiting, singing its serenade rich and
obscene to her, reciting the verses written in
pencil on its walls, quoting the fragments of
interminable literature that stopped it, the mur-
ders, the thefts, the wars that floated to the brim.

"I have to try," said Victoria. "You see I
haven't any baby carriage. I wouldn't know where
to put it. I haven't any husband to bring it a rattle
and play with it when it cried."

"I think you should have it," Fontana said
very quickly. "If it is Antony's baby, I mean I
think you should have it. I think it would be an
awful thing to send away a baby you and Antony
had made together."

I'll have to go out there now, said Victoria.
She stood up and held on to the back of the bench
and the room was hot as water on her face and it

was running cold as water down her spine. The pain was turning like a rag they were twisting in her. She put her hand on the wall and she said:

"I'll have to go out there a minute."

"I'll go with you," Fontana said, throwing her big hat down behind her. "You might faint somewhere alone."

When they came back Fontana sat down on the bench beside her, and the dog was sighing on the floor, wearily, wearily sighing, as if he knew now they never would be done.

"What did you take?" she said.

"Pills," said Victoria. "Six of them twelve times a day and it doesn't make any difference."

"You mustn't take any more," said Fontana. She picked up the fingers of Victoria's hand separately in her own small, nervous fingers. "You must have it. I think it would be fun to have it," she said.

"I couldn't bear having it," Victoria said. "It isn't Antony's, of course. It was never anything like that between us, you see. He has you all the time, he always has you, and I had no one. I used to think it was good to have no one, but when Antony talked about you I wanted some one. It happened the first time on the boat on the river. I don't know who it was exactly." Let her have the rag, dirtier, filthier, fouler. Draw the blinds, close the door, Fontana, a souse is passing singing a dirty ditty. You still have time to escape, a drunk is passing, reeling down one of the poorer streets you couldn't be found on at any time of day.

"And after that it happened very often," she said. "There were four or five young men I met with Antony or at Sorrel's lectures. It was never Antony," she said.

"Didn't you fall in love at all?" said Fontana.

"In love?" said Victoria, and she looked down at her fingers in Fontana's. "I must be very puritan. I hated every one. It becomes like a madness, to find some one you don't hate as much as you hated the one before."

"I've never hated it," said Fontana seriously. "I've done it a great deal, and it's always been so nice."

"I can't speak to them after," Victoria said. "As if we were accomplices in some unspeakable crime. We might as well have murdered something between us and were trying to hide the corpse from every one."

"I never did it with any one I didn't like," said Fontana.

"It's different," said Victoria. "When you've had a lot to drink, it's not a matter of choosing. Or anyway it's only the choice of being with some one all night or else going home alone," and she turned her head aside in fear that Fontana might suddenly see down into the cesspool of her heart. You have to be rich to do it, she was thinking, rich or else married. Poor and unmarried gives it a smell of something like misery; it doesn't sound like love any more. When you're poor you go around without a change of linen, asking for some kind of comfort and never getting it, watch-

ing the others that share it between them, going
arm in arm. You carry a great hunger for love
and you live so badly that you soil it if it ever
comes near you.

"Just the same," said Fontana, with her words
beginning to skip and hop again. "You must stop
taking the medicine. There are other things people
can do for you. They do it and it's over very
quickly and everything is just as good as before."

Her little ears lay close to her head, but the
ends of them were soft and thriftless. She did
not wear any stones in them or any rings on her
fingers, but there was a string of diamonds on one
wrist that went three times around.

"We're a bit hard up now," she said. She was
ready to laugh at any minute. "That's why Antony
went back. He's awfully good at making money
suddenly when we need it. I know a *sage-femme*,"
she said, "and we'll go and see her. She'll do
something very quick to you and it will be over
right away."

It was seven o'clock and Victoria locked the
door behind them. The car and the chauffeur
were waiting for Fontana a little beyond the door.
When she talked to the servant something altered
in Fontana's voice: the little lash of her class and
her ease was suddenly there like a lion-tamer's
whip come subtly to life in his hand. The Russian
dog came after them into the car and slouched
down beside them, incredibly bored, incredibly
clean, with his hair curled smooth as caracal and his
loose, tapering limbs bent under his pointed breast.

CHAPTER TWENTY-EIGHT

In the morning they went to see the *sage-femme* who had a little garden in front of her house. The garden began suddenly on the other side of the wall at the end of the rue d'Alésia: there was the gate in the sad, city-like wall, and without any warning of vine or grass at the entrance, the garden began suddenly to bloom on the other side. It started with rose-trees, and behind the roses was a Chinese *tilleul*, and up the face of the little house ran vines and vines of ghostly wistaria, white and purple like flowers in decay.

"Antony and I had this house once," Fontana said. "When we were first married we rented this little house for ourselves. We put a bathroom in it, but we could only light the geyser once a week because we were pretending we could live on what they paid Antony at the office. We put all my money in one bank and we tried to forget all about it. I used to make the toast for breakfast," Fontana said. They were on the doorstep, and the woman opened the door to them and asked them to come in.

The *sage-femme* was full of welcome at once at the sight of Fontana's hat, it was such a careless and wealthy hat, and Fontana began speaking French to her right away, quick, bright little words like a little bird hopping back and forth on the step. This had once been her house, she said, and down there in the corner of the garden we used to have supper in the summer, and we used to have doves in the attic, and she looked up laughing at the open *mansarde* window at the top, but there was no sign of a feather or even a streak of bird-lime any more.

"You moved in after me," Fontana said, and the woman as well was laughing at nothing whatsoever. It was all so simple and easy to do, so truly and superbly gay when there was enough money behind it. "They told me you did everything for ladies, and so well," said Fontana, making it up as she went along, and laughing. She really believed that any *sage-femme* in Paris would do it immediately for them: it was only a matter of asking for it, but she was so quick and innocent-looking that the woman never imagined for a minute. There was only a little uncertainty in the *sage-femme's* eye for the other one, for Victoria, who look tired enough to fall.

She took them into the house, and Fontana said:

"This is where Antony used to paint on Sundays, and this is where Antony used to walk up and down stairs, and this is where I cried for two hours the first time Horace came over and told Antony what he thought of him. He stood on the landing there and he looked at what Antony had been painting, and he said the man should be the

provider. He said Antony must provide the
money instead of painting the pictures. It didn't
make any difference when I said I had enough to
go around." Little drops of merriment were running along Fontana's lashes. In every room they
went into there was a bed for the mother and a
little bed for the baby that would come.

"I can take care of five mothers at a time,"
said the *sage-femme*, and Fontana said:

"This is where Antony used to shave in the
morning, and this is where he had his books, and
this is where people used to come." And this is
where Antony breathed, and spoke, and lived, and
the walls of the house can never be ordinary after,
said Fontana's laughter, skipping and jumping.
"And this is the room where we used to sleep,"
she said.

There were no clients in the house now. It was
not the season for babies, perhaps, but the beds
were there in preparation, and the *sage-femme's*
jubilant strength was waiting for cries that would
rip the roof off and for agony and toil. After she
had shown them it all, every nook and cranny and
how tidy and neat the birth would be, she took
them downstairs again to the parlour and showed
them her licence framed in gold and hanging over
the mantelpiece.

"Which lady is expecting the baby?" she said,
and Fontana looked at Victoria and laughed.

"This lady," she said. "But you see we don't
want the baby. We can't possibly have the baby
this time. We came to ask you to take it away."

This was a blow to the *sage-femme*, for she had shown them so much, even the taps of running water in the best room; she had really counted on them, figured the price she would ask, paid off several outstanding bills with it, and settled back in comfort for some time to come. In fact, they were taking the food out of her mouth for she had already spent the money. But Fontana was laughing again as if there were a funny side to it, and the woman started laughing.

"Oh, no, mesdames," she said with her stomach shaking. "I don't eat that kind of bread, I really don't!"

She kept on saying it while she laughed, saying it over and over like a little tune to set them marching down the garden and out the gate. There was almost a spark of hope in her eye at the last, as if she thought they might reconsider and have the baby after all.

"Come back and see me when the time comes," she said, "but for anything else, oh, no, indeed! *Je ne mange pas de ce pain-là.*"

They sat down in the car again with the dog stretched out like a suave, bored duke beside them, and Fontana's laughter ran up and down the windows.

"We'll go to the canal boat on the river," she said, giving the sharp little hops of her orders to the man in front. "We'll see Michel. Michel knows everything. I went to the rue Blomet one night last week with Michel and it was very hot upstairs against the ceiling and we walked around

watching the blacks downstairs at it in frenzy to
the music. They were playing 'I likes a man what
takes his time', and the blacks were packed tight
downstairs, the women wearing that pink they
like, and Michel said 'My God, but the blacks are
dirty! They're dirty all over with civilization.'
And afterwards," said Fontana, "when we were
in the car there was a streak of black on his face,
and I licked my handkerchief and wiped it off,
and I said it was probably civilization, and that
was why it came off so easily he said."

It was the back seat of any kind of vehicle which
affected him in this way, Fontana said, even the
backside of the canal boat did this to him, as if he
were at a loss for conversation. Usually she pre-
ferred the weather to this, but the weather had
very few alternatives: there was good and bad
and then you came to an end. She believed he
would have been disconcerted if she had said,
"did you happen to be out this evening when
that one small yellow cloud was trying to break off
from the main body?" For like all Frenchmen,
he had no sense of humour, only a lewd and
brutal sense of wit.

Michel knew of another *sage-femme*, one who
lived near the Odéon with the trams going by in
innocence just outside the windows. She lived
three flights up in the dark and on every flight
there was the smell of brussels sprouts, left over
from the winter-time, perhaps, but strong and
rank in the unswept, sagging stairs. And this one
had a reputation, he said: she had been known to

time and again, she was really in business for it; there wouldn't be any trouble about her as long as you paid the price she asked you.

"If it's Michel's baby," said Fontana, going breathless up the stairs, "we'll have to pay any price. We couldn't possibly have Michel's baby. You couldn't even dress it as a baby, with all that bawdiness in its blood."

But Victoria sat suddenly down in the middle of the stairs.

"I think I'm going to be sick again," she said. "It's the smell of everything cooking."

The *sage-femme* was as thin as a rake, poor woman, and her rooms were very shabby; business could not have been going at all well that year. The hair on her head and the bones in her neck and the old grey dress that she had been waiting in with the shutters closed at the window, were all as good as a warning given. She was prepared for anything, she was ready for dishonesty or treachery; she was prepared to bear witness even to death. She had no time for Fontana's skipping talk or her laughter, for she wanted the words said out at once in the semi-dark of the parlour, spoken in undertones for fear of the walls overhearing. She had seen so much that was secret rot and secret disease and suppuration carried month after month in silence, hidden away in shame from all eyes except hers, and now she had no patience left for words that came to nothing. She wanted it said, and the figure stated and accepted once and for all, and the money paid her in advance. Victoria told her what it was and the spark of interest came into her eye and she nodded.

"You'll have to sign a paper first," she said to Victoria.

"What kind of a paper?" Victoria said.

"A paper saying you won't use my name and that you'll call in a doctor when it begins coming," said the *sage-femme*. "He'll have you taken to the hospital and they'll finish it off there. But before I do a thing, you have to pay the money and you have to sign the paper."

"Is it sure to help me?" said Victoria, but the woman gave no sign that she had heard her. She sat with her long, grey face unflickering, her soiled hands folded over, her eyes sombre and small and sly.

"How much will it be?" said Victoria, with misgiving. I haven't any choice, she was thinking. It will have to be this or else nothing at all. The door was open into the other room and she could see a bare table standing there, a wide, bare, kitchen table standing on the stained planks of the floor. "How much will it be?" Victoria said, but Fontana jumped up from her chair and the *sage-femme* started in suspicion.

"What's the matter with you?" she said.

"I think it's rather dangerous," said Fontana, smiling bright and young. She is older than I am, Victoria thought, but nothing has ever come to take the youth away. "Isn't it very dangerous?" Fontana said.

"I do it all the time," said the *sage-femme* in

her lowered voice. And isn't it very dangerous, Victoria thought looking at Fontana's face, to carry it all with you, all of your youth, year after year, to take it with you? Because when it goes, then it must all go at once from you, you will suddenly have to put it down somewhere. "I've always done it," the *sage-femme* said. "I have *artistes* from the Opéra Comique. I have first-class people." For a moment it seemed that first-class people could not possibly have anything to do with death.

"But have you ever had any accidents?" said Fontana, smiling. She stood there with her nice, little dress freshly starched, her eyes wide open, really expecting the *sage-femme* to answer her with the truth. You are older than me, Fontana, but you are my daughter. Your head only comes to my shoulder and your teeth are a little crooked with honesty.

"Not when the doctor's called in," said the *sage-femme* scarcely audibly. "That's why you have to sign the paper."

Fontana began laughing a little, and she turned to the *sage-femme* laughing, and all the girls who had ever come into the place, the chambermaids from cheap hotels, and the girls from the Bon Marché and the nougat-stands in the travelling fairs, and the girls who must dance at Bobino or the Empire for a living, cheaply painted and cheaply paid; and all the others, the nameless ones *sans domicile fixe* and *sans profession*, with their heels walked sideways, like Victoria's, and their

faces walked long and bony like horses' faces, all
of them came forbidden and unbidden out of the
darkness of the corners and gathered there around
them. Victoria rose from her chair as if to wave
them back from where they had come, or to stand
between them and Fontana, but they paid no heed
to the signs she made, they crowded close one
behind the other. Their teeth and their breaths
were bad and they were wearing champagne-
coloured stockings over the veins and the ankle-
bones and the discolorations of their flesh. Their
bones were big and their skin was coarse, and they
twisted their skirts like servants. And there must
be something better than this, said Fontana drawing back from the sight of them in the place, there
must be something better. She held on to Victoria's hand and she was shaking her head in the
big hat and laughing at the *sage-femme*. There
must be something better somewhere else, the
thing that was brimming in her eyes was saying.
They were out the door, they were on the landing,
and behind them in the silence of the *sage-femme's*
rooms they could hear the dripping, the endless
dripping of the life-blood as it left the bodies of
those others; the unceasing drip of the stream as
it left the wide, bare table and fell, drop by drop,
to the planks beneath it, dripping and dripping on
for ever like a finger tapping quickly on the floor.

CHAPTER TWENTY-NINE

Sorrel came into the shop in the pale, summery morning, light as a maid on his sandalled feet, and carrying a roll of fresh-printed posters under his arm.

"Take the old ones down, Victoria," he said. "Get a sponge, darling, and get the old ones off the glass. These have to be up some time today. I promised the auto*MO*bile people." Waal, I'll be switched, said the tails of his skirts, the hay ain't pitched. He opened the posters out flat on the floor, kneeling down as quick as a young man without a crack in his joints still. "Take the old ones down, Victoria." Victoria climbed up on the poets' bench near the window and started ripping the old ones out. "I got something off," he said, standing below her and smiling up. His eyes were utterly guileless, utterly baffled, as though he scarcely understood the ins and the outs of it. "They gave me quite a reduction on the price of the car in exchange for a little advertising."

The posters were opened out flat on the floor and Victoria read the words printed on them: they seemed far and undimensional, but scrupulous, like a country and its landscape looked down on from the air. First there was the strong block-printing in black saying that on Saturday night next at eight-thirty Sorrel would speak at the Salle des Etudiants on "La Débâcle de l'Homme Moderne", and beneath it, in smaller letters, but quite clear, was printed "Sorrel drives a Tressex" —there was nothing more to it than that.

"We'll put it on every poster for the next six months," said Sorrel with the distraught, wild, smiling bewilderment wandering in perplexity from eye to mouth, from feature to feature across his countenance. It might have had nothing to do with business; it was only a quiet, generous agreement to which the brotherhood of man had come. "I'm getting the car this afternoon," he said. "It has the knee-action drive and the airflow body. The English claim it's English and the Americans say it's American, and the Germans say they did it first, but all I know is she makes a hundred and thirty kilometres an hour, and you don't know you're moving!" He was laughing now, with the Adam's apple jerking in his neck. "Why, at that rate," he said, "a fellow can get down south over-night!" Can get to the olive trees and the sparse, bare hills and the way things were in Cyprus, can go back fast through the years, back to the resurrection and the divinity of youth, to the courage which cast out, and the fervour of youth which advances in the wilderness as a forest-fire advances, the flames as tall as men and running forward hand in hand.

"Take the old ones down, Victoria!" Sorrel said, and he did not stop speaking in fear of what ques-

tions might be put him. How old are you, Victoria
might say to him if he stopped, and he would have
to answer I'm sixty and I can't take it barefoot
across the thorns as I used to. Thistles are mules'
fodder, and the long, bare hills with the mistral
laying waste on them are fit habitation for sheep
but not for men.

He was saying, "Matilde and Talanger and I
are going to run down to Toulon the day after tomorrow." It's been a hard winter, he was saying,
and a very trying spring. It's going to be a very
hot summer, he was saying. "We'll leave you to
carry on the works for a little while without us,
Victoria dear. You and Estelle will have to keep
tabs on the others. And about the printing-press,
dear," he was saying, "we'll get at that in the fall,
together. Every one needs a bit of a change of
scenery this time of the year."

But Victoria said:

"The thing is, I'll have to be going away, Sorrel.
There're a lot of reasons. One of them is I'm ill,
I'll have to have an operation. I want to talk to you
some time when you could sit down and listen.
I've a lot of things I have to say."

The smile went suddenly thin and acid in Sorrel's face; it was drawn up lipless in fear under his
hawklike nose.

"Ho, ho," he said, laughing high, "so you're
like all these American ladies! You *must* have an
operation. You *must* have your appendix out because every one's doing it this year, or you must
have Dr. Freud or Dr. Jung or Dr. Somebodyelse

306

look inside you and tell you what's happening to your soul! Oh, you Americans!" he said, shaking his head back and forth with the venomous resignation of his laughter. "You'll be the death of me! It's just the big national complaint that's biting you, Victoria!" he said. "You've gone and let the heat get on your nerves! You ought to manage better. You ought to keep the door of the shop open just as soon as the sun starts shining on the glass," said Sorrel, throwing the shop-door open into the street. "And then open the door into the courtyard in back and that gives you a nice breeze all day long! Don't just sit there thinking how hot you are! Do something about it! Open a door or two and let the fresh air in!"

Don't let the heat get on your nerves, he was saying still when Peri came down the street, walking with intention in his short, Greek dress and carrying a worn, tan suitcase in his hand. Peri came in through the open door and put his suitcase down on the bench, and Sorrel turned his head from the sight of it. It was a poor man's bag without any labels on to say where it had been, and Sorrel kneeled down on the floor so that he need not see it; he began rolling up the posters again, and he was humming hastily in his throat, hastily, hastily doing up the posters, with his little tune humming in unconcern. But here he was trapped in the shop with the door closed fast behind Peri, and Peri's face in menace reflected in the two long glasses in the room.

Peri did not stir nor speak; he stood there, just

within the shop, his eyes moving animal-bright
and quick from under his ambush, looking sometimes at Sorrel and sometimes at Victoria with the
faint, yellow-edged smile on his face and his short,
thick arms crossed over. Victoria flattened the new
poster over the glass of the window, and Sorrel
stood up again on his light, nimble feet. He was
carrying the roll of posters, fragrant with printer's
ink, under his arm, and he was ready now, he
would be off to other places. He was settling his
tunic on his shoulders and getting ready to pass
Peri and go out the door.

"I may need your help this evening," he said to
Peri in a tentative, frail voice. His eyes were bewildered with their longing not to see; he did not
want to see the suitcase sitting there on the bench,
he could not bear to see it. "I want to put these
posters up along the boulevards tonight," he said,
but his voice was failing. He dared not see Victoria's face because of the decision that must be
there now. There was no one to stand between
him and what Peri was about to say.

"Tonight," said Peri with his arms still crossed,
"we'll be out of your sight, and this time it will be
for ever. The others are waiting for me at the
station, all of them, Cina and Gabrielle and Arthur
and the children. We're going to Italy. We're
through with you and your sweat-shop," said Peri,
and his voice was rising. "You and Matilde and
Estelle and Edmond with your grand cars and your
vacations all summer! We're through with you!
You can rot in hell with your American dollars,"

he said, and he added all the imprecations he could think of at the moment. "You can have your filthy American money," he said, "but I've cleared your colony out! They follow *me*," he said, and he struck his chest a blow with his fist. "When I move on, your colony moves with me!"

"And what a colony!" said Estelle in contempt, only she was not there to say it. "Watch out at the customs, Peri! They'll think you're a fur-bearing animal when you try to cross the frontier!"

And Matilde cried out: "How dare you raise your voice to Sorrel! You, Peri, you lout, you servant!" Only she was not there to fling Peri out the door with her anger. Sorrel was there alone, there was no shelter to which he could turn, no woman to stand as shield before him and take the blows that fell now on his naked breast. Sorrel was alone, with the colony departed from him and the accumulation of its rancour raining down upon him. Oh dear, oh dear, said the frail perplexity of his collapse, I must have left my 'brelly to home, Victoria, and Victoria jumped down off the poets' bench and walked toward Peri.

"You've said enough now. Don't say any more. You'll miss your train," she said.

But the rage of it was not to be stilled now that it had burst from him at last. It thundered in the little shop, it quivered like a wind in the curtains that had been so formally painted with the images of man's activity. Peri kept his hands fast in his armpits as if he might make use of them if he once let go. But how he had kept within him all those years

309

the foul stream of his impotence was the greatest wonder of all; how he had contained it with only the faintest murmurings of its presence overheard. In such a flood it came from his mouth, in such virulence as if the blood itself had curdled in his veins.

"You won't get anybody else in a hurry!" he shouted; and the cords in his neck stood out like rope lashed down. "I'll tell everybody wherever I go what kind of a *salaud* you are! Raking the dollars in like any dirty *patron* and not letting any of us get a squint at them! What did any of us others get out of your filthy museum deal, and who put it over for you? You weren't the one who was in here in the shop passing flattery out free of charge! And who's going to ride in your lousy car?" shouted Peri with his hair shaken down in his eyes. "Vaudeville dancers, not poets, I tell you! The poets and philosophers are too decent to be seen in company with you!"

Victoria stepped forward and touched his arm, and across the window-glass the posters were saying "Sorrel Drives a Tressex".

"Please go," said Victoria. "Please go."

He waited a minute to say some more, and then he went out in such anger that he left the suitcase behind him. Victoria put it quickly out the door and called his name after him down the street. He came back through the few people there were, his eyes glazed over, and he took it up as a blind man might have taken it, feeling for the handle along the edge. His lips were moving still with the words he had left unspoken: he must carry them off un-

said with him to the third-class waiting-room of
the station, to Cina and Gabrielle and Arthur in his
helmet of hair, to Hippolytus and Athenia and
Prosperine and Bishinka waiting in their poor
tunics, waiting will-less for the next thing that
would come.

He went off and he did not see how Sorrel began
crying, crying terribly, like a woman whose pride
has been ravaged and whose pity for the violation
has blighted for a little while a small, enduring,
womanly world. The tears ran down the rugged
places of his face and he did not seek to wipe them
away with his hand. He turned and went back
into the darkness where the stairs were, behind the
curtain, where no one from the street could see him
crying. And coldly, quietly Victoria was saying,
This must be some kind of an end for him, it is the
end of one thing he tried to establish. But quick
as light flashing through the empty shop, Estelle's
voice cried out in piercing contempt "Do you
think he gives a good God damn about them? He's
seen too many of them come and go. He'll have
the place to himself now and a little peace and
quiet. Do you think he cares, Victoria? *Il s'en fout,
il s'en fout royalement*," she said.

Victoria stood motionless in the shop, listening
to the sound of his crying and to the strangely living, the unheard voice of Estelle speaking out. She
could not lift the curtain and go out to him, she
could no longer go to him and put her arms around
him. He was crying alone, without any one, in the
dark.

CHAPTER THIRTY

Outside the boughs were heavy and rich with great, black-seeming clusters of leaves in the evening. They cast an endless dusk on the walls of the house and into the room even in June, even with the windows open to the garden. The chill of it ran down Fontana's spine when the servant brought her to Victoria's door, but she did not speak of it. She came in with the Russian dog behind her and she called very merrily out, "Here's music for your ears, Victoria John"; and she closed the door behind her. Her voice was eager from having looked an hour for Victoria: she had been to the shop after it was closed, and she had waited at the Métro door for her to come up the steps, and she had driven a long way to where she was. She sat down quickly on the side of the bed, and she had a small, white straw hat with a feather on it tilted over one eye, and she said:

"I've got a doctor who will do it. I've fixed it up with him. He puts you to sleep and when you wake up it's over."

But instead of these words being the end of it all, it seemed to Victoria as soon as they were said that this was only the beginning. She sat up in

bed with her man's shirt and her old, brown skirt
on her and she said:

"You're so good to me without any reason for
being so good. Why do you do it?"

"I'm not good," Fontana said, and she began
to laugh. "But we like each other, don't we?"

"I like you," said Victoria, and she felt shy at
saying anything so simply out. "We've said a lot
to each other, but we've never said anything really."

"I know," Fontana said. "I wanted to ask you
in the middle of the night if you're afraid of being
hurt. I'm such an awful coward."

"Yes, I'm afraid," Victoria said. "I hate it.
But there are other things I have to tell you. You
see, I'm leaving Sorrel and I haven't any money.
I couldn't possibly pay a doctor. How could I
pay one? I shall have to ask you to lend me money.
And when I am well I will work and pay you back.
Only people must have promised you things like
this before, and it always comes to nothing."

"You lie down, Victoria John," said Fontana,
"and I'll lie down beside you."

The lordly dog saw that she had put her hat
aside and he laid his long, white forepaws on the
bed and drew himself up as well. The three of
them laid there quiet a moment and then Fontana
turned her head on the pillow and looked out the
open window at the trees with their branches
strong and dark in the evening.

"Did Antony ever come here?" she said because
of the difference it would make in the place.

"Antony brought me home at night," said

313

Victoria, "but he never walked through the garden and he never came in here. The last time," she said, and she heard her own voice tremble with courage in her throat, "the last time he brought me home I was drunk and he put a lot of money in my handbag. He must have taken the boat to New York a few days after that. I didn't see him again and then I had your letter saying he was gone. It was a great deal of money," said Victoria in shame. "There were thousands and thousands."

"Yes," said Fontana, " Antony sold a horse. He sold the horse in the country and he drove into Paris with the money."

"I never tried to find him and give it back," Victoria said. It was the time of evening for voices of children to be heard playing in the street, but there were no voices. There were only the trees growing sombre and heavy in the grass outside. "I gave the money to two little Russian women who lived in the next room. They'd been starving there for years," she said. "They wanted to go to Monte Carlo and I helped them climb out their window at night without the landlady knowing. They hated her and they went that way so they wouldn't have to pay."

"Antony was to cable the money to Horace. That's why we sold the horse," said Fontana. She lay there in the gathering dark, her short, thick hair pushed back from her brow with her quick, small-wristed hand. Her feet were near the dog on the bed, the slippers kicked off them and fallen, and the little silken toes curled up against his hair.

"I thought you had so much that it couldn't possibly matter," said Victoria. "Or perhaps I didn't think about it. I just did what I wanted to do with it. I don't believe I thought at all."

"Antony told me that he gave it away," Fontana said; and the room was going dark now. "He said he forgot and gave it away to some one. Things had been going not so well for Horace, and we had to do what we could to help him out. But it doesn't matter now," she said. "It doesn't matter. Antony's made money every time he's gone over."

"Yes, it matters," Victoria said. "I owe you that money."

"No," said Fontana, "nobody owes it to any one. It's just something that happened." The darkness was filling the room and the three women on the mantelpiece were not looking any more. The dark that came in through the windows was blotting the stains and the dust and the poverty out. "It's other things," said Fontana as if she had just finished laughing or was just about to begin again. "Things that happen to Antony whether I'm with him or not, things that happen inside him." She lay on the bed in the darkness trying to tell Victoria what their life was, but there were no words that could say it: when he came into a room he took the burden of it over and every other woman had to carry the burden of living alone; he made the flowers grow in spring, they looked in through the window and saw his face; he made the crows fly straight and the willows weep for love by the rivers. "When Antony comes back from America it's like beginning life all over again, every time it's like that. Everything stops and waits for him while he's in America. I stop thinking, and nothing grows any taller. But it's the other things," said Fontana. "The ones that happen inside him. I see them happening and there's nothing I can do."

Victoria touched Fontana's hand where it lay beside her in the dark.

"What about you?" she said. "What happens inside of you?"

"Oh, nothing, nothing at all," said Fontana, laughing. "Absolutely nothing. I made up my mind from the beginning that I wouldn't let them get me, I mean none of the things that put their arms around you and get you down in the end. I would be very sly with everything, I would be very cunning from absolutely the crack of dawn until going to bed at night. I made up my mind to outwit things as fast as they came up, one after another. But I would do it incredibly as Rimbaud did it. Not a niche left open in the armour."

I am so old, so old, thought Victoria sadly. This little woman is my child, but I will never tell her. The young, untired voice of Fontana was fresh as a bird's call in the dark.

"When I went to school on the Hudson, I began deciding it. I wanted to wear high heels then because I knew there was something lovely and lewd in a little girl with black silk stockings on and high heels throwing what there was to the front and the back to the winds. That was the picture of carelessness I wanted to carry up and down the corridors at school and show it off at the windows if I thought any one was passing. I took it to garden-parties after I came out, with my hair curled and an organdie hat on top of the whole thing, and I always wore it like a miniature on a ribbon between my breasts so that no one could see it until they married me. I made a nice little picture-book of myself, absolutely indelible. But as for me, myself, I made up my mind early: I would laugh hard like a hyena rather than ever let them find out."

"Find out what?" said Victoria, and Fontana burst into laughter.

"I don't know," she said, laughing; "that's just it. I don't really know. Sometimes I think it's that if I let the outside come off I'll find I'm really crying underneath, I mean making a terrible display like an hysterical woman throwing things in a room. We have so many people come to see us, always very fevered and gay, more and more people all the time because when a thing like that gets started you can never tell it to stop. More and more people come driving out until we have to come into Paris to escape them. It's very silly, isn't it?" said Fontana.

"You and Antony could go away together," said Victoria.

"We always have to come back in a little while because Antony's a good son," said Fontana. "But when we're alone Antony paints and I make

people. I found out I could make people, marvellously cool people, out of clay. I've put some out
at Rambouillet around the fireplace and the pool,
you'll see them when you come there. They're very
soothing and nice with big, flat limbs and shoulders.
Everything's waiting out there, everything in abey-
ance until he comes back. There are three hundred
and thirty-six hours in a fortnight," she said.
"Do you like fishing? We can go fishing out there
in the streams together when the weather's bad."

"We'll do this, that, and the other thing together," said Fontana, and she leaned up on her
elbow, laughing. "When Antony comes back we'll
drive down to Havre or Cherbourg or wherever it
is and meet him." The smell of her perfume when
she stirred was like a garden suddenly flowering in
the dark.

"What if I stayed the night here?" she said;
and the dog's jaws cried as he yawned at the end
of the bed in darkness.

"It's not clean here," said Victoria.

"Oh yes," said Fontana. "It's lovely here. It's
lovely. Every corner smells of night." She sat
up, small and darker against the darkness of the
open window. "Boris will have to have a nightgown," she said. "He always sleeps in a nightgown or else his nose runs in the morning."

She jumped out of bed in her stockinged feet.

"Where would the light be?" she said.

"It's gas," said Victoria, getting up. "I'll find
some matches and light it."

"Oh, lovely!" said Fontana. "Like a tropic
butterfly!"

318

"I only have a shirt left," said Victoria from the closet. "How would a shirt do for Boris?"

Fontana took the workman's shirt and passed it over Boris's head and drew his long, white, delicate arms through the dangling sleeves. She buttoned the cuffs of it at his wrists and the collar over at his throat, and there sat Boris upright on the sagging bed, the pure white blade of his muzzle lifted, his eyes gone deep in grief for the outrage that had been done him, for the bitter injury they had dealt his long, svelte, languid bones.

There he sat on the bed like a clown in the shirt she had put on him, afraid to stir in this unwonted, workman's thing. And Fontana stood crying with laughter before him, laughing and laughing until she was weak with her laughter, and she flung her arms around Victoria and clung to her for breath. He was such a ludicrous figure of grief with his noble, cynical being buttoned up to the neck in this alien garment that Fontana could not get over the sight of him. She clung laughing to Victoria until the tears ran out of her eyes.

"Oh, Boris, Boris!" she cried out; and the two of them stood rocking with laughter, swaying like drunken women before the poor, white, injured dog.

"Let's put the tunic on him," Victoria said at last, but they did not stop laughing. "It would be much better if he wore Matilde's silk tunic. That would give him back his pride."

But the shirt was warmer so they left it on him. Victoria turned the gas out and they laid down on the narrow bed together. Fontana was laughing still, and she put her arm around Victoria's neck, and they went to sleep abruptly and still smiling, as if some kind of peace had been suddenly and at the same instant given to their hearts.

The doctor was driving his own car before them up the Champs Elysées, and they were following in Fontana's car, following him through the gliding traffic to the other end of Paris where the *cliniques* and the cemeteries dwell together. They were following him through the warm, silky morning as a thread pursues a needle's eye.

"When you wake up," Fontana said, "I'll be in the room waiting. It'll be exactly like any other day. It will be the way it was waking up together in your room, only Boris won't be there with his shirt on." She was laughing, and she opened the paper up, and she said, "Look, it's June twenty-fourth, nineteen-thirty-four", and suddenly they both saw it written across the top of the Paris-American paper: it was written "Prominent Young Club Man Cuts Veins In Father's Office", and in smaller letters below: "Antony Lister Takes Own Life. Wall Street Losses Rumoured."

The sun was shining on the Petit and on the Grand Palais; it was running like riches down the windows of the car.

"Don't cry. Antony said you never cried," said Fontana, a small, clear voice picking it up and putting it together and going on with it for ever.

AFTERWORD

Kay Boyle's life, for much of her early fiction, was the catafalque on which she was to hang her fiction. Born in St Paul, Minnesota in 1902, she started her career as a writer at the age of six. With her family, at first quite well-to-do, she travelled abroad and was educated by her cultivated mother. At nineteen she married a young French engineer she had met in Cincinnati where the family was then living. After a year of work in New York for the editor of *Broom*, Lola Ridge, she and her husband went to France on borrowed money in 1923. It was a significant move, an important move. It provided the young writer with what were to be the sources of her fiction for some time to come. Everything served her creative purposes: her life with her husband's family in Brittany (*Plagued by the Nightingale*, 1931), her love affair with editor-poet Ernest Walsh (*Year Before Last*, 1932) and the book we are fortunate now to have back in print with this edition, *My Next Bride*, first published in New York in 1934.

My Next Bride is a departure from the fictional mode used in Kay Boyle's two earlier novels. Her heroine, Victoria, is a third version of the closely autobiographical Bridget and Hannah who inhabited *Plagued by the Nightingale* and *Year Before Last*, but in many ways she is a more inventive and imaginative one. Unlike her forerunners Victoria is, at twenty, unmarried, has never been, and talks of herself as a virgin while she worries about being left a spinster. Then, at a drunken party which she cannot recall, she becomes pregnant and is forced to undergo the misery of an abortion. The pregnancy is part of Kay Boyle's own history, as is Victoria's decision to go to work for Sorrel in his store, but Victoria's childless state is fiction. In truth the child Talanger in the colony is not Kay Boyle's daughter Sharon but the "slant-eyed, impudent, gold-face girl", whom we believe we can recognize from the photograph in Boyle's autobiographical *Being Geniuses Together* as Raymond Duncan's daughter.

Straight from life, of course, is Kay Boyle's portrait of the idealistic yet fraudulent colony founded by Sorrel and his wife, the dancer Ida, who has died before the novel begins. The colony forms the core of the novel; Boyle has used it to support her muckraking revelations of human misuse under which she herself suffered. Sorrel is Raymond Duncan in every detail, enslaving all those idealists who came to live under his manipulatory charm and his elevated but ultimately debasing ideals about the good life. And straight from life, as well, is the portrait of Antony Lister, drawn from Kay Boyle's second husband, the American Laurence Vail. Antony is married to wealthy dilettante Fontana, a rather fancy name that Kay Boyle has given to Peggy Guggenheim, Vail's first wife.

My Next Bride is not an eventful novel. Instead of plot, almost to the last page, it substitutes a poetic and impressionistic style, which blurs the edges of character and event and gives us instead a Manet-like portrait of a young American's life in Paris in the early Thirties. Its descriptions are often veiled and hazy, like much of Antony's conversation, determinedly allusive and clouded. At times the novel seems to be awash in a sea of suggestion rather than contained in concrete detail. At other times we are allowed to see, in painfully accurate particulars, what Kay Boyle wishes us not to miss: the looks of Peri the Greek, the day-to-day existence of actors Estelle and Edmund, the physical appearance of Sorrel, and Victoria's landlady, and the two pathetic Russian ladies who inhabit her boarding house.

What does happen in the novel is that Victoria, virgin-American-puritan, grows up. She experiences a series of maturing shocks from the fakery and pretensions of the colony, homesickness, hunger, need, overwork, unwanted pregnancy, the revelation of harsh reality behind hyperbolic appearance. She comes face to face with her extreme youth: "To be young is to be filled with mercy and patience, having lost nothing yet not knowing even of the bereavement there can be without death coming, nor knowing that to be young is to see mercifully." She learns about her true relationship to her native country: ... "to be American is to be puritan, to be American is to stand outside and watch, or else to abandon oneself forever to whatever is. Words out of a book, like whiskey taken, or a painting seen with anguish, the love of those so pure that the moment comes close and falls like fruit upon the mouth." An expatriate who comes to France to paint, Victoria discovers the price of homesickness when a basket of food arrives from Antony for the two Russians: "America, she said in silence, touching the boxes of what had grown there, I want to go back to you. I want a father with a voice like baked beans to put his arms around me. I want a mother warm as cornbread to wash my ears at night."

My Next Bride begins with a wonderfully gothic scene, a tone that will disappear as the novel progresses, only to be resurrected on the last pages. Victoria arrives from Montreal, intent on getting a job in Paris and painting there, determined to live on the outskirts of the city. At Neuilly she happens into the boarding house ruled by a blind landlady: "She came lifting her own weight from the obscurity, bearing her own flesh forward like a burden, manipulating as if under water the speechless, slow advance." Downstairs there are the two Russian sisters, survivors of the Revolution against aristocrats: "Poverty had made grotesques of them, for in their ladies' bearing and their speech there was no difference, but they were living in the shadow of what had happened somewhere else, a long time past, when their fur jackets and their boots and stays were new." The historic house is decaying: "The trees here are as old as your country", the monstrous flesh of the landlady seems to be saying to Victoria. "The walls are ready to fall away in disrepair. The stairway has carried down the footsteps of young men too sick to ever remount them. There has been war and invasion in this place, and women running blind up the stairs hearing their men were dead." Gothicism moves into intensely poignant moments with the Russian ladies, starving yet gallant in their airs and pretences, who are brought to desperation and a search for work they are not equipped to do. Their rescue runs parallel to Victoria's rescue from her illusions about the colony: the three lives have in common their expatriate status, their ladylikeness, and their unreal, brave aspirations.

Historians of utopian communities may well resort to this novel for Kay Boyle's disillusioned view of the colony Raymond Duncan estab-

lished in Paris in the late Twenties. We know
something of the facts about this colony
because Kay Boyle has given them to us in
Being Geniuses Together, in the autobiographical chapters she inserted into Robert
McAlmon's account of life in Paris in the
Twenties.

Kay Boyle was in Paris with her baby
daughter Sharon in the spring of 1928. At a tea
at which Gertrude Stein was present she met
Raymond Duncan: "He was a man of fifty or
so, lean and muscular, neat and scrupulously
well kept, with his long hair pinned in silky
grey braids in a crown around his small, eagle-
like head. One end of his elegant tunic
was flung across his left shoulder, and
his bare feet, in the simplest of thonged
sandals, were immaculately clean ... He
spoke with the flat twang of a Midwestern
farmer, and his corded, lean neck was that of
a man who has worked in the fields or on
the sea."

Duncan spoke glowingly of his colony in
Neuilly: "of the goats that were herded, their
bells ringing, through the alleys and by-ways of
Paris early every morning ... the children in his
colony would go out with their wooden bowls to
drink the fresh milk that the goatherd would
draw for them from the udders of his flock."
Robert McAlmon provides a report of Kay
Boyle's involvement with Duncan: "For a time
she was saleswoman for the Raymond Duncan

shops ... and she managed to sell quantities of hand-woven rugs, tunics, draperies ... She didn't get a percentage, however; only a small salary, but then Raymond Duncan was never a practical man. What could money mean to him when it was Kay who needed it?" Kay Boyle's motive for joining the colony had been guilt; she was residing in luxury with the Princess Dayang Muda, writing her biography. The Dayang Muda was Gladys Palmer (of Huntley-Palmer Biscuit fame) who had married the white rajah, a British subject, of Sarawah. Duncan offered her the theoretical pleasures of the simple, deprived, healthy life. She stayed with him for six months, leaving when she learned the truth behind his frauds. James Joyce too was taken in by Duncan's pretences, asking where the looms were that had produced the fine cloth he sold in his shop. "It was on the tip of my tongue to tell him", writes Boyle, "that the only weaving I'd seen in my time in the colony was my own art of weaving in and out and back and forth the worn-out collars and cuffs of the shirts" brought to her by writer-friends.

Kay Boyle has given her character Sorrel a dead wife who was once a famous dancer and teacher of dancing. This is a use of his sister Isadora for fictional purposes, as is the child Talanger, made of Sharon into Duncan's daughter. Kay Boyle's young, tender spirit is Victoria's and the shop is where it was in fact, accurately reproduced as are the activities and nature of the colony. Sorrel is Duncan, "clean as a swan in preparation, his hair smooth, his eyes mild as a woman's, his dignity in readiness for the Americans who came to tea". Victoria's disillusion is Kay Boyle's, and her inverted portrait of the colony which she offers to the wealthy American woman is a fantasy version of the truth: "Victoria went on speaking of the house in Neuilly as if it stood fair and clean in pride, with vegetables cooking in the broad white kitchen, and the women painting the scarves and weaving in the common room, and the men at work in peace and quiet carving the sandals out of the fresh, sweet slabs of leather." In this invented portrait of the sterile, deprived, dingy surroundings at the colony Victoria's disenchantment is complete. She leaves when, as it happened in life, Sorrel buys an elaborate motorcar with the money from his American patron and escapes with his mistress into the benignity of Southern France for a vacation.

Kay Boyle stopped short of some of the other horrors she witnessed at the colony when she allowed her fiction to end with Victoria's alliance with Fontana, Antony's wife, and Antony's curious, melodramatic, almost unaccountable suicide. In truth, Raymond Duncan did go South, taking Kay Boyle's daughter with him, and ultimately, because he would not give her back, Boyle was forced, in a bizarre move, to kidnap the child in order to get her back. Even more bizarre, and left out of the fiction, was what happened to Kay Boyle when she was freed for the time being of the care of her child. She writes (in *Being Geniuses Together*) that she "went off the deep end". She drank heavilyi and "consorted with this one and that one", enjoying none of her debauchery: "The puritanical conscience, with its little grey bonnet tied under its chin, kept me from taking with gusto all these fine experiences I was having at nightfall, and I went about trying to cleanse myself of the shame of them come the brutal light of day." The result Boyle records in the novel, Victoria's abortion.

At one point in the novel, Antony Lister declares to Victoria: "I like you, Victoria ... I like the way you don't say things." This is perhaps the secret to Boyle's winningly successful portrait of her heroine. Victoria's thoughts are fertile, suggestive, silently embroidering and elaborating upon the events which educate her into womanhood: her sensitive and understanding view of Antony's offers of his love, Sorrel, his colony and shop and the underlying selfishness of his idealism, her homesickness, her abortion, her understanding with Fontana at the end. Victoria's silences are illuminating for us, much more enlightening than talk would be. We know her better for them, and we ally ourselves with the shy, tender, quiet woman who achieves honesty, a vision of meaning in her life, and, as she reaches her majority, a strong sense of what she wishes her life not to be. She will not be Antony's next bride, she will be her own, fully-realized, emotionally mature woman. Or so we believe as the novel ends.

Doris Grumbach
Washington, 1985

The first Virago Modern Classic was published in London in 1978, launching a list dedicated to the celebration of women writers and to the rediscovery and reprinting of their works. While the series is called "Modern Classics" it is not true that these works of fiction are universally and equally considered "great," although that is often the case. Published with new critical and biographical introductions, books appear in the series for different reasons: sometimes for their importance in literary history; sometimes because they illuminate particular aspects of women's lives, both personal and public. They may be classics of comedy or storytelling; their interest can be historical, feminist, political, or literary. In any case, in their variety and richness they promise to confuse forever the question of what women's fiction is all about, while at the same time affirming a true female tradition in literature.

Initially, the Virago Modern Classics concentrated on English novels and short stories published in the early decades of the century. As the series has grown, it has broadened to include works of fiction from different centuries and from different countries, cultures, and literary traditions; there are books written by black women, by Catholic and Jewish women, by women of almost every English-speaking country, and there are several relevant novels by men.

Nearly 200 Virago Modern Classics will have been published in England by the end of 1985. During that same year, Penguin Books began to publish Virago Modern Classics in the United States, with the expectation of having some 40 titles from the series available by the end of 1986. Some of the earlier books in the series were published in the United States by The Dial Press.